TOBIN'S IN LAS VEGAS AND HE'S UP TO HIS OLD, OLD TRICKS . . .

'Her breasts were quite magnificent, full and firm, their dark, high-standing nipples altogether irresistible. At the touch of my mouth she flinched, then, as I began working on her, she braced her thighs tightly together and began to moan.

"That . . ." she sighed tremulously, "will get you into a lot of trouble . . . do you have any idea what that *does* to a girl?"

"No. What?"

"Keep going and you'll find out."

I kept going.'

Tobin in
Las Vegas
Stanley Morgan

Mayflower

Granada Publishing Limited
First published in 1975 by Mayflower Books Ltd
Frogmore, St Albans, Herts AL2 2NF

A Mayflower Original
Copyright © Stanley Morgan 1975
Made and printed in Great Britain by
Hazell Watson & Viney Ltd
Aylesbury, Bucks
Set in Linotype Plantin

To All My Young Friends Of The Gwernymynydd Club
With All Good Wishes and My Sincere Thanks
For Your Support

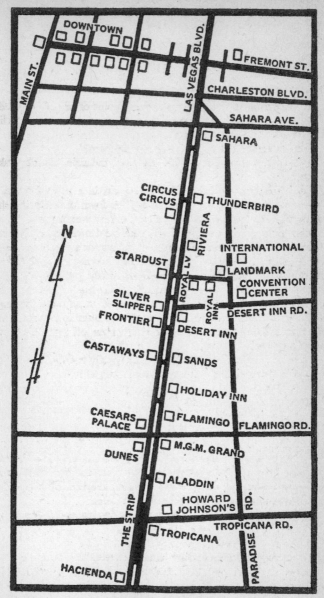

The Strip, Las Vegas

ONE

'Russ . . . !'

The urgency of Buzz's tone and the point of his elbow thudding into my arm jerked me from the kind of doze you slip into on a long, boring jet flight.

I opened my eyes and got him in focus. 'Mm?'

With a lascivious grin he nodded down the aisle. 'Quick – take a squint!'

As I was lumbered with the centre seat in a row of three, I had to lean over him, to my right, to peer down the aisle, but the sight that greeted me made the effort so very worthwhile.

Our airstew, a mind-bending blonde we'd nicknamed Steamy Mimi, was up on tip-toe, collecting a pillow for a passenger from the back of the deep overhead rack and showing us about ninetenths of her stupendous undercarriage in the process.

I mean, they really were the most fantastic legs – long, tapering columns of unimaginable delight, swathed in shimmering silk, legs that dreams were made of – and both Buzz and I had been dreaming about them ever since we'd taken off from Toronto four hours earlier.

'Man . . .' sighed Buzz, with a yearning only twenty-four hours of out-and-out celibacy can produce. 'I've *got* to have her.'

'Yes, Buzz.'

'She's driving me cuckoo!'

'She hasn't far to go.'

'Just *look* at those thighs!'

'I'm lookin' . . . I'm lookin' . . . !'

And then something incredible happened . . . and I really *was* looking. For Mimi dropped the pillow onto the floor and went into a crouch to retrieve it. Pow! A right old eyeful of little white knickers embroidered with dainty blue flowers.

'Jeezus!' gasped Buzz, shoving me away for a clearer view.

'Steady, son, you'll burst your seat belt.'

'I've got to *have* her . . . got to!'

'You mean up here – at thirty thousand feet?'

'Here . . . Los Angeles . . . Tahiti . . . Sydney . . . preferably all four.'

'You've got it bad, lad.'

'The worst.'

'Well, you'd better do something about it . . . get things moving for L.A.'

'Yeah,' he murmured, his eyes narrowing cunningly as he ogled Mimi's delectable chassis undulating down the aisle to the nearest galley. Now he grinned devilishly. 'No time to waste. We'll be in L.A. in an hour.'

'Fifty-five minutes.'

'Right!' he said decisively, slamming his fold-down table up into the seat in front. Then he was gone.

I settled back in my seat, grinning, trying to imagine what line he'd come up with to open the bidding. Whatever it was, I reckoned poor Mimi was already a gonner. There weren't too many birds who could resist the Malone charm when he shifted into high gear. One problem a big, blond, handsome hunk like Buzz did *not* have was pulling birds – especially on the tennis circuit. In fact there were times . . .

But I get ahead of myself. Here I am rabbiting on about him, and there you are wondering who I am and why we're heading for Sydney and forty-two other things. So I'd better slow up a touch and explain the situation.

My name is Tobin – Russ Tobin, a sort of six-foot, blue-eyed, brown-haired, twenty-six-year-old Englishman who is working his way around the world investigating life.

And my smitten mate is Buzz Malone, a six-foot-two, well-sculptured Australian pro-tennis player whom I met on the Miami–New York train a week ago and in the oddest circumstances imaginable.

Now I won't go into the fine detail of our adventure on the train and later in New York, that's already been recounted and would only confuse the present issue, but suffice it to say that we were finally chased over the Canadian border by a gang of crooks who thought we had in our possession something we didn't have in our possession, and we've just taken a much-needed breather in Toronto.

While there, however, Buzz received a telegram from his Australian agent telling him to get back home to Sydney for a tennis tournament, and he, Buzz, convinced me I should go back with him – assuring me that not only can he find me an odd job or two there to help keep body and soul together, but also that with the help of Lis little black book of telephone numbers I shall more than likely investigate myself into a coma within a week – a challenge I simply cannot resist.

So here we are aboard a Qantas Jumbo, four hours out of freezing Toronto and less than an hour away from our first drop-down in Los Angeles for juice, then it's up, up and away to scintillating Tahiti for a wickedly-promising over-night stop, then finally on to Sydney for . . . who knows?

Rest assured, however, that I shall keep you microscopically informed.

But aye, aye . . . what do we have here? Buzz is returning already, his countenance a picture of misery, shoulders slumped in utter dejection! Can it be that the irresistible Malone charm has finally copped out?

Heart-rendingly anguished, he swung into his seat and dropped down, all but wrenching the chair from its mountings.

'Well . . .?' I enquired solicitously.

'She's married.'

I laughed. 'Well . . .?'

'To the bloody captain!'

'Oh.'

'Can you believe it? There must be nine hundred airstews on this flying factory – and I had to pick the one that's hitched to the skipper!'

I shook my head solemnly. 'What a dirty shame.'

'They have no right . . . flashing everything at you like that when they're married to captains! I've a good mind to complain.'

'Do,' I nodded. 'When that form comes round for passengers' comments, you complain about that. I'll support you. Ah, it's not like the old days when all the stews had to be single. You knew where you were then. Granted, a stew may have been having it *off* with the skipper, but at least you stood an outside chance she'd fancy a change . . .'

'*A*men t'that,' drawled a gravelly, sleep-soaked voice in my left ear.

I turned to the tall, lanky sprawl in Western-style clothes who'd been slumped on his spine, Stetson tipped over his face, ever since Buzz and I had boarded.

Now he roused himself, rubbed sleep from his craggy, crumpled, tanned-leather countenance with a huge, horny hand and smacked his tongue against the roof of his mouth with an expres-

9

sion of extreme revulsion. 'Oh, man . . . tastes like th'inside of an old Hoover bag. Ah musta really tied one on.'

I grinned. 'You don't remember?'

He shook his head and regretted it. 'Nope,' he winced. 'Reckon Ah started Christmas Eve . . .'

'Six days ago?' I frowned.

'What date is it t'day?'

'The thirtieth.'

'Then it *was* six days ago.' He gave a rumbling chuckle. 'Hell's teeth, that was some party. Hey, would you guys excuse me, Ah gotta go let some out.'

We cleared the seats for him and he clambered across, finally straightening to a dishevelled six-four in his tooled-leather cowboy boots, a rugged, likeable character who'd obviously packed a thousand years of living into a rumbustious forty or so.

'Much 'bliged,' he nodded, then rolled away down the aisle towards the rear toilets, Stetson jammed on the back of his head and his crumpled cowboy shirt, cream piped in brown, hanging out of his trousers.

'And you think you've got troubles,' I said to Buzz as I sat down. 'I wouldn't swap my head for his plus a thousand acres of Texas.'

He grinned. 'I'd sure like to have been at that party.'

It was fifteen minutes before Wild Bill Hickock returned and when he did we barely recognized him. He'd had a wash, combed his abundant greying hair, straightened himself out and looked ten years younger. He slid us a lop-sided grin and excused himself for bothering us again.

When he was seated he pulled a packet of Lucky Strike from his breast pocket and gave us both one, then struck us a light in true cowboy style – cracking the matchhead with his thumb nail.

'The name's Foley . . . Henry Foley. But mah friends call me "Flush" – as in poker.'

'Russ Tobin,' I said, wiping smoke out of my eye. 'This is Buzz Malone. He's Australian. I'm English.'

'Glad to know you guys. Couldn't help overhearin' your observation on married airstews. Hell, it's got to where a guy doesn't know what he's lechin' anymore. You stoppin' in L.A.?'

'No, we're going on to Tahiti, then Australia. Buzz has a tennis tournament to play.'

'No kiddin'. You a pro, Buzz?'

Buzz told him he was and Flush grinned. 'Hear the game's got quite a female followin'?'

Buzz laughed. 'It's the only reason I play. What's your sport, Flush?'

Foley's smile deepened. 'Man, Ah never can make up my mind. When I'm playin' poker, that's it – nuthin' else matters. But when I'm not playin' poker . . .' he shrugged. 'Drinkin', I guess. An' talking about drinkin', I need one in the worst way – so let's have a close-up of that airstew that just broke Buzz's heart while we're doin' it.'

He reached up a long arm and tugged the service button set in the panel of controls overhead.

'Are you a professional gambler, Flush?' I asked him.

'No,' he said uncertainly, 'meanin' not *quite* full-time. I've got a small spread down in Oklahoma that requires mah attention a few days a year . . . run a few head a cattle and an oil-well or two . . .'

I laughed. 'You really mean it?'

'Sure, I mean it,' he grinned. 'Ain't you fellas heard of Oklahoma oil?'

'Oh, sure,' I said. 'It's just that I've never met a real live oil man before.'

'Well, here y'are lookin' right at one. And if you weren't both committed to Australia, I'd invite you over t'have a look round.'

'Well, that's very kind,' I said. 'Maybe we'll drop in on you one day. I may even come back from Australia this way and take you up on the offer.'

'Oh, you're not staying in Australia? What do you do for a living, Russ?'

'At the moment I'm taking a good look at the world – working at anything that comes along. Buzz is going to fix me up with some bread-and-butter jobs while he's playing tennis.'

'Well, now, Ah approve of that. Ah think a young fella *should* get out an' see the world before he set . . .'

He stopped, his eyes softening as he gazed in the direction of the galley. 'Oh, my . . . Ah do believe I know why poor ole Buzz's heart is broken. Hell's teeth, if I wouldn't swop a coupla mah oil-wells to be that captain for a night or two.'

I followed his gaze. Mimi was bearing down on us, her lovely brow raised in query at Flush. She came in very close, leaned across Buzz to cancel the call button on Flush's panel and stayed there, driving Buzz and me crosseyed with desire with the drift of her perfume.

'Yes, sir, what can I do for you?' she smiled, knowing damnwell what she already was doing for all three of us.

'Well, now . . .' drawled Flush, playing a little game. 'Ah wonder if it's possible t'have me a pillow, ma'am? One of them titchy li'l things outta the back a that rack up theyah?'

'A pillow . . . of course, sir.'

Up she went, straining on tip-toe. I glanced at Buzz. He *was* crosseyed, her thigh a millimetre from his and that fabulous bottom staring him straight in the eye.

I saw him flex his fingers as though fighting a desperate urge to grab it, to run his hands up her high-riding skirt into the dark, warm recess of heaven above, but instead he uttered a low, agonized groan and wiped sweat from his forehead.

'There you are, sir.'

'Well, thank yuh, ma'am, much obliged. An' do you happen to have one up there for mah friend here?'

She transferred her limpid pools to me and scuttled me with a knowing smile. 'You'd like one, too?'

'I'd . . . love one.'

Up she went again, this time actually touching Buzz's knee with her thigh. He snapped his eyes shut and gasped, 'Jeezus!' under his breath.

'Sorry,' she smiled at him, handing me the pillow. 'And how about you, sir – would you like one, too? Are you feeling all right?'

'F . . . fine,' he nodded, his hands grasping the arms of his seat as though about to be electrocuted.

Up she went for the third time, this time moving even closer to Buzz's side as she reached for a distant pillow, her blouse riding out of her skirt and exposing an inch or two of naked flesh not an inch or two from his nose.

'Ohhh . . .' he whimpered.

'Here you are, sir . . . will there be anything else?'

'Yes, ma'am,' said Flush. 'We'd all like a drink, if it's possible.'

'Of course. What would you like?'

You for a start, love, I thought.

'Bourbon and branch,' replied Flush.

I ordered vodka tonic.

12

Buzz had great difficulty ordering anything but finally managed brandy and soda.

As she departed, Buzz deflated with a piteous groan and jokingly fell forward and smashed his head on the seat in front. At least I think he was joking.

'It was *there* . . .! Only an inch from my face! So *close* . . .!'

'Now, Buzz, don't take on so,' commiserated Flush. 'Ah know how 'tis when the she-devils get yuh, but, hell, man, a few hours from now you'll be in Tahiti – an' I hear the pickin's are mighty plentiful out there.'

Buzz brightened noticeably, then slumped a little. 'Well, if we have to wait a few more hours, I guess we'll just have to wait.'

'What stoicism,' I grinned. 'What courageous forbearance. What . . . the HELL!'

Whhoooosshh!

Suddenly the giant plane lurched four miles to the left, shook itself like a terrier coming out of a bath, dropped stone-like a sickening two hundred feet, then just as suddenly righted itself and continued on as though nothing had happened.

And in the cathedral-sized cabin – chaos!

Screams rent the air, people floated off the floor, suddenly weightless, then crashed down onto it with terrible impact. Airstews came hurtling out the galleys accompanied by an avalanche of plastic crockery, dixie cups, bags of ice-cubes, miniature bottles of booze and a snow-storm of paper napkins. In an instant the immaculate, super-neat plane had become a dumping ground of trash and tangled bodies.

Quickly, though, with the realization that the plane had regained normal flight, the panic subsided. Exploding hysteria became relieved laughter and the fearsome happening became a huge, nervous joke. People shouted to one another, stranger communed with stranger and volunteered eagerly to help his neighbour.

An army of passengers descended on the galleys and in no time had the mess cleared away, despite the urgings of the airstews that they should heed the illuminated signs, retake their seats and fasten their safety belts.

For the passengers, though, safely delivered from the brink of Hell and now secure in the feel of a level flightdeck, it was carnival time and nobody was about to deny them the celebration. They whooped and shouted, laughed and clowned, each secretly wondering what had caused the mishap and afraid to wonder if it had in any way damaged the plane.

'Buzz . . .?'

'Yes, Russ?'

'Do me a favour . . . reach up and scrape my stomach off the ceiling.'

'That . . .' he sighed, 'was *very* nasty.'

The captain's voice crackled over the intercom, virtually incomprehensible in the cabin din, muttering something about violent air-thermals and air-pockets over the Grand Canyon.

'Are we over it?' I asked Flush.

I peered past him but it was too dark to see anything on the ground. The sky was a mantle of dark purple slashed with vermilion by the setting sun, but the earth lay in darkest shadow.

'Guess so,' nodded Flush. 'The thermals can be mighty tricky in these parts. There's some pre-tty rugged territory down there.'

Now there was another word from the captain, this time an imperative pronouncement that silenced the cabin incisively.

'Ladies and gentlemen, this is the captain . . . may I have your attention, *please* . . .'

The chatter petered out and the slightly Australian voice continued in an easier, more reassuring manner.

'Well, I've had the cabin reports and I'm delighted to hear no one was hurt in that little curfuffle back there. As for the plane, everything appears to be functioning just splendidly, so there's absolutely nothing for you to worry about. However . . . as this is a very long flight, in the interests of total safety I'm going to change our plans a little and instead of landing at Los Angeles as scheduled, I'm going to land at Las Vegas, which is only about fifteen minutes away . . .'

Flush Foley gave a start. His craggy countenance split in a gleeful grin and he let rip a subdued 'Yaaahhoooo!' and biffed the arm of his seat with his fist. 'Hot *damn*, now if that ain't the goldarndest stroke of good fortune! If that ain't Lady Luck slippin' me the sign mah time has come, I'm a crosseyed sidewinder! Great balls a fire, boys, that's where I'm headin' – li'l ole Vegas! One of the biggest poker tournaments of the year starts tonight at ten o'clock an' I thought I was gonna miss it. Well, paint me red an' call me Rusty, the fickle finger o' Fate sure seems to be pointin' Flush Foley in the direction of the fattest poker pot of the year. Hey, you fellas ever bin to Vegas?'

'No,' we told him.

'Oh ho!' he laughed and thumped me on the knee. 'Then you two ain't lived yet an' that's for sure. That is the *hottest*, most excitin' town in the whole of the U.S.A. After you've seen Vegas, any other place in the whole damn world seems about as lively as Nathan Coffen's Funeral Parlour.'

'I've heard about it, of course,' I said. 'Always fancied a visit.'

'Yeah, me too,' said Buzz, leaning forward eagerly. 'I heard everything's open twenty-four hours a day, is that right, Flush?'

Flush shook his head and fished out his Luckies, as though preparing for a lengthy discourse on the matter.

'Boys, I'll tell yuh . . . folks a lot more literate than I am have tried describin' Las Vegas but not one of them comes anywhere near the truth. You've gotta see it with your own two eyes. Vegas ain't so much super-luxurious hotels and a billion neon lights . . . it's a whole new experience, a grand slam kick in the head. So, my advice is just let go of any preconceived ideas you might have of a twenty-first-century gambling town and prepare to be amazed.'

I glanced at Buzz, saw the light of excitement in his eye and knew we'd be lucky to see Tahiti this side of July.

'O.K.,' said Flush, disappearing behind a cloud of smoke. 'A few pertinent facts about the town that's bin called everythin' from the Sodom an' Gomorrah of the twentieth century to "Lost Wages", Nevada . . . and a thousand less complimentary names in between.

'History – damn little. Apart from a straggle of hardy miners pickin' at a little gold and silver back in the 1880s, nuthin' much happened until 1905 when the Union Pacific set up a division point there, then the tent town started to grow.

'Then, in 1931, came legalized gambling – the match to the touch-paper, an' the boom's bin goin' on ever since.'

'That's its main attraction, then – gambling?' asked Buzz.

Foley laughed. 'Depends on your point of view, Buzz. Las Vegans like t'think of it as "The Entertainment Capital Of The World" – leastwise, that's what they call it. An' there's no gettin' away from it, they do pull in the greats of show business all year round – Sammy Davis Junior, Dean Martin, Tom Jones ... there's always some big names in town. But, of course, it's all a big come-on for the gambling. That's where the money's made. Money!' he laughed. 'Man, enough green stuff is bet across the Vegas tables every year to pay the damn U.S. defence bill! Seven billion dollars, some say, an' I reckon they're not far wrong.'

'Seven billion . . .!' I turned to Buzz. 'That's . . . over two thousand million pounds!'

'That's about the size of it,' nodded Flush. 'An' when you boys get there, you'll see how possible it is. There's just no escapin' it. You'll be tempted by a bank of one-arm bandits the moment yuh step offa this plane – they're there right in the airport terminal! And they'll be doggin' you everywhere you go after that – hotels, motels, drugstores, supermarkets, shops, restaurants . . . just about everywhere but the john – an' by God some folks even want them installed in there so's you can keep right on gambling while you're having a crap.

'But, of course, that's only *one* way t'go broke. You've also got poker, blackjack, roulette, baccarat, keno, craps . . . and if yuh don't fancy any of them ways to lose your shirt, you can always try the women!'

Buzz leaned closer still, his interest re-doubled. 'Women? Are they . . . plentiful?'

Flush guffawed. 'Like crows in a September corn field. I reckon there're more hookers, hustlers, birds and broads to the square mile in Vegas than any other town in the whole damn world. It's a natural law – where there's bread, there's broads, and in the same proportions. So, with seven billion dollars lyin' around loose . . .'

'Point taken,' Buzz croaked. 'Oh, boy . . .'

' 'Course, they're not *all* on the game, by any means,' continued Flush. 'Some are just kids who wander in from Los Angeles, which is only five hours' drive away, t'see what it's all about . . . some are divorcees who've come in for a quickie split . . . then there're bored housewives, genuine tourists . . . you name it, they're there. But it sure adds up to one heck of a lotta females.' He gave us a lop-sided grin. 'Now, I may be wrong, but I've got you fellas pointed more in the direction of broads than blackjack. You just don't come across as high-rollers t'me, right?'

I grinned and shook my head. 'Flush, when it comes to gambling, you are talking to the world's leading chicken. If I lost ten dollars in one evening I'd be miserable for a year.'

'Me too,' nodded Buzz, though not very convincingly.

'Well, you're both mighty lucky fellas. Gamblin' can be a terrible cross to bear. I could tell you some mighty sad tales about gambling losses that would break your hearts. Why, only this spring, back in March, a good buddy a mine dropped close to a million at the crap tables in one week-end.'

My mouth dropped open. 'A million dollars!'

Flush nodded. 'Sure thing. That ole' boy just went berserk down there – that's the way it can take yuh once you get going. Easiest thing in the world t'keep writing them markers and shoving them chips on the line – nuthin' to it at all.' He grinned suddenly. 'But mind what Ah told yuh about the women – they can take you for just as much in half the time when they put their connivin' minds to it.'

'We'll bear it in mind,' I said, winking at Buzz. 'Fortunately I'm almost broke to start with – not much chance of me losing a million. But we might not even get out of the airport terminal, what d'you think, Flush? They might just give us a meal while they're doing a quick check on the plane.'

'Well, it's possible, though I doubt it. These airline cats always underplay the damage angle to gentle the customers. But I've bin in worse bumps than that one back there and they've never had to check the plane. I reckon if Sonny Jim is setting down in Vegas instead of L.A., then somethin's dropped off this crate that didn't oughta have dropped off. Hell, L.A. is only another thirty minutes' flyin' time. It's gotta be pretty serious if he can't keep this thing in the air for another half hour.'

'Oh,' I said.

Buzz gulped.

'Heck, but don't take my word for it,' laughed Flush. 'I'm no damn air-mechanic. But I'll give you five-to-one right now you won't climb back on board this plane tonight.'

Buzz's eyes became sparklers. 'Really? Well, that means . . .'

Flush grinned. 'That means that you'll be accommodated overnight in a Vegas hotel and get your chance too for a good close-up view of "The Entertainment Capital of the World" – warts an' all.'

'You really think so?' laughed Buzz, winking at me.

17

Flush shrugged. 'Like I said – I'm offerin' five-to-one. Any takers?'

There were none. And it was just as well.

We'd have lost.

TWO

No sooner had we declined Flush's bet than the Jumbo began to descend, and once it started it came down with a rush.

Flush, looking out of his window, beckoned me over. 'There she is. Come an' take a look.'

I leaned across. Far below, a hand-sized cluster of brilliant multi-coloured jewels blazed like a cat's eye in a surrounding eternity of blackness.

'Quite a sight,' I said. 'It looks terribly lonely down there, Flush. What's out there in the blackness?'

'Desert,' he answered scathingly. 'Desert and mountains – the bleakest, rockiest sons-a-bitches you ever saw. Vegas is surrounded by them.'

I leaned back and let Buzz take a look. He gave a low whistle and grinned. 'Tobin, I can see the birds from here . . . thousands of them! They're waving to us!'

'They'll be wavin' more than their hankies at a coupla good-lookin' fellas like you,' smiled Flush. 'You two won't stay lonely long.'

'Care to put that in writing?' laughed Buzz, sitting back again.

'I'll do better 'n that. On this one I'll offer *twenty*-to-one. Hell, you guys just don't know what's gonna hit you down there. It's New Year's Eve tomorrow!'

'Is . . . that significant?' asked Buzz.

'Significant! It's only the hottest time in the whole Vegas calendar, is all. Over Christmas, Vegas dies – about th'only time it even pauses for breath. I guess it's because even the high-rollers are obliged t'spare a minute or two to their families over the festive season. But then, by golly, it all starts up again with a vengeance. All the hotels throw a blisterin' great wingding of a New Year's party and, brother, the sky's the limit. I reckon you fellas couldn't a dropped in at a livelier time.'

I looked at Buzz. 'You hear that, Buzz?'

'Yes, I heard that, Russell.'

'Buzz . . .'

'Yes, Russell?'

'I've been thinking . . .'

'I thought as much. So have I.'

'Oh . . . what have you been thinking, Buzz?'

'No, you first, Russ.'

'Well, I've been thinking that . . . even if the plane *doesn't* require extensive attention . . . couldn't we . . .'

'Sort of stay on for a couple of days . . . like over New Year?' I gasped. 'Now, how did you guess I was thinking that?'

''Cos I'm smart.'

'I'll allow that. And what were *you* thinking, Buzz?'

'Well, I was thinking . . . that even if the plane *doesn't* require extensive attention . . . couldn't we . . .'

'Sort of stay on for a couple of days . . . like over New Year?'

He shook his head. 'Incredible – and not a little bit disturbing – how you can read my mind like that.'

Flush let out a laugh. 'Heck, I'm beginnin' to feel sorry for those poor dames down there. Well, like I said, it's a chance in a life-time. You sure won't regret it. An' if you do decide to stay on, it'd be mah pleasure to show you the town a bit. The ver' least we can do is take a cab in together and I'll give you the general low-down on what goes on where – might save you an hour or two.'

'Well, that's very kind, Flush,' I said. 'We'd certainly appreciate it.'

'Hell, it's mah pleasure. Anyways, let's see what th'airline comes up with, then you can plan . . .'

This time a female interruption over the intercom. 'Ladies and gentlemen, we are now preparing to land at McCarran International Airport, Las Vegas . . . will you kindly ensure your seat belts are securely fastened and extinguish all smoking materials . . . thank you.'

As we came in on a low, lumbering circuit I caught a brief panoramic glimpse of the city, an oasis of exciting, beckoning light in a sea of forbidding darkness, radiating a plethora of promise and a magnetic attraction that was irresistible. Like a brilliant, garish fairground on the edge of a dark town, it blared out life, excitement, fun – and I couldn't wait to get into the vulgar, razzamatazz heart of it.

19

'Quite a circus,' mused Flush Foley, as though reading my thoughts. 'A monument to man's ingenuity . . . or stupidity, depending on your point of view. The Vegans who live here won't hear a word said against the place. They'll poke you in the eye with statistics – like there're 143 churches in Vegas which give it, per capita, more churches than in any other metropolis in the U.S.A. – in order to blind you to th' crap an' corruption that goes on *outside* the churches . . . and undoubtedly helps to *build* the churches.'

He laughed, jovially cynical. 'Hell, they may as well be honest an' admit it's a neon-lit lunatic asylum an' a green-felt jungle an' all th'other nasty names it's collected, because it don't take a very high intellect to detect the truth.'

'You sound as though you secretly hate the place, Flush,' I said.

'Me – I got mixed feelin's about it, Russ. I know the ole lady for what she is – a ruthless old whore in fancy get-up – but, dang it, she *can* be fun. I get together here once in a while with some good old buddies and we have ourselves a ball . . . lose a few bucks or win a few, it don't matter. Then we go home an' work for some more. Hell, I don't come to see the lights an' the sights, I come for the company . . . and I sure as hades don't come expectin' to win! That's a mug's game. There's a local sayin' here that sums it up very neatly . . . the kindest favour a tourist can do for himself when he gets off the plane in Vegas is to step back inta the propellers. He'll save himself an awful lotta grief.'

Buzz and I laughed.

'But surely some of them do win?' I said.

'Oh, sure . . . about ten per cent, leavin' ninety per cent that always lose. The house *always* wins, Russ.'

'It does?'

He shrugged. 'Of course. Who d'you think pays for these multi-million-dollar hotel-casinos.'

'Mm, see your point.'

'Y'see, gambling's the only thing they make money on. The restaurants lose money . . . the dinner shows lose money . . . the hotel rooms lose money. Not so much nowadays as a few years ago when you could book a good room, see a first-class show *and* eat a big dinner for practically nothing – the big corporations have changed all that now – but it's still the gamblin' that brings in the big bread.'

'Where d'you stand the best chance of winning?' grinned Buzz.

Flush turned to the window and pointed out at the huge engine cowling. 'Right there, buddy – take a header inta that soon as you get off. Seriously . . .' he shrugged. 'Blackjack, I guess, though there's not much in it. And for the best chance of *losin'* – try the slots. There's just no *way* of beating them. Give you a tip, though . . . every sixth machine in any casino is primed to pay out more jackpots than th'others – it's just another come-on. Problem is . . .' he laughed, unhooking his seat-belt as the sign went off, '. . . finding the first machine!'

The doll with the golden syrup voice was on the intercom again. 'Ladies and gentlemen . . . please make your way into the main terminal and remain there with your stewardess. In a very short while you will be informed of the captain's decision regarding onward flight. It may be necessary to ground the aircraft overnight, in which case all those passengers who wish to remain in Las Vegas overnight will be provided with complimentary accommodation at a first-class hotel. For those passengers whose final destination is Los Angeles, there is a United Airways flight leaving here at eleven o'clock this evening and they may continue their journey aboard that plane.

'Each passenger will, in any event, be personally consulted by our Traffic Manager inside the terminal. Please make sure to take all your hand luggage and personal belongings with you. Thank you.'

'You're *more* than welcome, sweetheart,' replied Flush, tipping his Stetson. 'You just don't know what a big, big favour you've done your Uncle Flush.'

'Big tournament, hm?' I asked him.

'One of the biggest. Thirty guys all stakin' five thousand dollars each – winner takes all.'

'Wow . . . a hundred and fifty thousand dollars!'

'Right on,' he grinned. 'And *Ah* intend bein' that guy.'

'How about the other twenty-nine?'

He pulled a face. 'That's th'only trouble – *they* intend bein' that guy, too.'

We got our stuff together and shuffled down the crowded, mile-long aisle, passed through a door and into a carpeted passenger tunnel which fed us straight into the terminal.

It was a huge round room, ringed by big picture windows that looked out on the runways. It was carpeted wall-to-wall in red, had an extensive, round information desk in its centre, and, on the left, a red-carpeted tunnel that led, so a sign said, to everywhere, including the city itself.

The noise hit us immediately – the metallic crash of a hundred slot-machine handles and the sound of coins cascading into the catchment trays, emanating from a bank of one-arm bandits on our left.

'There yuh go!' grinned Flush. 'The pressure's on already.'

We strolled closer and watched the action. Every machine was occupied, some punters playing two and three machines at a time, feeding nickels into the slots from paper cups as fast as they could go, yanking the handle and moving on to the next machine before the tumblers of the first had stopped, hardly seeming to care whether they'd won or not.

'Don't let those little ole nickels fool yuh,' advised Flush. 'You can still get through a whole mess a money with them. An unpractised arm can get through a two-dollar roll of nickels in about two minutes, and when yuh git warmed up you can halve that time easy. Work it out – two dollars a minute . . . one hundred an' twenty dollars an hour . . . that's about fifteen hundred bucks in a twelve-hour session!'

I laughed. 'But nobody would play for twelve hours, surely?'

He grinned and pulled his nose. 'Russ . . . you'll see some mighty strange sights in these Vegas casinos . . . old dames dressed damn-near in rags, sittin' on stools at the slots because they're too exhausted t'stand, some wearin' gloves on account of they've got blisters. Yep, they play for twelve hours at a stretch. An' a word of warnin' – don't ever try to move in on one of their machines while they're playin' – they're likely to open your head with a roll of nickels!'

'About losing fifteen hundred dollars in a twelve-hour session,' said Buzz. 'That's assuming, of course, that they don't *win* anything. They must win something.'

'Oh, sure they do – listen them nickels shooting into the trays. But just watch what happens to them afterwards.'

Buzz nodded. 'They go back into the machine?'

'Straight back in. Think about it, Buzz . . . you say to yourself

I'm gonna change two dollars inta nickels and play the machines – an' that's it, no more. So you win five bucks. That's taken about two minutes. Are you gonna be satisfied playin' for just two minutes? No, sir, you want more action, And all around you jackpot bells are ringin' and people are whoopin' for joy 'cause they just won maybe twenty, fifty dollars . . . like hell you're gonna quit. Anyway, what good is five dollars – and all in piddlin' nickels? Are you gonna go back to the change girl and cash 'em in? No, sir, you ain't. So you say to yourself "It's their money, anyway – I'll try for the jackpot" . . .'

Buzz laughed. 'And back it all goes in the machine.'

'Yuh got it. They're the devil's own piggy-banks – pure sucker bait. Why, some of them casinos gross twenty . . . fifty thousand dollars a week from their slots alone – and that's just chicken feed.'

'I'm beginning to get the picture,' I said.

Flush grinned. 'Russ, you'd do well to remember the Vegas punter's prayer: "Please God, help me break even" – 'cause that's really the best you can hope to do. If you come outta Vegas with the same money you took in, then, believe me, you've beaten the house.'

At that moment an ear-splitting shriek jolted the room and a bell began a raucous jangle. At a machine far down one of the rows, coins exploded into a catchment tray and with each spewing gush of nickels a good-looking girl in jeans let rip a holler of delight and leapt in the air, clapping her hands.

'I got it . . . I got it . . . !'

'Well,' said Buzz, 'there's one happy winner.'

'Oh, there're lots of them,' acknowledged Flush. 'It's the pot winners that keep all the others hopin' and playin'. Look at 'em all go, now . . . pullin' twice as hard! But I wonder how much she *put* in that machine to get out twenty-five?'

'Shall I go and ask her?' said Buzz, winking at me.

'Sure, why not.'

Buzz approached the girl who was frantically scooping the huge pile of nickels into paper cups as though she had one minute to catch her plane. Several had fallen on the floor, so by way of introducing himself, Buzz picked them up for her.

She flashed him a suspicious look, but this quickly turned to a smile of thanks and then he was talking to her.

A moment later Steamy Mimi was at my elbow and I quickly forgot Buzz.

'Would you gentlemen kindly join my group over by the desk? We're ready to make an announcement.'

'Yes, certainly.' I turned and called to Buzz who reluctantly said goodbye to the girl and came back.

'Heck, I'd hardly got going . . .'

'Mimi wants us over at the desk.'

'Well . . .?' asked Flush.

Buzz nodded. 'Yep, she's three dollars down on the evening. That jackpot just saved her room rent.'

'There yuh go,' sighed Flush. 'And I reckon she'll *still* put it all back.'

We wandered over to the centre desk and joined Mimi's group of maybe twenty passengers, and as we approached, a young official in TWA uniform detached himself from a telephone and came towards us, consulting a clip-board.

'Rightee-ho . . .' he said, flashing us all a welcoming smile. 'Well, it looks as though some of you folks are going to enjoy an obligatory night on the town, courtesy of Qantas. There's nothing seriously wrong with the plane – just a couple of things that got shook up in that air pocket – but of course Captain Hardacre wants everything perfect for the onward flight to Sydney.

'First off, let me apologize on his behalf for any inconvenience this delay might cause you and assure you that Sydney has been informed – so any folks meeting you will be notified in good time.

'Now, I'll take you one at a time and tell you what has been arranged for you. Mister and Mrs. Kopeck . . . your flight was due to terminate at Los Angeles. Do you wish to take the eleven o'clock United Airways flight from here tonight . . .?'

He ran quickly through the list, coming to Buzz and me about half-way down.

'Mister Malone and Mister Tobin, passengers for Sydney . . .' he gave us a grin. 'Any objections to spending a night in Las Vegas, gentlemen? No, I thought perhaps you wouldn't have. O.K., we've booked you a twin-room in the Sahara Hotel – right on the Strip. Sorry about the twin, but it's New Year and accommodation is very scarce. Do you have any objections to sharing?'

We told him we didn't.

'Fine. Well, enjoy your stay, we'll let you know by phone early tomorrow morning about take-off time . . .'

'Erm . . .' said Buzz.

'Yes, sir?'

'If we . . . wanted to stay on for a couple of days, could that be arranged?'

The guy laughed. 'Yes, sir, it could. Let me know when you want to leave and I'll hunt up a flight from L.A. . . .'

'Well,' Buzz glanced at me. 'We'd like to stay for New Year. Could we fly out on the first of January?'

'Sure thing. I'll arrange that and get in touch with you at the Sahara sometime tomorrow. O.K.? Now . . . Mister Foley . . . you were heading for L.A., sir . . .'

Flush grinned and shook his head. 'No, sir, I was really headin' for right here. That li'l ruckus up there did me a big favour – saved me flyin' all the way to L.A. and back agin.'

'Good for you,' smiled TWA. 'Well, we had provisionally booked you into the Sahara, too, in case . . .'

Flush nodded. 'I'll take it and thanks a lot.'

'And I cancel your flight to L.A., right?'

'Right.'

'Fine . . . one very satisfied customer. Next . . .'

'Well, now . . .' said Flush, drawing Buzz and me aside, 'ain't that just dandy. The poker tourny is takin' place at the Thunderbird, right next door to the Sahara. Reckon we can collect our bags and vamoose, fellas, what d'you say? No sense in hangin' around here any longer. Buzz . . . would you just like to go an' check it's O.K. with Miss Mimi . . .?'

He was off like a greased bullet, collected a lovely smile and a handshake from her and returned.

'Sends her fondest love to you both and says you're free to collect your bags and vamoose – her very words.'

We started down the long exit tunnel, reached its end, turned left and were confronted by another corridor at least four miles in length but providing a travelling walk-way. We stepped onto this and killed time with more discussion about one-arm bandits.

'They're not all nickel machines, though, are they, Flush?' I asked.

'Heck, no . . . there're dime machines, quarter machines and some huge eight-footers that swallow silver "Ike" dollars or

25

paper "Washingtons". Now, on them you can *really* shift a fortune . . . though it's also possible to win five-thousand-dollar jackpots . . . in theory, anyway.'

'What's the Sahara Hotel like, Flush?' asked Buzz, changing the subject.

'Nice. One of the older hotels – meanin' it was built more than three weeks ago – but just as comfortable as most of the new luxury showpieces.'

'That TWA chap said it was right on the "Strip". What's the Strip – a nudist complex?'

'Yep,' laughed Flush, 'but not the way you mean. No, the Strip is *the* street in Vegas, the lush, plush backbone of the town where you find all the super-de-luxe hotels. Its official name is Las Vegas Boulevard South, but I can't ever remember anyone callin' it that. It's about three miles long, runs south to north and straight into downtown Vegas and Casino Centre – better known as "Glitter Gulch". That's the "poorer" part a town – not so ritzy but ten times brighter than the Strip.

'The Sahara is the last big hotel on the Strip, right at the north end, so we'll be ridin' right along it – give yuh a chance to see everythin'.'

'Great.'

We came to the end of the moving walk-way and stepped off, passed through a lobby of shops and snackbars on a lower level, having descended by escalator, and finally emerged into the luggage hall in time to collect our bags from a carousel.

A couple of minutes later we were climbing into a taxi at the terminal exit.

'Sahara,' Flush told him and we were off.

'A heck of a sight warmer than Toronto,' I observed.

The driver heard me and grinned. 'Man, this is freezing! Down to fifty tonight.'

'It was thirty in Toronto,' I insisted.

'Be warmer tomorrow, though – up around sixty.'

'Nice,' said Flush. To us he said, 'This place is five-star hell in the summer – hot enough to bake biscuits on the sidewalk an' I ain't kiddin'. On top of the Sahara they have one a them *elec*tronic temperature signs – an' last August that baby showed a hundred and ten three weeks runnin'.'

Buzz laughed. 'Sounds like the Australian outback.'

'But cooler at night, though, I suppose?' I asked Flush.

26

'Oh, sure . . . maybe all the way down to ninety-nine – if yuh were lucky!'

'Wow . . . how do people stand it?'

'They stay indoors. Every place yuh go in Vegas is air-conditioned down to around sixty. That keeps the punters inside. 'Course, it's not so bad around the swimpools – all the hotels have got one or more. Seem t'recall the Sahara's got two, though I never did set foot in either one of 'em myself. Sure don't come to Vegas t'take mah clothes off – leastwise not to swim!'

While he was talking I was peering out of the window, waiting to be overwhelmed by my first sight of the glittering Strip with its fabulous hotel-casinos, but so far I was positively underwhelmed by the landscape. Here, the outskirts of the town looked desolate, neglected, more like a building site than a settled metropolis, just a few low concrete buildings here and there, separated by vacant lots of stony desert scrub. Very disappointing.

I turned to Buzz and was about to pull a disparaging face when suddenly the taxi swung out from behind a huge truck and raced ahead. A few minutes more and we were approaching a junction and there it all began to happen.

On our left there appeared a towering, T-shaped illuminated sign, perhaps a hundred feet high, proclaiming the name TROPICANA, and advertising in its centre panels FOLIES BERGERE and XAVIER CUGAT and his Orchestra.

And beyond the sign – a long, low, beautiful hotel, fronted by a spectacular, illuminated fountain, sculptured in white concrete in the form of a double tulip, the inner bell rising from the outer, the whole embraced by gushing white water that rose in frothing jets from its centre and cascaded from every petal.

'The Tropicana,' I murmured, in awe, realizing I'd almost done Las Vegas the most terrible injustice.

'Also known as the Tiffany of Las Vegas,' nodded Flush. 'It's a beauty. Furnished throughout in French Provincial . . . and their tropical gardens are reckoned to be the most beautiful in the world. They should be – the landscaping cost over a million bucks. And so does every new version of the Folies Bergère! Men, you should *see* those costumes and stage sets.'

Now we swung out of the junction and onto a broad and beautiful dual-carriageway – and immediately we were in the thick of it. Las Vegas Boulevard South . . . the famous Strip. We were blinded, pulverized, devastated by an overwhelming world of light. Lights, lights, lights, of every description . . . street lights, traffic lights, car headlights, and eight billion miles of neon, ten times brighter than the Blackpool Illuminations, a trillion signs each vying for attention . . . advertising hotels, motels, wedding chapels, restaurants, snack bars, food stores, liquor stores, drug stores, fly me, drive him, buy this, drink that . . .

Buzz summed it all up rather succinctly. 'Fuck . . . in' hell!'

'Welcome to the Strip,' laughed Flush. 'We may be gaudy but, by God, we're bright. Over on your left . . . the famous Dunes Hotel – lavish girlie show, The Casino de Paris. If it's tits you're after, that's the place to find 'em – and just about everythin' else you could want, same as in all the other hotels you'll see. That's hotel policy along the Strip – get the punters inside an' keep 'em there. Provide everythin' they could possibly need under one roof from soup to nuts an' there's no reason for them t'step outside.

'Every hotel provides colour T.V. in a beautiful room, a swim-pool or two, restaurants, snackbars, drug store, barber shop, fur salon, jewellery store, candy and magazine counter, clothing store . . . every damn thing a body could need while they're gamblin' away their life's savings, the car, the house and the kids. Who *says* us Yanks ain't smart?'

He winked at the driver in the mirror and the driver guffawed. 'Oh, we're smart all right. I'm so damn smart I sizzle here in the summer an' freeze my balls off in the winter when I could be pushin' cab in beautiful, balmy California.'

'So why doncha?' said Flush.

The driver shook his head. 'Must be the kick I get drivin' all them big winners back to the airport.'

This time Flush guffawed. 'O.K., you guys, you think you've seen a hotel or two, hm? Well, you ain't . . . but there's one comin' up right now on your left . . . Caesar's Palace. Now, *that's* a hotel!'

Buzz and I just gaped, disbelieving what we were seeing.

'Don' that defy description?' grinned Flush.

Well, it did, but I'll have a go.

Imagine an area several city blocks vast and bulldoze it flat. Fence this in on two sides with lines of delicate white arches, twenty feet high, backed by white-stone tracery. In front of these lay walks of emerald grass, and into these plant slender, towering cypress trees, creating twin avenues of breathtaking beauty. Now, between these avenues, landscape a fabulous, one-hundred-yard-long lily pond containing four fountains that shoot illuminated water fifty feet into the air, and when you've done that you've just *started* to build the forecourt of the Caesar's Palace Hotel. Add to all this white marble statuary, a profusion of exotic plant life, and a multi-million-dollar hotel faced with matching, delicate white-stone tracery and . . .

Well, I could go on for another nine pages, but I think maybe you're beginning to get the idea. Think 'MONEY' and you won't be far off. I mean *millions* of money, untold millions, lavishly spent by people with enormous flare for the ultra-spectacular, to whom no detail is unimportant, and for whom no architectural or ethnic theme is sacred. French Provincial, Ancient Rome, Classical Arabia . . . they'll have a go at anything.

This is Las Vegas.

Every foot of the way down that three-mile Strip Buzz and I had our mouths open, gaping at another dozen hotel-casinos that equally defy description.

Firstly, on our right and diagonally opposite Caesar's Palace – the new MGM Grand, a two-thousand-room city with a porti-coed entrance that could have sheltered Caesar's army from the Vegas noon-day sun.

Then, also on the right, the Flamingo . . . the Holiday Inn . . . the Sands . . . the Desert Inn. Now over to the left of the Strip for the New Frontier and the Silver Slipper. Right again for the Royal Las Vegas . . . left again for the Stardust and the un-believable Circus Circus Hotel, fronted by a fantastic mock candy-striped Big Top, constructed in concrete! Right again for the Riviera and the long, low and very illuminated Thunderbird . . . and finally to the end of the Strip and to the Sahara, poised on the right at the junction of the Strip and Sahara Avenue.

But, of course, those were just the hotels! Interspersed be-tween them was a mass of highly-illuminated lesser stuff – shops, restaurants, motels, gas stations, drug stores . . . you name it, it was there, contributing to what I reckoned *then* must surely be the brightest street in the world.

But then I hadn't yet seen Glitter Gulch in *downtown* Vegas.

Anyway, back to the Sahara – really rather a sober-looking member of the elite compared to places like Caesar's Palace and the Stardust.

The taxi drove into the forecourt and drew up under a rigid

canopy, and before we got out a porter was there with a trolley for the luggage.

Refusing a contribution from us, Flush paid off the cab and ushered us in through swing doors and into ... bedlam.

Being conditioned to entering the quiet refinement of 'normal' hotels, it came as nothing less than a shock to find ourselves thrust bang into the heart of a rumbustious gambling casino, which happened, almost incidentally, to incorporate the reception desk of a hotel.

To our left, the casino sprawled away two or three hundred feet, a riot of noise, colour and feverish activity, crowded with punters at the blackjack tables, craps tables and the slot machines.

Over on the right a Wheel of Fortune was in action, its leather tongue rippling the pegs like a football rattle. Also on the right, yet another bank of slot machines ... and also the long reception desk.

With an air of total familiarity, Flush led us to it and hailed a balding receptionist in a tomato-red blazer.

'Max, you ole sonofagun, how you bin?'

'Same as last time,' grinned Max. 'Overworked and grossly underpaid.'

'Coupla buddies of mine off the plane,' said Flush. 'You should have some late bookings for us through TWA ... Malone and Tobin.'

'Sure we got bookings for yuh – two broom closets and a john. What else can you expect at New Year?'

Max went down the desk and returned with some forms, asking Buzz and me for our passports.

While he was checking them and filling in forms, Buzz and I were gaping around the casino, grinning at the noise, the ferocity of the action.

'What time does all this come to a grinding halt?' I asked Flush.

He laughed. 'Never. I told yuh, they're open twenty-four hours a day. Heck, I still don't think you fellas have got the Vegas picture. Look ...' he swept a finger round the casino, 'you see any windows in this place?'

'No ...'

'Don't bother lookin' – there ain't any. Nor in any other casino, either. No windows ... and no clocks. Nothin' to remind the punter what time it is. That's Las Vegas ... the only truly twenty-four-hour city in the world. You want a beefburger in that coffee shop at five in the mornin' – yuh got it.'

I laughed. 'When do the staff sleep?'

'Three shifts – eight hours on, sixteen off.' He shrugged. 'Simple.'

'Here y'are, gents,' said Max, 'just sign your John Henries here and the Sahara's all yours. You're all in the small tower, same floor . . . nice view of the Strip from your rooms. Just follow the porter, he'll show you where.'

'How do we change travellers' cheques?' I asked him.

He pointed down the casino. 'At the cashier's window. And if you've got too much to carry around, we'll rent you a safety-deposit box – free. I'd advise it.'

I said to Buzz. 'We'd better change some now, we can't even tip the porter.'

'I'll come down with you,' said Flush. 'I'm flatter 'n a dollar pancake.'

'Enjoy your stay, gents,' said Max. 'Anythin' you want, just holla.'

We wandered down the casino, passing the blackjack tables. On our left was a raised bar area with a small stage on which a girl singer was belting out 'What Are You Doing The Rest Of Your Life' to a dozen young fellas who looked as though she was what they had in mind.

We moved on, and passed, again on our left, the baccarat table, the aristocrat of any casino, ostentatiously roped off from the rest of the room and set beneath a stately canopy exuding an aura of smug hauteur, like a duchess at a dog race. Fine in the South of France where the clientele dressed like dukes and duchesses, but I couldn't help feeling that the guy sprawled across this one in a hideous Hawaiian shirt and chewing a kingsize cigar was blitzing the ritzy image a bit.

We reached the cashier's window, a long, grilled counter attended by four females all working flat out changing travellers' cheques, bills and plastic chips. Small lines of customers were waiting at each window, so we joined one and had another look around.

Directly in front of the cage were the crap tables.

Even though I'd spent that hairy two weeks with Stud Ryder in and around the casino on Paradise Island and got to know quite a bit about gambling, craps was the one game that had always eluded me.

To a beginner it can seem extremely complicated because there are so many different ways to bet and the action is very fast. There's a Pass Line bet ... Don't Pass Line ... Come ... Don't Come ... Odds ... Place ... Field ... Proposition ... and Hard Way bet – and all at different odds! How the dealer manages to compute the wins and losses, rake in, pay out and keep the game going almost continually just beats me.

Now, as we stood waiting our turn, their voices behind me came as a continuous recitation of totally unintelligible directives ... '... place your come and field bets, ladies and gentlemen. Four. Point's four. Anyone wants odds on the hard one? Seven the winner! Pay the front line. Bets down he's coming out again. Nine! The field loses. New shooter coming out. Bets down. Coming out ... get the odds on eleven ... six! The point is six ... nine – and the point is six. Place your come and field bets ...' on and on and on. They could have been talking Martian.

From our position at the cage I saw that the casino was L-shaped, as spacious round the bend as on the straight. Beyond the dice tables stretched a vast bank of slot machines, maybe a couple of hundred, and beyond them was the poker area, its tables filled to capacity.

Over on my left was an entertainment lounge, an area of tables and chairs facing a raised stage, open to the casino though separated by a rope barrier. The current entertainment, according to the billboard, featured The Drifters, a comedian named Pete Barbutti, and a couple of other acts, though at that moment nothing was happening at all. Perhaps an act had just finished.

Facing us and a little to our right was the entrance to the dinner-show room, the Congo Room, currently featuring comedian Buddy Hackett.

This double form of entertainment was, I later discovered, common to all the Strip hotels – a big, big name starring in the show room, and some excellent, though lesser, names in the free lounge shows.

To give you an idea of the talent then playing Las Vegas, I'd noticed on our drive from the airport that Petula Clark and Anthony Newley were double-billing at Caesar's Palace; Bobby Gentry was playing the Desert Inn; the Riviera was proudly presenting Dean Martin; Danny Thomas was occupying the Copa Room at the Sands; and Vic Damone was wooing them at the New Frontier.

As Flush said – no wonder the dinner shows lose money. You'd have to sell an awful lot of Southern Fried Chicken to pay Tom Jones for two performances a night.

Anyway – back to us.

I cashed two hundred dollars – all the money I had this side of the Atlantic. I had a bit tucked away in the bank in England, but even that was diminishing fast, and one of these days I'd have to stay put in one place for more than a week or two and re-charge the Tobin coffers.

Buzz, who was considerably better heeled, cashed five hundred dollars and turned from the cage with a grin. 'Now I feel more human.'

'How're yuh gonna blow it?' asked Flush. 'Craps . . . black-jack?'

Buzz shook his head. 'Birds – let's find some.'

We headed back towards the reception desk where our porter was impatiently waiting for us.

'This way, gents.'

He led off with his trolley, past the Wheel of Fortune and the bank of slots, towards a corridor at the end of the room . . . but we didn't reach it.

'Russ . . . !'

It was Buzz, ten yards behind, staring up at a monstrous slot machine at least eight feet tall, its handle three feet long with a huge black knob on the end, the size of a coconut.

'Will you look at this!' he laughed. 'Must be the granddaddy of 'em all!'

'They're the ones I told you about,' said Flush. 'The dollar machines – take either a silver "Ike" or a paper Washington.'

Buzz shook his head. 'I've just got to have a go on this.'

'Buzz . . .' I warned.

'Just one, mate, just one.'

He pulled out his roll of notes, peeled off a single dollar, and stuffed the rest back in his pocket.

'Just feed it into the slot there,' said Flush. 'The devil will do the rest.'

Grinning like a schoolkid, Buzz gingerly fed the tip of the note into the opening of the slot, expecting, I suspect, to have to shove it all the way home. But, as though it smelled the presence of money, the machine awoke instantly, jerked alive, then slowly . . . silently . . . smooth as satin . . . sucked the note from his fingers and swallowed it whole.

'Ugh,' Buzz grimaced. 'That was obscene.'

'Well go on – pull the handle.'

Buzz laughed. 'I don't think I dare. I've got a feeling a big steel fist will shoot out and thump me for trying to get my money back.'

Nevertheless he took hold of the huge handle by its giant knob and slowly drew it down. It was like a road barrier descending.

Click.

The machinery whirred into action, sending the four reels of fruit spinning . . . then . . . chunk . . . chunk . . . chunk . . . chunk. All stopped.

Two cherries!

He'd won!

Clatter . . . clatter. Into the catchment tray dropped two big silver dollars, the first I'd ever seen.

Buzz let out a whoop and scooped them out. 'Well, how about that! A hundred percent profit already!'

Flush grinned. 'An' if you've got any sense, you'll quit now while you're ahead.'

'Boy, do these feel good,' said Buzz, weighing the dollars in his hand. 'Now, that's what I call a coin.'

'You'll be feelin' a lot of them in the next coupla days,' said Flush. 'Every casino restaurant and coffee shop will slip you a couple in your change.' He tapped his head. 'It's all part of the big con. Silver dollars are too damn heavy to carry around in your pocket, so the temptation is to get rid of 'em in the first available machine. And, gents, you will note that this machine just *happens* to be . . . right outside the coffee shop, there.'

Buzz laughed. 'Well, I'll be damned.'

'Yessir, you most likely will be – same as everyone else. Come on, you guys, the porter looks meaner 'n a burro with a burr.'

We followed the porter at a half-run down the long corridor towards the elevators.

'Out there,' said Flush, pointing to the windows on our right, 'are the swimpools – as crowded as the casino during the summer . . . and on your left, here – The House of Lords – one of the best restaurants in town. If yuh decide to eat there, just tell the maître d' that Flush Foley sent yuh . . . an' he'll probably throw you out!'

It was a very long corridor, accommodating some beautiful shops: magazine and souvenir, women's clothing, men's clothing, hairdressers, candy counter, fur salon, antiques, jewellery, and even an indoor amusement arcade – everything, as Flush had said, a guest could need.

One of two elevators took us up to the sixth floor. Two right turns and the porter was showing Buzz and me into Room 1623 (a quaint number for the sixth floor but I'm sure they had their reasons), and it was a beauty – decorated in orange and white, with white-oak furniture, two easy chairs, huge reading lamps and a coloured T.V. And, of course, its own bathroom.

As the porter left, Flush popped his head in. 'Everythin' O.K.?'

'Terrific,' we said.

'Well, see you fellas later. I've gotta move to the Thunderbird kinda fast. Play it cool, chaps,' he grinned, putting on an English accent, '. . . an' watch out for them wooden nickels.'

'Thanks a million, Flush,' said Buzz. 'And good luck in the tournament. Keep us posted.'

'Will do. So long.'

Buzz closed the door and heaved a sigh of contentment. 'Well, son . . . we're here.'

'In wild Las Vegas. Never thought I'd see it.'

He crossed to the window, drew back the orange drapes, cranked open one part of the four-part window and hung out on his elbows. I went to the other end and did the same. Being on the extreme right side of the hotel, we were now looking back on the Strip though from some considerable distance, the Sahara complex being extremely deep.

In front of us stretched a huge empty lot of desert scrub, land worth untold millions on which, one day, yet another super-deluxe hotel would be built.

Over to our right, perhaps a quarter of a mile away, we could see the candy-striped confection of the Circus Circus Hotel, also our next-door neighbour, the Thunderbird; but the rest of the hotels along the Strip were lost in the glittering, flickering amazement of neon.

Over to our left, perhaps a mile away along a secondary road running parallel to the Strip, stood two more hotels – the immense Hilton International and the Landmark, the latter designed in the shape of an electric torch standing on its base.

Unbelievable.

For quite a while Buzz and I just stared at it all, trying to absorb the enormity of the operation – the cost, the nerve, the imagination that had built this Disneyland for adults slap in the middle of the most hostile, Godforsaken desert country imaginable. Then, with a disbelieving shake of his head, he chuckled, 'I'll tell you, mate, only the Yanks could have done it. Can you imagine a Pom building Circus Circus or Caesar's Palace?'

I laughed. 'If the English had built the Strip it would've finished up looking like New Brighton front. The casinos would be open from ten in the morning till six at night, with two hours off for lunch. "Wot – tea and sandwiches at *nine* o'clock at night! Oh, no, love – can't get the staff you know. Come back at ten tomorrow . . . no, sorry, tomorrow's Wednesday, we're closed all day Wednesday." '

'Right,' laughed Buzz. 'And on Thursday they'd be out of bread! Well, come on, son, let's get tarted up and get out of here. I want an eyeful of all this.'

We unpacked quickly, then Buzz went into the bathroom for a shower.

'Hey, mate . . . !'

I went to the door.

'Just look at this . . . four plastic drinking glasses – all individually wrapped in sanitized paper for your personal comfort . . . and an ice-bucket! This is a twenty-seven star hotel!'

'I'm going to try the tele, see what's on. Hurry up, eh.'

I returned to the bedroom.

'Hey, Buzz . . . there's a notice here advertising free gambling lessons on T.V.'

'Do I need lessons to shove a dollar bill in a Big Bertha! I tell you, I felt a distinct affinity with that machine. I reckon winning first time was an omen!'

I groaned. 'And that's just what the management *wants* you to reckon.'

'No, man, I've got a feeling. I think Big Bertha's going to cough up a dollar or two for Buzz before we leave Vegas.'

'Sure, she is – and I think Buzz is going to cough up a dollar or three to Big Bertha. Buzz . . . you're getting hooked!'

His reply was lost in the rush of water, but I think it was rude.

I sat on the bed, thinking how easy it would be to get hooked on gambling in Vegas, surrounded by it all the time as you were. Me I wasn't worried about. With only a little over two hundred dollars in the kitty the problem took care of itself.

But Buzz . . . he was pretty loaded. He'd had a good tennis tour before I'd met him on the New York train and I reckon he had a fair old wad on him. I just hoped he didn't get bitten by the bug. The thought of a Big Bertha breaking him was not nice to contemplate.

Well, as things turned out, I wasn't far wrong – just in one minor direction.

Big Bertha didn't break Buzz . . . Buzz knocked the hell out of a Big Bertha!

But that wasn't until the *following* night.

First let me tell you about this one!

THREE

With all due modesty, as we stepped out of that hotel room we did look *pre*-tty snazzy. Buzz had on a green weave jacket, a lighter green shirt, pale biscuit tie and matching slacks. And I was wearing a deep-brown jacket with oatmeal accessories and dark tie.

A very sexy-looking duo.

That we were non-American probably stood out a mile, because we both wear our hair longer than most Americans, who, apart from the hippies, do generally tend more towards short-back-and-sides. And whether or not it was our hair-length that finally got us into so much trouble, I don't know, but it's a possibility. Then again, with our luck, we'd have probably landed in it even if we'd been bald! We seem to have that sort of luck.

Anyway, there we were, strolling out of the Sahara feeling ready for anything.

'Where to first?' Buzz asked.

'Why not just start walking and see what comes?'

'Yeah, why not?'

We crossed the Sahara forecourt and got onto the Strip, and once again had to stop and stare in amazement.

37

'Good God, just look at it,' gasped Buzz. 'How many bulbs d'you reckon are in that lot?'

I shook my head. 'Billions.'

I wasn't far wrong. We learned later that a whole army of men is employed along the Strip, just to replace burned-out bulbs. Long hours, the guy complained, but at least the work was light. Yes, well . . .

We started walking.

It's not only the only way to really *see* the place, it is also the only way to get very sore feet.

After half an hour, Buzz came to a sudden halt. 'I need a drink . . . and I also need a cab. My dogs are killing me.'

Actually we hadn't done badly. We'd passed the Thunderbird, Circus Circus, Riviera, had stood for five minutes watching the fantastic lighting programme of the Stardust sign, had dawdled at the Silver Slipper admiring its giant revolving silver slipper sign, and were now standing beneath the tallest free-standing sign in the world – the two-hundred-foot colossus of the New Frontier.

And we were beat.

Buzz stuck two fingers in his mouth and let go an ear-piercer, and eight cabs came to a screeching halt.

Five minutes later we were driving down the fountained approach to Caesar's Palace and drawing up at the opulent front door.

'Welcome to the pad,' said Buzz, pausing on the top step to look back down the avenue of fountains. 'Come in and meet the gang.'

'Sounds like you've quite a party going on.'

'No, just a few of the lads in for a quiet poker session.'

The joke became hilarious as we crossed the small foyer and were suddenly confronted by the casino. To a man there were nine trillion people jammed in there.

'*Holy* . . .' gaped Buzz. 'Hey, somebody's gate-crashed!'

The room was endless and unbelievably opulent, its ceiling a cascade of chandeliers, a palace from wall to distant wall – though whether Caesar would have approved is another matter.

For one thing the noise was fearsome, a far – and deafening – cry from old Julius's pad, even on the Ides of March when he was getting the knife from the lads.

It emanated from the hearty yanking of a thousand slot-

machine handles, from coins crashing into tin trays, from bells
ringing, punters laughing, shouting, cursing, and from dealers
cracking their commands at a multitude of betting tables.

It was pure, plush mayhem.

'Not much like the Winter Gardens, Hoylake!' I grinned.

He laughed. 'Shall we risk a plunge?'

'Plunge on, I'm right behind you!'

We descended several steps into the casino, at once feeling like
members of the Liverpool Kop at a Cup Final, and slowly ad-
vanced across the vast room, taking in sights and sounds,
snatches of conversation, facial contortions, clothes, hair-styles
and the shape of bodies. Here alone was a source of endless entertainment and it didn't cost a cent.

Buzz turned, grinned, and nodded to a tall, slender Negress
adorned with a flaming red Afro hairdo that changed to green as
it reached her forehead, her eyelashes three inches long and
battery-powered ear-rings that flashed on and off.

I laughed . . . dug Buzz on the arm. 'The waitress!'

She was beautiful . . . attired in a micro toga outfit, white
trimmed with gold, one shoulder bare, her hair piled in a cone.

'And another . . .!' he pointed. 'The place is lousy with 'em!
And to think we wasted an hour getting here!'

On the far side of the room we entered an arcade of exquisite
shops. Buzz stopped, let out a guffaw. 'Blimey – only the Yanks
could think *that* up, too!'

'What?'

'The name of that coffee shop – the "Noshorium"! Christ,
Caesar must be worn out turning in his bloody grave.'

We strolled down the arcade, admiring the merchandise – the
clothes, the fur salon, the jewellery shop.

Then, at the souvenir shop, they went and spoiled it all.

Again Buzz stopped and clutched my arm. 'Hey . . . can you
believe *that* . . . in *here*?'

It was, unbelievably, a display of clear-plastic lavatory seats,
embedded with U.S. coins . . . dollar bills . . . coloured butter-
flies.

I burst out laughing. 'The Glory That Was Rome. Mark
Antony would have a bleeding fit.'

'Come on, I need a drink!'

We returned to the casino, our eyes now bulging constantly
at the wealth of femininity that surrounded us . . . waitresses

and Keno girls in micro-skirted get-ups, neck-lines plunging to the navel ... punters, hunters, hookers and lookers, tall, short, thin, fat; smart, scraggy, svelte and baggy, and of every race, colour, religion and inclination you could put a name to.

'Russ ...' Buzz's voice came to me as a hoarse, tremulous whimper.

'Yes, Buzz?'

'I think I shall go blind. Did you ever *see* so many birds in one place?'

'Only in Snowdon's aviary.'

'Look ... the blonde over there ...!'

'The brunette over there ...!'

'Dig the red-head in the kaftan!'

'I'd love to – after the belter in the purple T-shirt.'

'Let's find a bar ... I need to sit down!'

'This way.'

Well, we found it ... I mean, there just *had* to be a Cleopatra's Barge, didn't there?

Only it wasn't *just* a stupendously decorated fifty-foot replica of the old girl's boat with a massive, gold, enormously-boobed figurehead of Cleo herself jutting out from the prow over the walk-way, but the whole damn thing was a cocktail bar actually floating in a tank of water! I swear it!

And furthermore, it was moving – gently rolling, motivated, I presumed, by some hidden hydraulic device.

On board, beneath a raised sail, a five-piece combo was bashing out 'Honeysuckle Rose' for the entertainment of the customers seated not only on the boat, but also on the 'dock', while a battery of Nubian-inspired waitresses, every one a busty beauty, served the drinks.

'My sainted aunt ...' chuckled Buzz. 'If Cleo could clap her eyes on this, she'd stick that asp up her knickers and chuck herself overboard. Come on, son, let's have a giggle.'

To board the ship, it was necessary to go through the dock area, and as we entered it we were approached by a tall, dark-haired lass in a long, white, flowing, one-shouldered Egyptian gown that showed up her knockers a treat. She flashed us a smile that lit up the room.

'Hi! You'd like a drink?'

'And a trip up your Nile,' grinned Buzz.

Her smile faltered.

'I mean . . . we'd like to sit on the barge,' he added quickly.

'Oh!' Her smile returned. She glanced across at the boat. 'Yes, there's a table there . . . go right through.'

We made our way between the tables, crossed the gangplank, and were greeted by another dark-haired beauty wearing enough mascara to re-paint the boat.

'Hi . . . table for two?'

'Yes,' said Buzz. 'Cleo sent us – said to mention her name for a good seat.'

She sighed wearily. 'If I had a dollar for every time that's been cracked, I'd own the joint. This way . . .'

'Charmed,' Buzz winked at me.

She gave us a table by the rail, overlooking the dock.

'What can I get you?'

'Two returns to Cairo,' said Buzz, purposely annoying her.

'Sir . . .' she sighed.

'I know, you're busy. O.K., scotch for me . . .'

'Vodka tonic,' I told her.

She departed.

'Pleasant soul,' remarked Buzz. 'If I didn't know she hadn't any on, I'd say *she* had an asp up her knickers.'

I gave him a cigarette, lit up, and turned to give the tables on the dock the once over.

'Buzz . . .' I said, looking beyond the walk-way to the entrance of a Japanese restaurant, 'correct me if I'm wrong, but I do not recall an Ah So Steak House ever featuring in the history of ancient Rome.'

'Sure it did. Caesar owned it. And as he crumpled to the floor, having got the chop from the lads, in his dying gasp he left the place to them.'

'He did?'

'Sure. He looked up at them and croaked, "And Ah So's to you lot, too." '

'Rude, that . . . hey . . .'

He nodded. 'I've seen them . . . the two over by the lotus pillar?'

'Not bad, hm?'

'Coupla flaming tigers, mate.'

A fitting description. They were both coloured girls, café-au-lait with two big lumps of sugar, very lithe and very pretty, both dressed in jeans and T-shirts, one orange, one green.

They were laughing a lot, displaying magnificent teeth, toying with their drinks like their hearts weren't really in it while sweeping the room for talent with their dark, limpid eyes.

They'd seen us all right.

'Very nice,' murmured Buzz. 'They're certainly hunting.'

'Worth a drink for a closer look?'

'Sure, why not? Anything's better than drinking with you all night.'

'Agreed. Who goes over?'

'You spotted them first.'

'Knickers. We'll toss for it.'

'I've got a better idea. We'll send a note over with the waitress.'

'The man's a genius.'

I fished out an old dry-cleaning ticket and wrote on the back: 'We're sailing in three minutes – would you care to join us on a cruise round the Mediteranean? Russ Tobin – Captain.'

At that moment Egyptian Joyce returned with our drinks. 'That'll be three dollars.'

'Miss, would you be very kind and deliver this note to the two young ladies sitting over there by the pillar?'

She shrugged.

I gave her four dollars and away she went.

We followed her progress. She handed the girls the note, turned and nodded in our direction. The one in the orange T-shirt took it, read it, laughed, showed it to her pal . . . then they looked over and gave us a little wave.

'We're in,' gulped Buzz.

'Blimey.'

'Hey up, they're coming.'

They sauntered across the gangplank, moving easily, very relaxed. Buzz stood up, I followed . . . turned. Crikey, they were nearly as tall as me! Lithe, slender, sensuous creatures, narrow hips and terrific breasts, their nipples showing clearly beneath their thin cotton shirts.

The one in the orange was in the lead.

'Hi,' she smiled, her eyes flickering lazily between Buzz and me.

'Thank you for coming,' grinned Buzz, his cool up around four hundred degrees Centigrade. 'We'd have come over personally but we wanted to give you a chance to refuse.'

'Hey, now . . .' she laughed, turning to her pal, 'that was nice. This is Josie Jones . . . I'm Angela Woolfit.'

I'll bet, I thought.

She looked between us. 'And which of you two is the guy that can't spell?'

'Mm?' I said. 'I wrote the note.'

'You're Captain Russ Tobin, hm?' she grinned. 'Some captain – can't even spell Mediterranean. It has two "r"s.'

'Oh.'

'I'm Buzz Malone,' he said, offering his hand. 'Won't you sit down?'

'Well . . .' said Josie, 'as it's likely to be a long trip . . .'

We sat, Josie on my left, Angela on my right, very close. Strange, isn't it, in looks there was nothing to choose between them, they were both very attractive girls, similar in build and style, yet straight off I knew it was going to be Angela and me.

'You're English, hm?' she asked, accepting a cigarette.

'I am – Buzz is Australian.'

Josie gave a gasp. 'Australian! Well, whadya know! I was over there only last year!'

Buzz laughed. 'Good God, were you really? Where? Doing what?'

'Water skiing . . . surfing! I belong to the California Cresters team, we did a world tour – *and* beat the pants off you!'

'Well, I'll be damned. Were you in Sydney?'

'Of course . . .!'

'That's my home town! Well, I'll be damned . . .'

Which pretty well took care of those two! Within the space of one drink they were so close you couldn't have pried them apart with a crowbar . . . sport . . . sport . . . sport!

Angela pulled a face at me. 'You mad about sports, Tobin?'

'Only indoor.'

She laughed. 'I see.'

'I mean . . . snooker, Scrabble – that sort of thing.'

Her eyes flashed. 'Yeah, I'll bet. Tell me, what are you two doing in Vegas? Is this your first visit? What d'you think of it? Isn't it the craziest town?'

'Well,' I laughed, 'we only arrived a couple of hours ago . . . it *is* our first visit, and we're not even supposed to be here. We were flying from Toronto to Sydney, with a drop-down in Los

Angeles, but we hit an air-pocket over the Grand Canyon that shook us up a bit . . .'

'And here you are.'

'And here we are . . . thanking whoever put that air-pocket up there for putting it up there because we are having a great time. And, yes, it *is* the craziest, most incredible . . . unbelievable . . . well . . .'

'Lost for words?'

'Yes . . . but would you like another drink?'

'Lord, Ah tho't you'd *nevah* ask.'

We managed to get Egyptian Joyce back again and ordered four more – the girls were drinking Singapore Slings, tall orange jobs they sucked up through straws. Then we settled back again into the chat – Buzz and Josie kibitzing with each other about the relative merits of the American and Australian surfing teams, Angela and I playing visual games with each other, everything nice and easy but making steady progress, as it should be on vacation with so little time to waste on long drawn-out preliminaries and with so many more worthwhile things to do.

'Tell me about you,' I said. 'How long have you two been here?'

She held up two long, elegant fingers. 'Two days – though we didn't come together. We just met at the motel.'

'You came in for the New Year?'

She grinned. 'What else?'

'Have you been here before?'

'About nine thousand times.' She laughed. 'Well, maybe six hundred. I live in L.A. This is our local playground.'

'So I hear.'

'Forbidden City. This is where all the bored housewives come to buy two dollarsworth of wickedness at the slots . . . and all the bored husbands come to play James Bond for a couple of days.'

I laughed. 'Is that true?'

'Sure, it's true. It's an exciting, naughty town.'

'Really naughty?'

Her eyes half-closed. '*Very* naughty. How . . . long are you staying – until the plane is ready, I guess?' she said, seeming to change the subject.

'No, Buzz and I have decided to stay on an extra day, for New

44

Year. We'll be leaving on the evening of the first, I imagine. TWA is arranging a flight.'

'Only two days. Not nearly enough time to see everything. There's a lot more to Vegas than just the Strip, you know. You heard about Glitter Gulch?'

'Downtown Vegas, yes, we heard about it.'

She laughed. 'You think the Strip is bright! Wait till you see Fremont Street.'

'I'd like to,' I said pointedly. 'How d'you fancy being an innocent's guide for an evening?'

She shrugged and glanced at Josie who had overheard us and now asked Buzz, 'Would you like that?'

'What – a foursome? Sure, I'd like it. You girls can help keep us out of trouble.'

'Oh?' grinned Josie. 'Are you in the habit of getting into it?'

'Well . . .' Buzz scratched his nose, 'it has been known.'

'We'll do our best,' said Josie, 'but no guarantees.'

'I should hope not,' laughed Buzz.

The drinks arrived and we drifted back into separate conversation.

'What do you do in L.A.?' I asked Angela.

She paused to suck up some Singapore Sling, pursing her beautiful, soft, warm, moist and mobile mouth most sexily around the straw and I thought what a crime to waste all that on a straw.

Her eyes flicked up, catching me watching her mouth, and the slow, amused smile she gave tripled my heartbeat, causing me to wonder whether the sexuality of the suck had been unconscious or blatantly premeditated.

'Oh,' she said lightly, 'I'm just a plain old secretary for a real estate company.'

'That's rich.'

'What is?'

'You . . . being a plain old anything. Do you like it?'

'What . . .? Oh, the job . . .' she shrugged. 'A girl's got to eat.'

'I know the feeling. As you Americans say – I've been there.'

'Doing what?'

'All sorts of things. Right now I'm touring the world, investigating life.'

'For any particular reason?'

Somehow, I felt compelled to lie. 'I'm . . . writing a book.'
Buzz choked on his drink.

Her eyes lit up. 'You're an author!'

'Well . . .'

'Well, you've certainly come to the right place for material.'

'You obviously know Vegas very well.'

'I ought to – the number of times I've been here.'

'Maybe you can give me some pointers?'

She took hold of the straw again and pursed for another suck.
'Sure, what d'you want to know?'

'Well . . . is it really as wild as they make out?'

'Wilder,' she said, accepting another cigarette. 'You know, of
course, that the Mob really started Las Vegas, don't you?'

'The Mafia? Is that really true?'

'Sure, it's true. It really was a nothing town until Bugsy
Siegel moved in in 1946 and built the "fabulous" Flamingo.
That was the beginning of the big time, though there were a
couple of hotels here before the Flamingo. Poor old Bugsy . . .
he didn't live long enough to see much progress, though.'

'Why, what happened to him?'

'He was bumped off by "the boys" in 1947 – at his home in
Beverly Hills.'

'Whatever for?'

'He went berserk on the Flamingo, cost the Mob a lot of
money. So they shot him through the window while he was
watching T.V.'

'Good God . . . boy, it's hard to believe they exist outside
fiction. And do they still run Vegas?'

She shrugged. 'Who knows? Most of the big hotels are owned
by huge corporations nowadays, but who's behind these corporations is anybody's guess. There is *one* hotel reputed to be still
owned by the Mob, though . . .'

'Oh, which one's that?'

Her slow smile was a tease. 'The one you're sitting in right
now.'

'Th . . . this one? Caesar's Palace?'

'Sure.'

Instinctively I glanced around, expecting to see 'Horse Face'
Licavoli and Jake 'Greasy Thumb' Guzik lurking in the shadows,
armpits bulging, watching the action through reptilian slits.

Angela laughed. 'You realize, of course, that you've just contributed about twelve dollars to the Mafia coffers, don't you?'

'Blimey! Hey, Buzz . . .'

He stuck his fag in the corner of his mouth and drawled, 'Take it easy, Blue Eyes, I intend hittin' the boys later where it really hoits – right in the Big Bertha. I'm gonna knock the stilts from un'er their Vegas operation or my name ain't One-Arm Malone!'

'Buzz has accepted the big dollar slots as a personal challenge,' I explained to the girls.

Angela nodded. 'And I'm sure the casino bosses will be delighted to hear it. There *are* easier ways of getting rid of your money, Buzz – like setting fire to it – but not many.'

'Never you mind,' insisted Buzz. 'I've got an affinity with those things. I'm going to make them cough up *something*.'

'Well, hang on to your air-ticket,' smiled Angela. 'It's a long, wet walk to Sydney.'

The conversation broke up again, Angela and I talking about gambling, the Mob . . . and finally getting around to the inevitable . . . sex.

'How wide open is Las Vegas regarding . . . well, girls,' I asked her.

'As the proverbial barn door,' she smiled. 'Two things Vegas has in greater quantity than any other city – money and the availability of sex. There isn't any particular district for it, not like most big cities, it's just all over. They do say that over ten percent of the resident population is engaged in it – one way or another.'

'Ten percent!'

'Sure . . . bartenders, cab drivers, bellhops, pit bosses . . . you name him, he can find you a girl. And if you're a high roller – a big gambler – he'll find you two – on the house.'

'Call girls, I suppose?'

'Not necessarily. A lot of the chorus girls and cocktail waitresses in these hotels will . . .' she grinned, '. . . "put out", as they say, for a high roller – as a favour to the management. In some places, show girls have to sit in the lounge for an hour before each performance to "pretty up the room", as it's called. What they're really doing is whetting the appetites of the punters who have just seen them on the stage practically nude. It's just another way of bringing in business.'

'And do these girls *have* to "put out"?'

'No-o-o,' she drawled, cynically. 'They can refuse. But if they do, they've got to watch out the door doesn't hit 'em between the shoulder blades on their way out!'

'Good God, they get the boot?'

'There's always a dozen more waiting outside to take their place.'

'Why – for the money? Do they earn good money?'

'Good?' she laughed. 'Probably the most lucrative job in Vegas is cocktail waitress in one of the Strip hotels. The basic salary isn't much – only a few dollars a day – but they can earn ten times as much in tips. The best position is in the "pit", where the drinks are free for the gamblers. There's so much money lying around there, a punter will throw anything onto her tray – especially when he's winning. I know a couple of pit girls who make a thousand . . . two thousand bucks a week regularly.'

I gaped. 'Two thou . . . good God, that's seven hundred pounds a week!'

'In any currency, it's a *lot* of bread. I must say I've been kinda tempted to try the job myself, but . . . well, I don't care for all the strings that go with it. When I "put out", I need to like the guy I'm putting out for – not die the death when he sheds his clothes.'

'Y . . . yes, quite . . .' I said, getting all choked up at the prospect. 'Er . . .'

'The more attractive girls,' she went on, as though nothing had happened, 'operate from phone calls from the pit bosses. They entertain the high rollers while the casino is emptying their pockets. They stand beside the punter and encourage him to bet – and also steal his chips at the same time. They've got to be careful, though . . . naturally the gambler wouldn't like it but neither do the pit bosses – on account of she's stealing money eventually destined for the house.'

I laughed and shook my head. 'Boy, how the other half lives . . . and I thought I'd been around. Vegas makes me feel this is my first day out in the world. Fascinating, though.'

'Oh, the stories I could tell you about this place . . . you could fill a library, never mind a book. One of the most famous "pit girls" ever was a chick named Ruth Walker – she used to operate from the old El Rancho Vegas Hotel before it burned down in 1960.

She started as a cigarette girl and within two years owned a fabulous home, a new Cadillac, countless fur stoles and a 20,000 dollar mink. Ruth used to earn around 10,000 dollars a month back in *those* days.'

'What . . . just from encouraging men to gamble?'

'Well, there's gambling and gambling, honey. These cookies thought nothing of dropping 100,000 bucks at the tables over a week-end.'

I winced. 'Angela, you're talking Monopoly money.'

'Oh, a hundred grand isn't all that much in Vegas. One Mississippi gambler paid for Ruth's home *and* spent a quarter of a million dollars on her besides. And I'll tell you . . .' she said, sucking up the last of the Singapore Sling, 'one of the Strip Hotels had their best-ever casino turn-over last month . . . like to guess how much bread changed hands . . .?'

I shook my head. 'Not the vaguest.'

'Seven million dollars . . .'

I groaned.

'. . . and most of it was lost by just *five* men. An Arab oil prince dropped a cool million and a quarter . . . a Japanese executive contributed another million . . . and the rest was donated by three Oklahoma oilmen.'

'Bloo . . . dy hell!' This was Buzz, who had caught the conversation. 'No wonder oil quadrupled last year.'

'You know,' I sighed, 'I've got the feeling that if we stayed in Vegas for six months we'd only just scratch the surface of what goes on here. I'm already beginning to feel battered by the enormity of the operation . . . and this has all sprouted in the last – what – only thirty years?'

Angela nodded. 'And it's getting bigger all the time. One of the next hotels to go up will be the Mark Antony – same group as Caesar's Palace . . .'

'Naturally,' I grinned. 'And where are they going to build that?'

'On the present Thunderbird site – and probably extending over the empty lot between the Thunderbird and the Sahara.'

'We know it well,' smiled Buzz. 'Our room overlooks it.'

'And I suppose . . .' I said, '. . . that the Mark Antony will be the biggest, tallest, longest, deepest, most extravagantly luxurious pad on the Strip?'

Angela was nodding before I'd finished. 'Sure – for at least a month. But there are two more being planned now – the McCarran International and The Las Vegas Hostelry. God *knows* what they'll be like. As of this moment the MGM Grand is billed as the largest resort hotel *in the world*, but I wouldn't give much for its chances in another year or two. The way things are going, Caesar's Palace is going to end up looking like a Downtown fleabag!'

'Angela – another drink?'

'Well . . . if we're going to show you guys Downtown, couldn't we save it till then?'

'Sure. Josie, how about you?'

'I agree. Let's hit the road. But first . . . a quick call at the Powder Room.'

'I'll second that,' said Buzz.

We parted company at the door of the ladies' loo and made our way to the gents'.

'Well, mate,' grinned Buzz, zipping down. 'What d'you reckon?'

'I think things are going *extremely* well. How are things with Josie?'

'Promising,' he nodded. 'Christ, she's had her hand on my knee for ten minutes.'

'Oh-*ho*-di-ho-di-ho . . . well, how're we going to play it?'

'In our inimitable style, Tobin – by ear. We'll have a little playaround in Glitter Gulch, spend a few bob on them, and see what transpires . . .'

'Yeah, Buzz, about that . . .'

'Yes, mate?'

'Hell, I hate to bring it up, you've been so damned generous already, but after hearing about those guys losing seven million, I do feel inordinately bare-assed with only two hundred and something to last me for two nights. I was wondering . . .'

'Say no more,' he commanded, giving it a shake and zipping up. 'Two hundred is bloody ridiculous for two nights in this town. See how you go, mate, and when you want some more – shout.'

'As an *advance*, let's make it clear. As soon as I get to Sydney I'll wire England and . . .'

'Tobin, will you shut up. Hell, if I hadn't met you I'd have been home by now and missed all this fun. I *owe* you, son . . .'

'Well, balls, but thanks a lot. Oh, boy . . . if this ain't going to be the best New Year I ever spent, my name's not Russell "Greasy Thumb" Tobin.'

'Kin-ky,' he frowned.

FOUR

The girls emerged from the loo all spruced up and ready for action, Angela now wearing a fresh squirt of scent that clobbered me between the eyes and made me her slave for the night.

'You . . .' I said, offering my arm, 'smell divine. What's it called?'

' "Lunatic Asylum",' she cracked. 'It's supposed to drive men nuts.'

'You know something . . . it works.'

'Good,' she laughed, taking my arm.

We walked back through the crowded casino section and hailed a waiting cab. One lovely thing about Vegas, there are eighteen taxis to every person which makes a nice change from the reverse London ratio. Then we were riding back along the Strip towards the Downtown section.

'With all this money floating around,' I said to Angela, 'I suppose there's a never-ending campaign by crooks and con-artists to relieve the casinos of it the easy way.'

'Oh, sure. All the casinos have their own security cops.'

'Has there ever been a big casino robbery?' Buzz asked.

She shook her head. 'If there has, it never leaked out – the casino bosses would see to that in case it encouraged others to try. The big problem – for the crooks – is the desert. Once you're out of Vegas there's just nowhere to hide. The cops can throw up road-blocks in minutes, then you've had it.'

'How about a helicopter?' I suggested.

She shrugged. 'I guess the same thing applies. It's nearly three hundred miles to L.A. – and with radar and their own helicopters, the cops could pick you off before you'd gone ten miles.'

'Tough,' I said. 'Buzz, we'll have to think of somethin' else.'

'It's a cinch, Blue Eyes . . . we don't *leave* town, see? After the heist we stay here and double the money gamblin', then leave respectable.'

'And what if we lose it all back?'

'Then we hit 'em again! It could go on forever but think of the fun we'd have losin' *their* money!'

I grinned, and said to Angela, 'How about conmen? I imagine there're one or two around?'

'One or two thousand, the place is swarming with them, though they usually try conning the tourists rather than the casinos. There was one team, though, that tried to "fix" a craps table – and almost succeeded. A couple of them, posing as repair men, actually took a table out of a casino! Then they installed a metal plate under it and returned it. A couple of nights later two other members of the gang went in – one of them in a high-powered battery wheelchair which he plugged into the table, creating an electro-magnetic field, then the other guy slipped a pair of loaded dice into the game and they were all set to clean up.'

'Ingenious,' I grinned.

'What happened?' asked Buzz.

She laughed. 'Well, before they could get going, the electric connection developed a short . . . and the table began to get hot! And it got so hot the dealers couldn't even pick up the silver dollars! Then it started to smoke and that was when the crooks decided it was time for a diplomatic withdrawal. They didn't make it, though . . . they were caught before they reached the door.'

'E for Effort, by golly,' said Buzz. 'Vegas must be a heck of a temptation for a dedicated pro.'

'Oh, they still manage to cream off hundreds of thousands of dollars a year,' Angela went on. 'In all sorts of ways – from milking slot machines to employing waitresses to steal chips.'

'She just pinches them off the tables?' I asked.

'Sure . . . some of them use adhesive on the bottom of an empty glass. They put the glass down on, say, a hundred-dollar chip and walk off with it – probably head straight for the powder room and hand it over to an accomplice or stash it away till later. Any method you can put a mind to – they use.'

Buzz shook his head. 'A hairy old town, Russell.'

'Yeah, I reckon I'd last about three minutes here by myself. Angela, I think I'll employ you as bodyguard until we get back on the plane.'

'It's a deal,' she laughed. 'Whatever you do, don't go buying any "infallible gambling systems".'

Buzz frowned. 'Aw, come on – they don't really expect to sell an infallible gambling system.'

'Ha! You'd be *amazed* at what they do sell people – from vacant building lots to shares in a Strip hotel. This is Sucker Town, U.S.A. and as long as you've got a dollar in your pocket, there'll be somebody trying to separate you from it – one way or another.'

'Well, thanks for the tip,' he said. 'We'll keep our eyes open.' He winked at me. 'Here are two suckers that're going to disappoint them very badly.'

Oh, boy . . . how wrong can a guy *be*!

But that sad, sad story I'll get to later.

We had now passed the Sahara Hotel and were running into a part of town ten points lower on the Posh Scale than the Strip, an area of blousy, haphazard, low-storeyed buildings with none of the chic luxury we'd so far encountered.

A block or two more and suddenly we were in the thick of it – a street ablaze with neon, an eye-blasting hurdy-gurdy of a thoroughfare, sizzling with flashing, blinking, winking, rippling light. Glitter Gulch, Nevada . . . the brightest, brassiest, razziest street in the world.

'What time do the lights come on?' winced Buzz. '*Holy* cow, would you just *look* at that lot!'

We paid the cab and stood on the pavement, Buzz and I gawping about us like a couple of country boys, staring up at the huge Golden Nugget sign . . . along the street to where the famous fifty-foot neon cowboy was waving us into the Pioneer Club . . . and everywhere there were signs . . . signs . . . signs, a bewildering maze of them, advertising everything your heart could desire . . . food, loans, wigs, motel, hotel, free parking . . . topless dancers, lucky jackpots, souvenirs, win, win . . . WIN!

'Would you like to see all of this from the air?' Angela asked mysteriously. 'Come . . .'

We followed.

'Helicopter?' I asked her.

She grinned. 'Nope.'

'Aeroplane?'

'Nope.'

'Hot air balloon?'

'Nope.'

'Springs?'

She laughed. 'Nope.'

'You don't talk much, do you?'

'Nope.'

Behind us, Buzz was pursuing the same line of questioning with an equally evasive Josie.

We walked along Fremont Street and turned suddenly into the entrance of the Mint Hotel. Again, as in the Strip hotels, it was straight into casino bedlam . . . slot machines, blackjack tables, Wheels of Fortune, bewildering the mind that so much gambling could go on in so many places twenty-four hours a day. Didn't these people ever get sick of yanking slot handles, throwing dice, checking Keno tickets . . .?

'Over here,' ordered Angela.

We crossed the casino and finally came to a halt at what I presumed was an elevator.

'Prepare to have your mind blown,' she commanded.

'You're too late – it was blown the moment I smelled that perfume.'

'That was the object of the exercise.'

The elevator door opened, operated from inside by an old guy on a stool. It was a very small elevator. Six people came out; we four got in and it was almost full.

The doors behind me closed.

'Face that way,' said Angela, pointing towards the doors.

'I'd rather face you.'

'Do as you're told – face that way.'

I shrugged, pretending huff. 'O.K., if that's the way you feel.'

As I turned, she pinched my bottom.

The elevator started its slow climb . . . then suddenly there were no doors in front of us any more . . . no building! Just a glassed-in view of Glitter Gulch. The elevator was climbing up the outside of the hotel!

Buzz chuckled. 'Well, I'll be damned . . .'

I turned to Angela. 'Tricky, that. Got any more surprises up your sleeve?'

'If I told you, it wouldn't be a surprise, would it? Watch the view.'

Up . . . and up . . . twenty-five storeys to an ever widening panorama of dazzling Las Vegas.

A moment later and we were inside the Top Of The Mint restaurant, in its Embassy Room, a place for drinking and dancing and sitting by the huge windows and watching the view below.

'Fancy a drink here?' asked Angela.

'I fancy everything here,' I told her and this time got a pinch on the arm.

We took a table by the windows, ordered drinks, ogled the spectacular view of the whole of Las Vegas at night, and listened to the group enjoying itself with 'Stardust'.

'The Ambassador Room is through there,' said Angela, pointing through an arched way. 'It's one of the best restaurants in town.'

'Is that a hint?' I grinned. 'Have you girls had dinner?'

They said no.

I looked at Buzz. 'What about it?'

'Fine – I could eat the hind leg of an old desert mule.'

I asked Angela: 'Do they serve hind leg of old desert mule?'

'That happens to be the Chef's Special . . . also Fillet of Rattler and Pack Horse à la Bourguignonne.'

'Right,' I said, 'if it's with chips, you're on – but only if you dance with me.'

She heaved a resigned sigh. 'God, the things women have to do for a meal.'

Out on the floor she turned suddenly and slipped into me, smooth as silk.

'Wow,' I gasped.

'What's the matter?' she smiled, knowing damn well.

'You're the matter. You feel too good.'

'Too good for what?'

'Your own safety.'

Incredibly, she moved even closer. 'Tell me about it.'

'Angela, don't do that.'

'What?'

'Breathe in my ear like that.'

'I've got to breathe somewhere – and my nose happens to *be* here.'

'I know where your nose is.'

'Don't you like it?'

'Don't be ridiculous.'

'Well, then . . .'

'If you persist, I cannot be held responsible for my behaviour.' She chuckled warmly. 'Su-per.'

I glanced over at Buzz, finding him and Josie similarly welded together. As he turned, he caught my eye and grinned like a cornered cougar, telling me he was home and dry . . . well, at least home.

'You're some dancer, Tobin,' drawled Angela. 'Great lead. We haven't moved a yard from the table yet.'

'Saves all that walking back when they finish.'

She grinned and gave me a hug. 'I'm very glad we met tonight. It's fun.'

'Yes, it is. It's also been highly instructive. I reckon I've learned more about Las Vegas in the past hour than most people learn ever.'

'Oh, there's a lot more I could tell you.'

'Well . . . the night is young . . . and I'm in no hurry to get to bed.'

It was, I swear, an innocent remark, but she took wonderful advantage of it. After the briefest, contrived pause she raised her cheek from my shoulder and frowned at me.

'I beg your pardon?'

I grinned at her expression. 'I said . . . I'm in no hurry to get to bed.'

'Wow,' she huffed, returning to my shoulder. 'Boy, do *you* know how to annihilate a girl's confidence. I have heard some put-downs in my time, but never . . .'

'Angela . . .'

'So – O.K., maybe a fella doesn't fancy a certain chick, but there are ways of *telling* her . . .'

'*Ang*ela . . .'

'I mean, what sort of gentleman comes right out – socko! – and tells her he's in no hurry to . . .'

'Angela . . .!'

'No, no, don't apologize, *please*! I get the message, loud and . . .'

'You devil . . .' I tickled her ribs and buckled her knees.

'Yow . . .! No, it's no good trying to get round me, you've done it now . . . and I thought all Englishmen were supposed to be gentlemen . . .'

'We are . . . we are! It's just that . . well, we move a little slower than other fellas.'

'So, it's true . . . you really *are* so cold-blooded, hm? Maybe American girls are too much woman for you.'

'Well, *no*, it's . . .'

'Maybe an Eskimo bird is more your meat – take about a week to thaw out.'

I narrow-eyed her. 'Lady, you . . . are asking for trouble.'

'Ha!'

'I'm warning you . . .'

'Double ha!'

'Right, you've had it . . .'

'I have? I mean, was that it? You know, I didn't feel a . . . yow! stop doing that!'

'I *mean* . . . that before the night is too much older, you will have cause to reverse your opinion about Englishmen.'

'Well, now . . .' she softened right up and crept into my ear again. '. . . that's better. Only a little, though – talk is very cheap.'

'There'll be no more talk on the matter.'

'Oh, now he's the strong, silent type.'

'Shut up and dance.'

'Oh,' she sighed, 'so masterful . . .'

She started working on me, then, just for the hell of it, just to show me what a girl can do to a man when she really puts her mind to it, caressing my chest with her breasts and doing the damndest things with her loins.

It worked.

Up came Herc with one hell of a rush, so hard and fast she exploded an appalled gasp and jerked her hips away. 'Oh . . . you bad boy.'

'Come back here.'

'Certainly not.'

I slid my hand low down on her waist and pulled her in hard. She didn't resist. 'That . . .' she chuckled in my ear, '. . . is obscene.'

'It's your fault.'

'Me . . .! What did I do?'

'Don't move away! Stay right where you are, I'll be arrested.'

Giggling, she thrust hard against him, groaning softly. 'Wow . . .'

'We'd . . . better sit down,' I croaked. 'You've got me in a right old mess.'

'*Can* you sit down? I mean, without stabbing yourself in the heart.'

'Don't exaggerate.'

'Who's exaggerating! My God, if that was neon-lit you'd outshine the New Frontier sign!'

'Fun-nee. It's all right for you girls . . .'

She laughed. 'It's perfect for us girls.'

'Look . . . dance towards the table, f'Pete'sake.'

'Nope . . . I'm going to abandon you right here and let all the other women in the room see what I've got myself.'

My grip tightened. 'Don't you dare! Now, move – thataway!'

Chuckling at my discomfort, she allowed herself to be aimed in the direction of the table, and, as we reached it, I went into a sneaky half-bend and flopped into the chair.

She landed in the one on my left, still highly amused. I gave her a mock scowl which temporarily brought on another bout of giggling, but then, suddenly, she was no longer laughing but was looking at me with misty wonderment that pulled me up sharp and tripped my heart into tumultuous action.

'Wow,' she gasped.

'Wow what?'

'Wow you.'

'Yes . . . wow you, too.'

'Some turn-on, hm?' Her pink tongue flicked nervously across dry lips. 'May I have a cigarette?'

I gave her one, and as I held my lighter to it, her eyes came up to meet mine. 'You really hungry?'

'I . . . couldn't eat a thing.'

'Not anything?'

God, that smile.

'Well . . . nothing that'd be on the menu.'

'You're naughty.'

'Ha!'

'Do you . . . want to go all through the charade of dinner?'

I grinned, heart pounding. 'Do you?'

'No.'

I glanced across at Buzz, sandwiched hard to Josie.

'I'm sure Josie won't mind,' said Angela.

'No – and I wouldn't say Buzz's mind is on Chicken à la Kiev

58

right now, either. Still . . . we'd better wait until they come back, hm?'

'That could take an hour, the way they're going at it.'

'True. So, what do we do – leave a note?'

'Why not dance over and tell them?'

'What a splendid idea.'

I swallowed my drink, stood up, and Angela came in for the kill again.

It took three taps on Buzz's shoulder to get him out of Josie's neck, and about three full seconds before he recognized me.

'Oh, hi . . .'

'How you doing?'

His grin told me.

'Look, Buzz . . . we . . . Angela and I . . . we sort of thought we might kind of skip dinner and . . . well, she wants to show me the town and . . . well, if you two don't mind . . . we thought we . . .'

Buzz conferred with Josie. 'One thing about Tobin, when he's got something to say, he says it – straight out – no beating about the bush. *Do* we mind if these two desert us?'

'Which two?' grinned Josie.

'Off you go,' he said, slipping a wink to me. 'I reckon I'll be safe enough.'

'Wanna bet?' growled Josie.

'See you later, then.'

'Much,' said Josie, moving Buzz back to where he'd been.

Five minutes later Angela and I were in a cab, heading across town.

FIVE

From the moment we entered her motel room Angela took charge of the proceedings in a manner that *should* have told me this was no casual, light-hearted, holiday bed-time story, a simple collision of souls hell-bent on screwing the pants off each other. But then a chap's mind does tend to get a little clouded to reality on these occasions.

All you see is a highly-desirable, nice-to-be-with piece of ultra-feminine crumpet and a hugely inviting double bed, and everything else disappears from view.

59

Hookers, of course – even amateur, week-end ones – rely on this sexual blindness to attain their profitable ends, knowing that if they play their man right he'll hand over the keys to Fort Knox, provided he believes he's getting his money's worth.

And so, dear Angela, presumably misreading me as a man of considerable substance, went into a routine befitting my imagined bankroll, a planned programme of sexual delight so miraculously exciting that, blunt-witted though I was, I should have realized it was all too good to be true.

Oh, don't get me wrong – these things *do* happen as perfectly and effortlessly as this, especially on holiday when time is of the essence. But it has been my experience that they do tend to happen that little bit more slowly. A more normal, uncommercial outcome to the liaison would have been dinner with Buzz and Josie, then an hour or so messing about the casinos before finally drifting towards the motel, know what I mean? I'm sure you do.

However, there I was, gazing around the room while she was locking the door behind us, my old ticker breaking into a gallop at the sight of the sumptuous double bed and my mind filled with nothing but the thought of getting her into it.

'There,' she said, with a 'home-at-last' smile. 'How d'you like it?'

Any way it comes, love, I thought.

'It's lovely,' I said, giving it another glance, the room I mean.

But next moment I stopped looking at the room because Angela stepped in front of me, snaked her arms around my neck, and thrust her dear little pubic mound into me.

'And it's all ours,' she murmured huskily, her eyelids drooping and her mouth going all soft and loose in preparation for the assault.

Then in she came, hungry as a lame lioness, smothering my mouth with hers, filling it with her hot, frantic tongue, sucking my lips into her scalding orifice, then releasing them and again driving in with her tongue. It was akin to kissing a milking machine and extremely disturbing.

She chuckled and ground her loins against old surging Herc. 'Boy, it certainly doesn't take you long.'

'You're *surprised*?'

'No . . . I had you pegged as a hotpants.'

'Really?'

'Yes, really.'

60

'And just *when* did you . . .'

'Soon as you walked onto the dock at Caesar's Palace.'

'That soon, hm?'

'Huh, you send out waves as subtle as a mule kick in the stomach.'

I grinned. 'And maybe it takes one hotpants to know another?'

Her eyes went all sleepy again. 'I think you know by now there's no maybe about it . . .' And then she came at me out of the sun again.

After three or four hours of this she broke away, gasping.

'Wow!' I panted. 'I thought you didn't fancy the idea of dinner.'

'*That* . . . was just hors-d'oeuvres,' she murmured threateningly. 'Wait till you see what I've got lined up for the main course.'

'Suddenly,' I croaked, 'I'm very hungry.'

'Really?'

'Truly.'

'Famished?'

'Starved.'

She grinned, very wickedly. 'You asked for it.'

She stepped away, eyeing me with mock threat and nodding to herself, as though selecting a particular battle plan, then made a slow circuit of the room, switching off all but one small table lamp, then she returned to me, a panther padding out of the gloom, and once more full-Nelson-ed me.

'Do you like games?'

'What sort of games?'

She cocked a brow. 'Oh, there are some you don't like?'

I grinned. 'None that I've come across so far.'

'Good.'

'How about you?'

'Uh-uh, this is your party. It's what you want.'

'I don't play like that. It has to be what *we* want.'

She shrugged. 'O.K., then that's your kind of game.' She nodded towards the sideboard. 'Go fix us a couple of drinks while I do a few things, they're in the cupboard.'

With a final peck on the mouth, she slid from my arms and went into the bathroom, closing the door.

I sidled to the sideboard, got out the booze, and while pouring a couple, glanced up and found myself smiling at me in the mirror.

Well, sport, I thought, here we go again. Incredible . . . how adroitly it can and does happen, in any town, any country. Be it China or Chelmsford, Borneo or Bournemouth, birds are birds and men are men and ever the twain shall meet, thank God.

Love indeed does conquer all. Come civil strife, political combat, religious dispute or ethnic argument, the one confrontation that would always come out on top of the popularity polls and help keep the world in one piece was this one – man to woman.

Women, if only the daft politicians would realize it, were the *answer* to world peace. Right, lads, we're having a spot of trouble with Russia this week, so I'm sending the entire Foreign Office over to make love to two thousand Russian women – and they're sending their lot over here to do the same.

By heck, they'd come back wiser in one respect, at least – they'd realize that basically there isn't a ha'p'orth of difference between the Russians and ourselves. For regardless of race, colour, creed and ideology, a woman in bed is a woman in bed is a woman in bed . . . and bless 'em, every one.

'Cheers,' I said to myself. 'Here's to closer international relations through freer intercourse.'

'That'll get you locked up,' she said from the doorway.

I turned . . . and went funny in the head. Well, you would, wouldn't you?

She was stark naked.

Strange, isn't it, that even though you can clearly imagine how they're going to look when they've peeled off those almost see-through, skin-tight clothes, the final revelation always clouts you under the heart and turns your legs to jelly.

She was beautiful, superbly built, a really prime offering of perfect birdhood, standing there with consummate confidence, showing me the lot.

A smoky smile broke on her wide mouth and she started towards me, sauntering with exaggerated languor, perfectly relaxed and very much in control.

'You should see your face,' she laughed. 'First time you've ever seen a naked woman?'

'Not . . . quite.'

'I'll bet.'

She reached me, took the glass from my hand and set it down, then attacked my jacket and tie.

'Do I suit?'

'P . . . perfectly.'

'Does my naked proximity disturb you?'

I gulped. 'Not in the least.'

She threw the jacket and tie onto a chair and started on the shirt, very leisurely, brushing my naked chest with her warm breasts as she eased the shirt from my shoulders.

It was more than I could stand. I grabbed her, brought her hard against me, thrilling to the feel of her naked warmth.

'Steady, boy, we've got a long night ahead of us . . . haven't we?'

'We have if you say so.'

'Is that what you'd like?'

'That's what I'd like.'

'Then that's what you've got.'

She eased away and got working on my trousers, dropped them to the floor, tutting to herself at the sight of Herc doing his best to burst my shorts asunder. And then her hand was in there, holding, caressing, as she groaned 'Ohhh!' very softly, a sound that seemed an awful lot like pleasurable discovery.

'He's . . . very big,' she whispered.

'About average.'

'And *very* hard.'

'That I'll go along with.'

'So will I.'

Then suddenly . . . wwwhhoosshh! down went the shorts and she went with them, on her knees, and Herc disappeared from sight.

I gasped.

Her mouth was a cauldron, her tongue a fleet, feathery butterfly, leaping and dancing, probing and stroking, driving me bananas.

'Hey . . . aawwww!'

She looked up. 'You complaining?'

'Don't be daft.'

'Come . . .'

She abandoned that little game, came to her feet, took my hand and drew me to the bed, pushed me onto my back and for several minutes more continued doing what she'd been doing.

Then she stopped and came up, sprawled over me and prodded my nose with her fingertip.

'Hi . . .'

'Hi, yourself.'

'You like that?'

'It was wonderful.' I held her, caressed her. 'You have skin as soft as a pup's ear.'

She chuckled. 'Nobody ever told me that before.'

'Have you ever felt a pup's ear? All warm and velvety . . .'

'Yes, I've felt one.'

'Angela . . .?'

'Yes, Russell . . .'

'Roll over, it's my turn.'

She obeyed, lay completely relaxed, arms lightly by her sides, legs slightly parted. A lazy murmur. 'What are you going to do?'

'You.'

'I asked what, not who.'

'Just close your eyes and keep quiet, this may take a while.'

'This is supposed to be your treat, not mine.'

'This *is* mine. Shut your eyes and do as you're told.'

'Yes, master.'

Her breasts were quite magnificent, full and firm, their dark, high-standing nipples altogether irresistible. At the touch of my mouth she flinched, then, as I began working on her, she braced her thighs tightly together and began to moan.

'That . . .' she sighed tremulously, 'will get you into a lot of trouble . . . do you have any idea what that *does* to a girl?'

'No. What?'

'Keep going and you'll find out.'

I kept going.

Moments later the first shudder hit her . . . then a gasp . . . her arm flopped helplessly on the bed and her legs parted hungrily. 'Oh, baby . . .' Her anguish mounted . . . she writhed, reached for my head, pulled at my hair, clawed my shoulder, murmuring soft, plaintive groans, then suddenly she cried out, grabbed for my hand and drove it between her legs and was into her orgasm instantly, crying out, 'Oh . . .! oh . . .! OH . . .!' as she bucked and tossed and squeezed on my captive hand until I feared she'd shatter bone.

'OHHHH . . .!'

A huge, appalled gasp . . . and then she collapsed, lay there, breathing chaotically, her lovely breasts rising and falling, slowly winding down and finally coming to rest . . . replete.

Stillness enveloped the room. After a while she turned her face to me and regarded me sleepily through half-closed lids.

'That . . . was lovely.'

'Thought you liked it, somehow.'

'It was so good, it could get to be a habit. I *might* just fancy another.'

'Well, I'm always willing to lend a hand.'

She chuckled and squeezed her thighs together.

'Feel tired?' I asked her. 'Want a rest?'

She frowned. 'A rest! Ha! that was just a warm-up.' She came up, pushed at my shoulder. 'Lie down, now it's your turn,' and began raining fleeting kisses all over my body, tickling, making me laugh, then once more went in for the kill and quickly brought Herc up to full throbbing health and strength.

Then, without warning, she swung a long, lithe leg across me, took a sighter on Herc and slowly sat him to the limit, hard to the bone.

'OHHHH . . .!' she gasped. 'Oh . . . Tobin, if he's just average I'm glad as hell you're not abnormal! Anything bigger than this is just plain greed!'

Then she closed her eyes, wreathed a delicious smile and concentrated on enjoying him.

'You look very smug up there,' I laughed. 'You planning on staying long?'

'Until I get evicted. At least an hour, anyway.'

She lasted about three minutes. A sudden shudder . . . her eyes popped . . . and uncontrollably she was into another onslaught of climax.

'Y . . . you're doing it again!'

I laughed at her, at her wide-eyed expression. 'I'm not doing anything, I'm just lying here.'

'It's him . . . and he's your responsibility! Oh, God . . .' She began to rock. 'Oh, sweet Jesus, that is *beautiful* . . .!' Her head dropped forward, the rocking became a compulsive pelvic jerk, her fingers clawed the counterpane. Now she threw back her head, lips drawn, teeth bared, and then she was truly into it, gone, lost, prisoner of her own tumultuous passion, divine beneficiary of a second stupendous climax.

'OHHHHHHHHHH...!'

With a great shudder she came to a halt, paused, swayed, then slowly toppled onto my chest like a felled poplar, lay there panting and moaning, making me laugh with her sounds of exaggerated exhaustion.

'It's ... all right for you ...'

'It's beautiful for me.'

'... you're not having them!'

'My turn will come.'

'Ha! When – March ... April?'

'Whenever you say.'

She looked up at me. 'Huh, just like that, hm?'

'Ho! You don't *know* how hard I'm having to hold on!'

'Well, that's better. I was beginning to think I wasn't getting to you.'

'You got mighty close to me that time, I can tell you.'

'Well, that's O.K., then ... and thank you.' She pecked me on the cheek. 'Don't think it isn't appreciated.'

'You tired now?'

She heaved a wearisome sigh. 'You men really don't know too much about us gals, do you?'

'No,' I lied.

'You're lying. *You* know a lot about us ... and so you also know I'm still just getting warmed up.'

'I was only asking.'

'However ...' she continued, 'I do think a small pause for station identification would be rather nice right now. Fancy a drink?'

'Love one. Shall I get them?'

'You stay right where you are. I'm coming back – right back. Don't you *dare* go off the boil.'

Extricating herself with a comical wince, she got off the bed, collected the drinks and the cigarettes, then climbed back on, reseating herself with an expression of contrived agony, then broke into a delighted laugh.

'Hey, this is fun. I just hope you're having half as much as I'm having and if you're not, too bad. Here ... drink.'

With great difficulty I half sat up and took a swallow. 'That's enough ... down. You're not here to get drunk.'

She lit a cigarette and handed it to me, positioning an ashtray on my chest. 'What a wonderful way to spend an evening. And to think I used to waste my time in an armchair.'

'You look extremely comfortable up there.'

'Ever think how incredible it is that two people can meet and make this kind of music straight off?'

'I knew it was going to be good.'

'So did I,' she said. 'The vibes were all beautiful.'

'Vibes?'

'Vibrations . . . chemistry.'

'Ah, yes. I'm a great believer in vibes. We should listen to them all the time.'

'Positively,' she nodded, stealing my cigarette. 'Ever stop to think that complete strangers maybe do make the best lovers?'

'No,' I said, stealing it back again. 'But maybe you're right. Everything's new . . . fresh . . . unexpected.'

'Ah, you got it. Familiarity – the great annihilator of piquant passion.'

'Hey, that's very good. Did you just make it up?'

'Scout's honour.'

'What are you – a part-time psychologist or something?'

She grinned. 'Aren't we all. Don't we have to read people all the time?'

'Angela, you're absolutely right . . . and right now I'm enjoying the story immensely.'

'So am I,' she said, stubbing out the cigarette. 'So – shall we continue with Chapter Three?'

'Turn the page, love, I'm right with you.'

'That,' she said, wincing a little as she placed the ashtray on the bedside table, 'is no lie.'

Chapter Three ran to about fifteen fun pages of lighthearted dalliance, teasing titillation and rousing slap-and-tickle before coming to an exhilarating end.

After a brief breather, Chapter Four commenced in more serious vein and finished quickly in a thunderclap of unexpected violence – prelude, we both knew, to Chapter Five – the Grand Finale.

We were into it suddenly and with feverish intensity, like climbers racing for the summit after a long, laborious trudge, alive with new-found vigour, propelled by the vision of our goal. With a cry, Angela went backwards, legs aloft and chasm-wide, hauling me with her, onto her and into her, craving to be ravaged.

'Oh, baby . . . baby . . .!' she wailed.

'Jesus, I'm coming . . .!'

'Come . . . come!'

'Ooh! . . . Ahhhh!'

'Ohhhhh . . .!'

'*Wooooowwwwww* . . .!'

'My God . . . my *GOD* . . .!'

'YYOOOOOOWWWWW . . .!'

'Jesus, that's hot . . .'

'UUGGGGHHHHHHH . . .!'

'Oh, baby . . . baby . . .!'

'Mmmmmmuuuuuhhhhh!'

I collapsed.

'Aaaaawwwww . . .'

She went boneless.

And there we lay . . . for a very long time.

A drowsy murmur. 'What time is it?'

I turned from her and squinted at my watch on the bedside table. 'Just on seven. The sun's coming up . . . it's going to be a lovely day.'

A sleep-filled chuckle. 'After a night like that, who cares about the day?'

I snuggled into her, took her breast in my hand. 'It was good, hm?'

'They don't come any gooder. How much sleep have we had?'

'Two . . . three hours, give or take a wink.'

'That much, hm? she slurred, too exhausted to speak. 'Don't know 'bout you, but I'm not moving a limb for another six hours.'

'Well, that's not surprising, the way you go at it.'

'Huh!'

I cuddled her close and she wriggled backwards into me, bed-warm and delicious. 'Angela . . .'

'Mmm . . .?'

'Would you think me a pig if I went back to the hotel and checked with Buzz? I feel kind of . . . you know . . .'

'No, of course I don't mind. I told you, I'm not going to be any kind of company for the next six hours . . . maybe ten.'

'Hey, d'you realize what day this is?'

68

'June 17th?'

I laughed. 'It's New Year's Eve. You got any plans for tonight?'

'Nope.'

'Would you like to see the New Year in with me – maybe Buzz and Josie, too? There'll be eight million parties going on.'

'Sure . . . love to.'

'Lovely. Shall I pick you up here?'

Small thoughtful pause. 'No, how about Caesar's Palace . . . save you coming downtown. Meet you same place.'

'On the dock? Fine. What time . . . say, nine o'clock?'

'Beautiful.'

'Terrific.'

She was almost asleep, poor kid, and not surprising after the number she'd racked up. I swear she'd gone well into double figures.

I kissed her shoulder and slid out of bed, had a quick sluice and got dressed. As I was finishing, she opened one eye and murmured, 'Honey . . . could you do something for me?'

'Sure . . . what?'

'I'm low on funds. Could you lend me a little – just until I can get to the bank and cash a cheque?'

'Of course. How much d'you want?'

'Could you make it a couple of hundred? I'll need something new for tonight.'

Blimey, two hundred dollars! It was just about all I had!

'Erm . . .'

She frowned. 'You don't have two hundred on you?'

'Well, yes . . . it's just that . . .' I laughed, '. . . two hundred is all I've got!'

She opened the other eye. 'You mean *total*?'

She made me feel like a piker. 'Well, no, not *total* total . . . I've got plenty in England, but you see . . . well, it's a long story, and cut short I was trying to get by on next to nothing until I got to Australia with Buzz, then get some out from England. Oh, but don't worry about it, I can borrow some from him, he's got plenty.'

I reached into my pocket.

'Anyway,' I said, 'I'll be seeing you tonight, won't I . . .'

She didn't answer and I took her silence as dilemma – wanting the money but not wanting to inconvenience me.

'Now, don't worry,' I said, counting off two hundred and holding up the one remaining bill, a five. 'Look, I've got enough for cab fare . . .' I put the money on the bedside table and kissed her on the forehead. 'Sleep, you need it. See you on Cleo's dock at nine. I'll hang the "Don't Disturb" sign on the doorknob, O.K.?'

She gave a wan smile and held out her hand. 'Bye . . .'

'Bye.'

And then I left.

I didn't take a cab. I walked the mile or so back to the Sahara. It was a magnificent morning, cool and fresh, the winter sun coming up gold and bright in the cloudless eastern sky, dispelling the nip in the desert air and setting the windows in the tall hotels a-sparkle. A truly beautiful day.

Malone was not at home.

He woke me around eleven, clattering the key in the door, then, seeing I was awake, entered the room on all fours as though too weak to stand.

'Ohhhhhhhh . . .!' he groaned, crawling to his bedside and heaving himself with wildly exaggerated difficulty onto it, then collapsed in a state of flat-out exhaustion. 'Oh, Tobin . . . Tobin . . . let me die. Bury me deep on the lone prairie and leave my bones to the gophers . . .'

'Find yourself another grave, this one's already occupied.'

He managed a filthy chuckle. 'You too, hm? By *God*, we must've picked a couple of right ones. Ho . . . I've been screwed some in my short, sweet life, but never . . . *never* . . . like that.'

'You seeing her tonight?'

He flopped his head from side to side. 'Alas, no . . . she already had something lined up for New Year . . . then again, I reckon it's just as well. Another night like that and I'd be out of pro-tennis for good. I don't reckon I'd get far serving on my knees. How 'bout you . . . for tonight?'

'I'm meeting her at nine in Caesar's Palace. Hey, Buzz, I should have checked with you first. I sort of took it for granted . . .'

He flopped a limp hand at me. 'Don't worry 'bout a thing . . . the town's bulging with them. I'll find something . . .'

'Sure.'

We lapsed into silence. Then, with a laugh, I said, 'Buzz . . . I reckon it's a good thing we're only here for two nights. After a week of this we'd look so old and haggard the Australian Immigration people would claim we're travelling on someone else's passports ...' I turned my head. 'Buzz ...'

He was asleep.

Or dead.

SIX

The phone woke me at four that afternoon, otherwise we'd have slept right through New Year.

In a befuddled daze I fumbled for the receiver and managed to locate my ear.

'Mister Malone?' a male voice enquired.

'No, I'm the other one. Do you want Mister Malone?'

He laughed. 'Not necessarily, Mister Tobin. This is TWA. I'm calling to confirm your onward flight to Sydney. We've booked you on the internal United Airways flight to Los Angeles tomorrow evening, leaving Las Vegas at eleven. This will connect you with a Qantas 747 flight departing L.A. for Tahiti at two a.m., arriving Tahiti ...'

'Oh, just a minute, could I get a pen ...'

I tottered across the room and found one, then returned and jotted down the times on a Keno ticket.

'Well, that sounds fine, thank you very much.'

'Can you confirm for Mister Malone, too, sir, and I'll make out the tickets?'

'Well, he's ...' I glanced at Buzz, still flat out on his back, mouth open, '... he's out at the moment, but take it as confirmed, it'll be all right.'

'Right, sir, your tickets will be at the TWA desk in the Sahara lobby in an hour.'

I thanked him and replaced the receiver, then sat on the edge of Buzz's bed, tickled his nose with the Keno ticket and cooed in female falsetto, 'Wake up, Buzz, darling, I want you again ...'

He coughed, choked, groaned heartily and turned on his side. 'Aawwhhhmmmnnnyyyaammnnn ...'

'Aw, come on, Buzz, just one more time ...'

'Gotosleepwillyuhbaby ... there'sagoodgirl ...'

'Malone!' I whacked him on the ass.

'OW!' He sat up, blinking bewilderedly. 'Oh, fuck, it's you . . . and thank Christ for it. I thought it was . . . what is it?'

'It's four o'clock and that was TWA.'

'What was?'

'That was – that phone call.'

'Oh.' He frowned. 'Which phone call?'

'Never mind, son, I know you're poorly. They just called with the flight times. We fly to L.A. tomorrow night on that eleven o'clock flight and pick up a Jumbo to Tahiti in the wee small hours.'

'Fantastic,' he nodded, consumed with indifference. 'What time did you say it was?'

'Four.'

'Four when? What the hell day is it?'

'It's New Year's Eve, you daft bugger. Come on, I'm starved. I need a hamburger.'

The mention of food always brings Buzz round.

Five o'clock saw us straddling two stools in Sambo's on the Strip, nattily dressed, fully refreshed and ready for anything.

'Pity about Josie,' he remarked, eyeing the waitress who was at that moment crouching down to pick up a fallen spoon and displaying all God had given her and a bit more besides. 'Tobin, would yuh just look at that. I'd rather be in there than in jail, I can tell you.'

'Yes, I can see you are emotionally devastated by loss, Malone.'

He grinned and bit into his second Jumboburger, squirting juice onto his shirt-cuff. 'Well, you've got to spread yourself around a bit, mate, haven't you – especially here. Sad to contemplate, really . . . all this incredible crumpet and so little time. I reckon I'll come here for my hols next year. Imagine a month of *this*!'

I shuddered. 'Yes.'

It was a shudder of ecstasy.

'I'm beginning to realize now,' he continued, 'what delights of eye and mind must have greeted Captain Bligh and Fletcher Christian when they stepped ashore on Tahiti two hundred years ago. All that sun-tanned pulchritude and not a restriction in sight. And talking of Tahiti . . .'

I shut my eyes. 'Don't. Let's get out of Vegas first. I don't think I can cope with so much excitement.'

'Hee hee,' he chuckled, 'what a trip – Vegas *and* Tahiti in one go.'

'Anything else I can get you?' enquired the waitress, a cute little colt with red hair and a snub nose, very fanciable in her tight-fitting overall and plunging neckline.

'Well,' replied Buzz thoughtfully, 'something did cross my mind a few moments ago . . .' he gave her a sexy grin. 'How are *you* spending New Year's night, honey?'

She shrugged. 'Same as usual – with my husband. He's the chef. Now, anything else I can get you?'

'Apple pie,' muttered Buzz. 'With vanilla ice-cream.'

We left Sambo's about six and wandered north on the Strip. It was busier than London's Oxford Street on Christmas Eve and radiated the same intense festive excitement.

'Hell of a town,' observed Buzz, moved to these outbursts of poignant, poetic observation from time to time. 'Disneyland for adults is right. Tobin . . . I feel like a gamble.'

'Now, Buzz . . .'

'Aw, heck, come on, we can't spend a night in Vegas without a little flutter.'

'How little?'

'Not much . . . say a hundred.'

'You say a hundred, I'm flat broke.'

He frowned. 'I thought you had a bob or two.'

'I did. I lent it to Angela until she could get to the bank. She's paying me back tonight.'

'Oh. Well, hell, that's no problem . . . here . . .'

He produced a fat wallet but I stopped him. 'No, Buzz, it's all right. I can wait till nine.'

'Tobin, for Godsake will you stop worrying about money – it's only money.' He pulled out several twenties and stuffed them in my pocket.

'Well, thanks, Buzz, that makes eight million I owe you.'

'Eight million and six, don't think I'm not counting. Right, now that we're suitably primed, where're we going to break the house?'

We were approaching the junction of Flamingo Road. Diagonally opposite, on the far side of the Strip, sprawled the breathtaking spectacle of Caesar's Palace. And immediately on our right, set well back from the road beyond a vast car park, towered the gigantic MGM Grand.

'There,' nodded Buzz, indicating the MGM. 'I've just got to see that place.'

'Fine . . . and at nine I can nip across the road for Angela.'

He slapped his hands together. 'Right – let's take the joint.'

You do not simply enter the MGM Grand by walking through a door. No, sir, first you have to cross a moat, which separates the car park from the hotel, by way of an ornate footbridge. Then you have to pass beneath the immense covered way which serves as a protection from sun and rain while you're waiting for a taxi or disembarking from a taxi or doing whatever else you're doing out there.

Finally you reach a selection of glass doors, both swing and revolving types, and, having made your selection, you enter the hotel.

Here, just inside the door, you pause on the plush red carpet of a raised lobby and gape . . . at the magnitude of the room confronting you, because it is by far the hugest room you have ever seen, imagined, dreamed of or contemplated and ten times bigger than you'd have thought possible.

From end to end and side to side it is e . . . normous! It is also all-embracing, for it contains a Keno lounge, umpteen bars, shops, toilets etcetera, etcetera, etcetera, and, at its heart, a vast, slightly-sunken casino roughly the size of Yorkshire.

'Wooo . . . ow!' was Buzz's description of it, and I'll go along with that in-depth observation all the way. 'Just *look* at those slots! There must be ninety thousand of 'em!'

A slight exaggeration, but it's the impression that counts. Anyway, after the first thousand, who cares?

'Let's have a drink and absorb the place,' he suggested.

Slowly, like a couple of Pennine pig-farmers on a first-time trip to Paris, we strolled down the room, gawping about us at everything there was to see – white marble statuary, elegant Victorian furnishings, the lavish display of crystal chandeliers in the incredible, ornate ceiling, and the exquisite white marble balustrading that encircled the sunken casino.

Reaching the end of the room we discovered further amazements – no fewer than four restaurants, an endless corridor of banquet halls and public rooms, and an underground town of shops. This was no hotel – it was a city!

Retracing our steps we walked into an open bar area of small tables and leather chairs that overlooked the casino, and as we sat down a blonde waitress was there for our order.

'What'll it be, gentlemen?'

The way she was dressed – her!

Jesus, she was practically naked. It was a sort of red, micro-skirted bunny outfit and black fishnet tights, a fetching little ensemble that was likely to fetch her a whole lot of trouble from randy bastards like Malone and maybe that's why she was wearing it.

She bent down to remove a crumpled fag packet from our ashtray and gave us a splendid eyeful of a pair of quite sumptuous knockers, then came up quickly and caught us at it, rewarding our diligence with a sexy smile.

'I, er . . .' stammered Buzz, 'I think I'll have a . . . whatcha-callit . . .'

'Make that two,' I grinned.

'Two whatchacallits,' she nodded. 'On the rocks?'

'Beer,' laughed Buzz. 'I'll have a beer.'

'Still make it two,' I told her.

She about-turned on her stiletto heel and wriggled back to the bar, everything moving on well-greased bearings, knowing damn well we were watching the shim-sham of her little red satin knickers.

'Oh, Tobin . . .' groaned Buzz, 'it's no good, I'll have to immigrate. It's downright *sinful* to let all this fabulous crumpet go to waste. And it's all so willing! I mean, you wouldn't have to waste precious time warming it up. Just *look* at it down there . . .'

He nodded towards the swarming casino and I had to agree with him. Within my vision, without turning my head, I could see a dozen birds I'd be hard-put to say no to – some beautifully gowned for the New Year's evening, others in trousers and sweaters, all types, all sizes, all, apparently, available, just strolling around the place, toying with a slot machine here, betting a little there, all undoubtedly hunting for a playmate to help while away the night.

'How d'you fancy the waitress?' I asked him.

'Madly.'

'Why don't you have a go?'

'I was thinking about it.'

'Here's your chance, here she comes.'

75

She came, treating us to another stupendous eyeful as she bent to place the drinks on the table.

'There y'go, that'll be two dollars, please.'

Buzz beat me to it, handing her three. 'Excuse me asking, miss, but . . well, being a stranger in town . . . I was wondering if you'd be interested in . . . you see, my pal here has got a girl for tonight and I was wondering if you'd care to make up a foursome and . . .'

'Honey, I'd love to but I'm on here till four – there's too much money to be made New Year's in tips for socializin'. Maybe some other time.'

She wheeled away to serve another table, hardly wiggling at all.

'Mmmm . . .' frowned Buzz. 'So, if she's working all night, why the come-on in the first place?'

'You, er, didn't by any chance give her a substantial tip, did you?'

'Only a dollar.'

'On a two-dollar bill. That's not an ungenerous tip – fifty percent.'

'Yeah, well . . .' he looked at me and laughed. 'Oh, fuck off, Tobin, you're too damn smart. Well . . .' he raised his beer, '. . . here's to whatever the Fates bring us tonight, be it fame, fortune or high adventure.'

'Cheers. Personally, I'd settle for another evening of quiet domesticity – just like last night. Early to bed, early to rise . . . makes you bug-eyed with fatigue but what a way to expire.'

'Yeah, it's all right for you,' he said, handing me a cigarette. 'I've still got to find mine.'

'She'll happen,' I told him, breaking into song. 'Some enchant . . . ed evening . . . you will see a strang . . . er . . .'

'Well, I've certainly got the crowded room,' he laughed. 'Man, did you ever *see* such a seethe. And we had better join it, there's no action up here.'

We finished our beers, descended the three or four steps into the casino and plunged into the noise and excitement, the excitement of money, close and in huge amounts, oodles of it, lying scattered around on the betting tables and clattering in and out of the slot machines.

This, of course, is one of the big dangers of Las Vegas. You quickly get so accustomed to seeing so much money being handled with such apparent disdain that its value becomes meaningless.

Bills of whatever denomination become mere pieces of paper, chips seem just what they in fact are – pieces of plastic, and in consequence your betting becomes reckless. Chasing an initial loss, it is so easy to be gripped by a mindless, panicky determination to get it back, and, heedless of its true value, you throw in more pieces of paper and plastic, the extent of your loss becoming reality only when you're cleaned out and the feverish action stops. The process is incredibly painless.

For maybe half an hour Buzz and I toured the casino, pausing to watch the action at the Baccarat table, then the dice, blackjack and roulette tables, admiring the speed and incredible dexterity of the dealers and the unbelievable volume of money changing hands, mostly in the direction of the house. Mugs' games, every one. They had to be – how else was this fabulous room paid for?

Finally we arrived at the banks of slot machines and Buzz came to life. 'Now, then, this is my meat. Let's get some change.'

We approached a raised cubicle, reminiscent of a courtroom witness box and manned by a woman, and changed ten dollars each into nickels, receiving five two-dollar rolls of the small silver coins, worth about 2p each in English money.

Breaking open the rolls, we poured the nickels into big Dixie cups and returned to the machines.

'We'll take three each,' suggested Buzz. 'You clobber those three, and I'll murder these.'

The type of machine we'd chosen played up to five nickels at a time, giving the player five different ways of winning – or losing – when fully loaded. We decided, however, to start more cautiously and put in only one nickel at a time, see how things went.

'Ready?' said Buzz.

'Ready.'

'Just think,' he sighed, his eyes sweeping the room, 'in a couple of hours, all this could be ours.'

I laughed. 'I'm counting on it. Right, here goes, countdown and blast off ... five ... four ... three ... two ... one ... GO!'

In ... pull ... in ... pull ... in ... pull.

By the time I'd got the third nickel in the third machine the first one had stopped. Eureka! One cherry! I'd won two nickels back!

The other two machines coughed up nothing. Well, overall I'd only lost one.

In went the nickels again.

It was three or four minutes before Buzz hit a small win of ten, but then in quick succession we hit a whole series of twos, fives, tens and fifteens, the coins cascading boisterously into the trays and stirring the determination to increased effort.

'Too slow, too slow,' Buzz complained. 'I'm loading for bear!'

'Five at a time?'

'Five at a time. Right, me beauties, take that . . . and that . . . and that . . .'

There comes a point when you just *know* you're not going to break the house. I think it's when your plunging finger-tips touch cardboard instead of nickels. I stared disbelievingly into the empty Dixie cup, wondering who could have stolen my nickels without me knowing.

'Well,' I sighed, 'that's it.'

He frowned in mid-pull. 'You're bust?'

'Yep.'

He glanced at his own cup. 'Jesus . . . only six left. O.K. – one in each machine.'

We loaded . . . pulled.

'Close your eyes!' commanded Buzz, 'and prepare yourself for the sound of a thundering jackpot!'

Clunk . . . clunk . . . clunk . . . clunk . . . clunk . . . tinkle tinkle.

Two nickels popped out of the last machine.

We sighed again.

'O.K.,' he said, 'one final try each.'

In . . . pull . . . in . . . pull.

Clunk . . . . clunk.

'Mmmm,' said Buzz, staring woefully at his machine. 'Well, you can't expect to win *every* time, can you, mate?'

'No, not every time,' I agreed, reflecting that we'd both just lost four quid each in about ten minutes. 'Well, it could have been worse – we might have been playing Big Bertha.'

A strange incandescent light entered his eyes. 'Ah, yes . . . the Big Berthas . . .'

'Now, Buzz . . .'

'I noticed one by the main door as we came in . . . and there's another one over there.'

'Buzz, I'm sure there's a dozen in here, but . . .'

'Ah, mate, I've just *got* to have a little go on one.'

'You've *had* a little go on one – in the Sahara.'

'*And* doubled my money. I tell you, I have an affinity with them. I can't get close to these little piddlers, these are for women. The Big Berthas are a *man's* machine.'

'They gulp unisex money, son – and in vast quantities. It takes no longer to lose a dollar on them than a nickel on these.'

'Yeah, but think of hitting the jackpot! *Five thousand dollars* – against a mere hundred and fifty on these things.'

'*If* you hit the jackpot. I reckon you stand a better chance of laying that waitress tonight than pulling a pot out of one of those.'

'Well, maybe – but you never will if you don't try, will you? Look, tell you what I'll do – I'll bet one hundred dollars, not a cent more. I won't take any winnings out of the tray, and what's in there I'll cash in and keep. Hell, I've *got* to get fifty back, surely!'

'Well, yes, I reckon you should.'

'O.K., then, let's go.'

We went back to the change desk and he broke a hundred dollar bill down into crisp new George Washington singles, a lovely sight. Then we headed down the room to the nearest Big Bertha, a veritable giantess, eight feet high and four feet wide, offering a complex six-tumbler system, the four winning symbols appearing from either left or right on the six-symbol result.

Above, an illuminated panel proclaiming FIVE THOUSAND DOLLAR JACKPOT in bold white lettering on a gaudy red background, and the sight of it stirred Buzz to renewed determination.

'*That's* the baby I want,' he chuckled, riffling his wad of Washingtons. 'Right, Tobin, you're on the lever, I'll feed the brute. Ready?'

I reached up, gripped the huge black knob. 'Contact!'

'O.K. . . . here's to the wildest New Year of your life. Come on, now, Bertha, cough your old silver heart up for Buzz and Russell.'

Cracking off a single, he fed it gingerly into Bertha's orifice, and once again, sensing the stuff of life at its chromium threshold, the obscene machinery came alive, pursed its prurient lips . . . and sucked.

In went the Washington, smooth as a hot knife through butter.

Buzz raised his arm and dropped it commandingly. 'Fire one!' I pulled. Keeeeeerrrr . . . joink!

The six tumblers tumbled . . . and thunked to a halt.

Orange . . . Orange . . . Orange . . . Cherry . . . Watermelon . . . Bar.

Buzz gasped . . . there was a slight mechanical pause . . . then ker . . . pow! . . . ker . . . pow! . . . ker . . . pow! . . . ker . . . pow . . .! Like shells from an anti-tank gun, ten bright and shiny silver dollars battered down into the tray, making a racket they must have heard half-way across the room.

'Yaaaaaahhoooo!' laughed Buzz, thumping me on the arm. 'What did I tell you, Tobin – I've got an affinity with these babies! Ten back for one! Now, these are the odds I've been waiting for!'

Three men who were strolling in the vicinity changed course and came over to see what the excitement was about.

'Hit somethin' good?' enquired one, a red-haired guy about five foot one with a five-foot-two cigar clamped between his teeth. He reminded me of Barney Rubble out of The Flintstones.

'A ten first time out,' replied Buzz.

'Quit while you're ahead,' advised Barney. 'I lost fifty on this sonovabitch last year.'

'I'm playing one hundred, win or lose,' said Buzz, brandishing his wad. 'I've got a system.'

Barney turned to his pals and guffawed. 'The guy's gotta system. Tell the management, kid, they'll give yuh the penthouse suite for nuthin', just so long as you stay in here an' play it.'

'Number Two,' Buzz said determinedly, feeding in another Washington. 'Fire!'

Orange . . . Grape . . . Watermelon . . . Bar . . . Cherry . . . Orange.

Nothing.

Barney gave another chuckle. 'That your system? Man, you *gotta* tell the management, they'll feed you free, too!'

Buzz slid me a scowl and nodded. 'Number Three.'

In George slid.

Cherry . . . cherry . . . cherry . . . Bar . . . Grape . . . Watermelon.

'Jesus, he hit it!' cried Barney, dropping cigar ash all down his shirt.

Ker . . . pow! . . . Ker . . . pow! . . . Ker . . . pow! . . . the anti-tank gun blasted off ten more times.

Buzz was grinning so hard I thought his face might split. In went another Washington – fast.

Damn me, if he didn't cop another two cherries – five more silver Ikes. Things were going unbelievably well.

Another couple of small wins came in the next five dollars, and now we were beginning to attract some attention, for with every win our three spectators would let out a cheer, which, added to the crash of silver dollars and our own reaction, added up to rather a lot of noise.

Within another ten dollars we had collected as many more spectators, and by the time Buzz was half-way through his wad we were surrounded by a fair old crowd, all of which was lost on Buzz who had eyes and mind solely for Big Bertha and her treasure.

'How're we doing?' I asked him.

'We're doing all right, mate,' he murmured excitedly, casting an eye over the small mountain of dollars in the tray. 'I reckon we're well ahead. Right, come on, you big brassy bitch, cough up that big one!'

Excitement piled upon excitement in the next twenty or thirty pulls, each near-miss drawing a groan of sympathy from the crowd, and each win, no matter how small, producing a rousing cheer.

I was beginning to worry now about the commotion we were causing in case it was distracting the high-rollers at the tables. But then I reckoned that this was just the sort of excitement the management would revel in, so I abandoned concern for the high-rollers and concentrated on Buzz, experiencing a sudden and alarming sixth-sense certainty that, by God, he *was* going to pull the jackpot before he'd finished.

Crazy, I know, because a machine is just a machine, incapable of mood, of exuding promise, yet there was no getting away from the feeling that with every pull Buzz was getting closer and closer to the big one.

Another win of ten dollars quickly followed, bolstering my belief, but then hope began to slip away as ten dollars went in without reward. Again a surge of excitement with two more wins of five dollars in quick succession, yet by now Buzz was down to his last three or four Washingtons and the end was clearly in sight.

He looked at me with a wan grin. 'I'm sure we're still ahead, though, cock.'

'But not by five thousand.'

'No, not quite . . . maybe twenty or so.'

'Which is what we lost on the nickel machines, hm?'

'We-ell, it's been fun. We've had an hour's entertainment free.'

'That we have. O.K., stick 'em in and we'll have a drink. I'll have to pick up Angela in a few minutes.'

'O.K. . . . here we go, keep everything crossed.'

He fed in a Washington and lost it . . . lost another . . . and on the last one, as though Bertha felt sympathy for his position and wished to save him embarrassment, she disgorged a modest five.

'Well, that's it,' announced Buzz. 'All gone.'

'Hey, you quittin'?' asked Barney, shocked by the prospect. 'Hell, you've got a sackful of silver Ikes there.'

'We said we'd quit when we'd used the bills,' I explained. 'Otherwise, you know what happens.'

'Sure – but whatcha gonna do with them Ikes? – hire a truck ta take them home? Besides, yuh owe it to your public! Yuh gotta keep on playin'.'

Buzz laughed and looked at me. 'The man's right, you know.'

I had to laugh at him. I'd known all along he wouldn't stop when the Washingtons had gone. I mean, what *do* you do with a hundred and fifty silver dollars that weigh half a ton?

'O.K.,' I sighed, turning to the handle. 'Fire One when ready.'

'Number One loading!'

'Atta, boy . . .!' laughed Barney.

'When all this is gone,' I said, 'you fellas stick around. I'll be round with the hat.'

Barney shrugged. 'Hell, it's only money . . .'

'Yeah, mine,' muttered Buzz . . . and dropped in the dollar.

I don't know what happened next . . . at least I *do* but it's hard to describe except in terms like 'all hell let loose' and 'the roof fell in'. All I do know is that from somewhere up above a firebell suddenly exploded into deafening life and a terrific cheer went up and then Barney and his pals were jumping up and down and slapping Buzz on the shoulder and pumping his hand and everyone was yelling at him and at me and at each other and making one holy hell of a din and there was Buzz, white-faced and wide-eyed, staring at me with his mouth open as though he'd been punched in the belly and then the realization came to me that he'd won the bloody jackpot and I couldn't believe it because nobody *ever* wins a jackpot, leastwise not a mate and not a *five thousand dollar* jackpot and . . .

'Yuh did it! . . . yuh did it! . . . yuh *did* it!' Barney was yelling, as he grasped Buzz round the knees and jerked him off the ground. 'Christamighty, yuh hit the fuckin' *pot*! . . . an' I did it for yuh . . . didn't I do it for yuh? . . . didn't I tell yuh to keep on playin' . . .?'

'Yes . . . yes,' Buzz was muttering, blinking about him, stunned by the reality of the dream. 'But . . . where's the money . . . there's no money . . .'

'Yuh don't *get* no money on a jackpot!' shouted Barney. 'Christ, five thousand silver Ikes'd fill the goddamn room! Don't worry, the dame'll be here.'

'Dame?'

Suddenly she was there, right on cue, a hard-looking brunette in a mini-skirted red uniform, pushing through the crowd with all the grace of a stormtrooper, clutching a clip-board.

'O.K., O.K., let me through there . . . out of the way, *please*!'

She broke through into the clearing occupied by Buzz, Barney and his two pals, frowned at Buzz with a glower of innate suspicion and rapped, 'You the winner?'

'Sure, he's the winner!' laughed Barney, giving Buzz another crack on the shoulder. 'An' *I* did it for him! I told him to go on playin', didn't I, pal?'

'Yeah, yeah,' drawled the dame. 'So you're his agent. Collect your commission later, I wanna talk to *him*.'

Barney's face fell. 'Commission! I don't want no damn commission. I like the guy, I'm glad he won . . .'

'Yeah, sure, ain't we all.' With a sigh she turned to Buzz, checked the machine, then came back to Buzz. 'There are one or two formalities you have to go through, you'll have to come along to the office.'

'Formalities?' blinked Buzz, still in shock.

'Yeh, like talking to the Internal Revenue, they'll want their cut.'

Buzz's face crumpled. 'Internal Revenue! You mean . . . Income Tax?'

She shrugged. 'Call it what yuh like, they'll still want their cut. Now, I want your name, address, occupation, social security number . . . name?'

'Erm . . .' He couldn't remember it.

'You on vacation here?' she demanded, scribbling away.

'Er, yes . . . no . . . well, sort of forced stop-over. We were heading for Los Angeles but had to come down here for repairs.'

'Lucky old you,' she drawled, not giving a stuff. 'O.K., follow me to the office.'

She started off. Buzz made to follow, reached me, cracked a huge grin and squeezed my face in his hands. 'We *did* it, you old bastard! We hit the bugger!'

'You did it, cock, not me.'

'Bollocks, we share it – right down the line.'

'Ho, no we don't. I tried to stop you . . .'

'When? I don't remember you trying to stop me . . .'

The bird was back, sighing dramatically. '*Sir*, *would* you mind . . .'

'Yes, yes, I'm coming. Come on, mate . . .'

I looked at my watch. It was just on nine. 'Buzz, I've got to pick Angela up. You go along, I'll be back in a flash. Where shall I meet you?'

He turned to the girl. 'How long will this take?'

'Fifteen . . . twenty minutes – provided we *ever* get there,' she sighed, sounding as though she had another three hundred super-jackpots waiting to be checked.

'All right,' I said. 'I'll go and get Angela and come to the office. Where will he be, miss?'

She pointed to a distant door. 'In there.'

'See you there, then.'

'Be fast,' he said, turning to pump Barney's hand. 'I reckon I owe you something, mate.'

'Nah,' grinned Barney. 'Buy us a drink when you've finished in there.'

'You're on.'

And then he was off, tailing the girl through the crowd.

With his departure, the spectators surged in for a glimpse of the winning line, exclaimed joyfully, sighed enviously, then began to disperse, retiring with renewed hope on the visual evidence that it *could* be done.

'See yuh later?' waved Barney.

'Yes, sure.'

Then I got away fast.

Bubbling with excitement, I half-ran down the room, anxious to break the news to Angela and get back to Buzz. By *God*, what a thing to happen . . . *five thousand* dollars . . . more than two thousand pounds. A fortune! What would he do with it? Would he want to stay on in Vegas a few more days – cancel the tennis tournament maybe? Well, he'd certainly want me to stay with him. Blimey . . .

As I left the MGM and fell into a taxi, visions of wild possibilities crowded my mind . . . a penthouse suite in Caesar's Palace, every conceivable luxury at the touch of a button, girls, parties, girls, parties, girls, girls, girls . . .

No, don't get me wrong, I wasn't gearing myself up to spend Buzz's money, but knowing him as I did it was a foregone conclusion that this was the sort of thing *he* was planning right now and that he'd want me in the thick of it. All I was doing was preparing myself for the inevitable.

In less than three minutes I was paying off the cab outside Caesar's Palace and racing up the steps, grinning to myself at the thought of Angela's face when I broke the news to her – a gasp of disbelief, 'No!', a dozen bewildered questions, then we'd be hurrying back to Buzz.

Half-way across the casino I was suddenly smitten with the possibility that all would not go smoothly for him, that there'd be trouble, maybe because he wasn't American. Very sorry, sir, but the big jackpots are for residents only . . . foreigners are allowed a limited win of two hundred dollars only. Or . . . regretfully, sir, the income tax due on winnings of this nature runs to ninety five percent, you owe us four thousand five hundred dollars . . .

I shook away the premonition. If that was the case, Las Vegas would cease to function. The whole point of gambling here or anywhere *was* the possibility of taking home a big win. Granted, there would be tax and there might be some restrictions about taking it out of the country, but I doubted that Buzz was planning to take any out of the country, anyway!

Reassured that all must go well. I passed through the casino, crossed the Keno lounge and approached Cleo's barge, fully expecting Angela to be sitting there.

She wasn't.

I checked the time . . . eight minutes past nine. Ah, well, it was a rare bird that was punctual. She'd be here soon.

I entered the dock, found a table with a good view of the approaches from both sides, ordered a drink and thought some more about Buzz and his money.

I still couldn't believe he'd won it. Trouble was – Angela was now taking the edge off the occasion, destroying the momentum. Pity things can't always go as you envisage them. She *should* have been here, dammit . . .

I lit a fag, drank my drink, did some more thinking and checked my watch again . . . nine twenty. Yes, well now she was getting naughty. I can understand a bird wanting to be a *little* late, just to keep a lad on his toes, but twenty minutes . . .

'You all alone, honey?'

The voice entered my ear from the left, smooth as warm oil. I turned, came face-to-face with the biggest knockers I've seen in many a long day. My eyes travelled up . . . to a face that had seen a million bedroom ceilings, aged twenty going on fifty-four, a long-haired brunette who knew precisely where her youth and looks had gone, and was still chasing the same punishment.

'Erm . . .' I coughed. 'Well, no, as a matter of fact I'm waiting for someone.'

'A girl?'

I laughed. 'Yes.'

'Well, at least I'm not totally wasting my time. Been waiting long?'

'Er, no . . . no, actually she's not due for another few minutes.'

'We could get an awful lot done in a few minutes. Care to buy me a drink?'

'Well, I . . .'

'Might do no harm to get acquainted . . . for later, maybe?'

'Well, I . . .'

'Maybe she won't turn up at all, it has been known. Then what would you do for New Year's night?'

'Oh, she'll turn up all right.'

'Like me to keep an eye on you for a while – just in *case* she doesn't?'

'Well, no, thanks all the s . . .'

86

'We wouldn't have to travel far for a *real* good time. I've got a room here in the hotel. Are you staying here, too?'

'No . . . no, I'm not.'

'You look to me like a guy who knows a good time when he sees it . . .' she inhaled subtly, ballooning her incredible boobs in my face, '. . . and you just *know* they don't come any better than with Ellie Bell, don't you?'

'Er, yes, I . . . look, I'm sorry, but . . .'

She laughed and took me off the hook. 'That's all right, honey, the world is full of lonely men. I just liked the look of you, is all. Hear now, if you change your mind just ring room 440, I'll be around.'

'Yes, thank you . . .'

'You're welcome. Bye, now.'

She sauntered off, her eyes covering the room like radar sweeps, then changed direction and headed for another solo male on the far side of the dock.

Phew! I reckon a fella would end up with more than a New Year's hangover from Miss Dong Dong Bell!

Now, where in *hell* was bloody Angela? Half past nine and still no sign. An unpunctual bird always puts you in a terrible dilemma. How long *do* you wait?

You get angry and swear you'll wait twenty minutes – half an hour at the most, but after half an hour you start making excuses for her. Maybe she can't get a cab . . . maybe at that very moment she's racing up the front steps in a panic, utterly contrite, the victim of some mishap or other.

Fine! But how long *do* you wait? I thought about Buzz, who'd be out of the office by now and looking for me, thought about telephoning him, having him paged, explain the delay, but what if, while I was away at the phone, Angela turned up, saw I wasn't there, presumed the worst and buzzed off? Then I'd come back and wait pointlessly for another . . . oh, buggerit, why *couldn't* she have been on time?

I finished my drink in a gulp, angry now that all the joy of Buzz's win was dissipating. I wanted to be over there – with him. I could imagine how he was feeling, probably at the bar with Barney and his pals knocking a few back but looking round for me, thinking 'where's the silly cunt *got* to?'

Another time check . . . nine forty.

Well, another five minutes and that was it, not a second longer.

What could have *happened* to her? Then . . . an arresting thought. Whatever had happened to *her* had also happened to my two hundred dollars!

The thought was so arresting it damn-near stopped my heart! Doubt and suspicion flooded in. Could she . . . had she . . . was it possible I'd been taken? Just who *was* Angela Woolfit? – the secretary she purported to be? Or a hooker?

Maybe both, old son. You remember what she said about amateur, weekend hookers nipping in from L.A. for a quick kill? Yes . . . and now I came to think of it, it did seem funny that she wanted to borrow two hundred until she could get to the bank. Why would she have a cashing arrangement with a Vegas bank? If you came in for a week-end from L.A. you brought cash with you – or travellers' cheques. You just *didn't* negotiate a cashing arrangement with a local bank for a few hundred dollars.

Oh, bloody hell . . . seventy quid up the spout.

All right, it had been great, and if she'd stated her case I'd have been glad to . . . but seventy quid!

Ah well, you live and learn.

Really angry now, and dismayed, not only at having been conned but that she should have ruined the moment of Buzz's triumph, I made my way back across the casino and out to a waiting cab. But then, even as I was climbing into it, the thought came that I might have been doing the girl the most terrible injustice. What if she was ill? What if she'd mistaken the arrangements and was waiting at the *motel* for me? It was a long shot, to be sure, but she had been very sleepy at the time.

Well, I wouldn't be able to relax until I'd checked it out and as I was already in the cab . . . I gave the driver the name of her motel.

It was just on ten when I arrived and I was now very concerned at Buzz's likely concern for me, knowing he'd be baffled, flummoxed and quite possibly downright narked that I hadn't shown. I know I would have been, in his position.

'Can you wait?' I asked the driver. 'I won't be long.'

I trotted across the central courtyard, my heart lifting as I saw the light in her room, yet palpitating at the prospect of a coming row. For if Angela darling had just decided not to turn up . . .

I paused at her door, cleared my throat, girded my loins, and knocked.

Footsteps approached . . . the door opened on a chain and a hard, crumpled face regarded me ferociously through the crack.

Hell, had she conned somebody else? !

'Yeah . . .?'

'I, er, hm . . . may I please speak to Angela . . . please?'

He said nothing for about five seconds, which is a very long time to be glared at by threatening death. But then a frown of incomprehension dissolved the glower. 'Who?'

'Erm . . .' I glanced at the door number to make sure it was the right one. 'Angela . . . Miss Angela Woolfit? This is her room.'

'It is, huh?' Now a lecherous grin dissolved the puzzled frown. 'Man, I'll tell yuh, if there wus *any* broad in here, never mind Miss Angela Woolfit, I wouldn' be standin' here yackin' to you!'

'Yes, I . . . oh, you mean . . .'

'I mean she don't live here no more is what I mean. I moved in at two and believe me there wus no Miss Angela Woolfit occupyin' dese presmises at dat time.'

'Oh . . . well, I'm sorry to disturb you. I was under the impression that she . . .'

'She done a bunk of yuh, huh?'

'Oh, no! No, she . . .'

'My condolences. I know de feelin'. Happy New Year.'

He closed the door in my face.

Disconsolate, I crossed to the office, to make absolutely sure.

'Miss Woolfit?' He was a little fat guy in braces. 'Who are you, her husband?'

'No, no . . . just a friend. She was supposed to meet me tonight but didn't turn up. I just wanted to make sure she wasn't . . . ill or anything.'

'Looked as fit as a fiddle when she booked out at one. Nice-lookin' girl. Still, that's the kinda trouble yuh get from nice-lookin' girls. Want some advice – find yourself an ugly one, they *always* turn up, worst luck.'

'I might just do that.'

'Better still – gamble. That way yuh *know* you're gonna lose. Saves a lotta wonderin'. Happy New Year.'

Well, that was it. I can't say I felt a *whole* lot better for knowing, but at least it had cleared the air and now I could approach the business of enjoying myself with Buzz with a clear conscience.

Well, I'll be damned . . . I'd been hooked, right through the gizzard. Hee hee, one prize fish, neat as ninepence – or seventy quid. Well, the profit hadn't all been one-sided, not by a long chalk. She *had* been fabulous. No, taken all round, it had been worth every penny and isn't it amazing how easily you can talk yourself out of being a right bloody idiot?

The cab dropped me at the entrance to the MGM on the dot of ten fifteen and I sprinted through the doors like a man reborn, anxious to reach Buzz and share his excitement.

Slowing to a fast walk, I raked the room for sign of him, thinking he'd probably head for the bar lounge where we'd previously had the beers so he could keep an eye on the door.

But no Buzz.

On I went to the next bar area, scanned the casino, the slots, then headed for the scene of his triumph – Big Bertha.

Still no Buzz.

Well, now, surely to God he couldn't still be in that office! But at least they might be able to tell me where he'd gone.

I went to the door and knocked. It was opened by a young exec in a dark suit, teeth like snowdrops, hair parted with an axe.

'Yes, sir?'

'I'm looking for a friend of mine, Buzz Malone . . . he won the jackpot on Big Bertha early on.'

He frowned. 'Big Bertha?'

'Yes, the . . .' I turned and pointed. 'The big dollar slot machine.'

'Oh, yes, Mister Malone. He a friend of yours?'

I grinned. 'And working partner – I was pulling the handle. I had to nip over to Caesar's Palace and arranged to meet him back here, but I can't see him around anywhere. I take it he's still not in here?'

'No, he left the office about . . . oh, an hour ago. We didn't keep him long.'

My heart sank. 'Oh . . . well, would you know which way he went?'

He laughed. 'Yes – straight to the bar over there . . .' he pointed to the one we'd had the beers in, '. . . with three friends. Why don't you ask the waitress, maybe she can help you.'

'Thanks, I will.'

I went to the bar, glad Buzz had chosen this one because the waitress would remember him. At this point I wasn't *too* worried because I knew he'd be on the premises somewhere, it was just a matter of time. Maybe he'd nipped off to the loo the moment I'd walked in, though somehow I doubted Barney and the other two would have gone with him. Still, it was a possibility.

As I entered the open lounge, the waitress saw me and came over, hardly wiggling at all.

'Table, sir?'

'Er, no, love, I'm looking for my pal, you remember him – he asked you for a date.'

'Sure,' she smiled. 'But he's gone.'

'How long ago?'

'Oh . . . fifteen, twenty minutes.'

'Did he leave any message for me . . . my name's Tobin.'

She shook her head. 'Nope. Frankly, I don't think he had his mind on any Tobin at the time.' She grinned. 'Just my opinion.'

'Oh? Why – was he . . . drunk or something?'

She laughed. 'Not with alcohol. He only had one with his three friends, then they left. But then he . . . well, struck up conversation, as they say, with a girl . . . and after, oh, half an hour they left together.'

My heart hit my boots. 'A . . . girl?'

'Yeah, real good-looker – blonde, grey silk evening dress, expensive hair-do, the works. Real class.'

'Good God,' I gasped. 'And . . . did you see which way they went?'

'I think it was straight out of the main door.'

'Half an hour ago, hm?'

'About that.' She smiled, sympathetically. 'Wanna know something, I think you've lost him.'

I nodded. 'I think you're right. And he left no message.'

'You might try the reception desk, but I didn't see them head that way. Far as I can remember, they walked off towards the door.'

'Yes, well . . . thank you very much.'

'You're welcome.'

Drenched by a feeling of emptiness and disbelief, I headed for the desk, knowing there'd be no message, which there wasn't. Oh, boy . . . how quickly can your high spirits come a cropper. What a bloody turn-around in one short hour. Anger raged at the dirty trick Angela had pulled, screwing up a wonderful evening.

Oh, *fuck* it . . .'

Aimlessly I wandered towards the main entrance, all ebullience gone, despairing at the way life can so unexpectedly floor you at times. People! God save me from 'em.

'Cab, sir?' asked a major.

'No, thanks, I need the exercise.'

Across the intersection and along the Strip I went, heading towards downtown, seeing nothing, feeling nothing except anger and disappointment. Where in *hell* could Buzz be? Why hadn't he left a message? Who was the girl? Where had they gone? . . . dancing, drinking, to a show, to a party . . .?

Well, it was my own damn fault – or rather Angela's. No, dammit, it was mine for waiting so long. Putting myself in Buzz's position, if I hadn't turned up after an hour and a quarter I'd have reasoned what he obviously reasoned – that I'd got myself caught up with Angela and had decided to go it alone. I mean, an hour and a quarter is a very long time to get from Caesar's Palace to the MGM – a three-minute walk!

Ah, well . . . there was nothing to be done about it. There wasn't a snowball's chance of finding him in this town on New Year's Eve, they could be in any one of the twenty big hotels along the Strip or having a fling downtown . . . or even in L.A. by now, who knew?

Well, *I* certainly wasn't going to waste my evening looking for them, no, sir. Thanks to Buzz, I had a few dollars in my pocket, so I would forget about them forthwith and have myself a stupendous New Year's Eve, if necessary all on my own.

Right, Tobin – enough of the miseries! Shoulders back, chin up, and right-wheel in the Flamingo for a much-needed bracer. Who needs 'em? Who *needs* 'em?

I needed them.

How could I enjoy the spectacle of boisterous gaiety that confronted me in this hour before midnight on New Year's Eve without a mate to share it? How can you extract total pleasure from the sight of a marvellous-looking girl here, a belting figure there, without a pal's elbow to nudge? It's just not the same. That sort of thing's got to be accompanied by winks and leers and 'Cor!' and 'Jeezuschrist!' to be totally pleasurable.

I pushed my way into the Flamingo and finally managed to get close enough to the bar to order a drink. All about me was pandemonium – nine billion people standing elbow to elbow, excitedly waiting for midnight and the start of a brand New Year.

What *was* the hoo-ha all about, I reflected sourly. One minute into the New Year and they'd be doing – and would keep on doing – precisely what they were doing now. What was the big deal about sticking a new number on the end of the year? Hell was hell whatever the date!

Oh, this was ridiculous, I castigated myself, not at all like me to be so down in the mouth. Come on, Tobin, you've played it solo often enough in the past and enjoyed yourself. It's only an attitude of mind. Get with it, man, and feel the occasion. *Talk* to somebody!

I looked around. The only apparently solo person within range was a middle-aged drunk so obviously squiffed he was having trouble finding his mouth and looked in imminent danger of falling on his face. Well, any port in a storm . . .

'Not long now, hm?' I said cheerily.

His face came round slowly, searching for the source of sound, then finally located me, though probably in double-image.

'Beg pardon . . .?'

'I said not long now . . .'

He thought about it, weaving around like a run-down top while staring into his glass. 'She'll murder me . . . *murder* me . . .!'

'Oh. Are you in trouble?'

'Mm . . .? Lost it all,' he bleated plaintively, close to tears. 'Crapped out the whole damn wad . . . she'll kill, sure as . . . don' know what t'do . . . what am I gonna *do*?'

'Lost a bundle, hm?'

'Two . . . three grand . . . don' know how it happened . . . gotta get it back . . .' He suddenly brightened and regarded me with fresh interest. 'Say, pal, could yuh stake me to a small . . .'

I was off.

'Gotta light, honey?'

She'd stepped out in front of me, cigarette poised at her lips, the dark brown eyes above transmitting smoke signals of peace on earth and goodwill to all men. Not a bad-looker but badly shop-worn.

'Yes, sure.'

I snapped a light to the cigarette, noting the delicacy of her caress as she touched my hand in way of support, but the grubby nails did little to help her image.

'You all alone?' she enquired.

'No, I'm heading over there to meet a buddy.'

She smiled. 'Is he as good-looking as you?'

I laughed, for the first time, it seemed, in weeks. '*He* thinks he's a damn-sight better looking, but then he has a warped sense of judgement.'

'Maybe . . . we could all play together?'

'Erm, no, I . . .'

'I'd make it reasonable – rate and half, forty bucks for two. You'd save ten.'

'Well, that's very kind, but . . .'

'Full service, honey, anything your little heart desires . . .'

'I'm sure it would be quite delightful, but I'm afraid we're already accommodated.'

'Well, *bully* for you.'

'Excuse me.'

She excused me.

Well, at least I'd talked to somebody.

I wandered on, circuited the casino, pausing here and there to watch the action without really seeing it, just allowing myself to drift, to be buffeted by the crowd . . . and then I saw her.

Strange, isn't it, how in a room of ten thousand faces one can suddenly emerge from the blue and stop your heart.

She was sitting up in the bar area, at a small table with two chairs, looking out over the casino as though she was waiting for somebody and just about to get mad because somebody hadn't turned up yet.

She had a lovely face, big green eyes and a small nose, her light brown hair cut short and falling in soft waves just below her ears, a face that, but for one feature, would have been described as wholesome, cute, pretty. Her mouth, however, denied the misconception. It was the most adorably sensuous and kissable kisser I'd seen since Paradise Island.

In build, as far as I could see, she was what an American car-dealer would call 'compact' – well-proportioned but not over-abundant in luxuries, but with a mouth like that who cared?

Not, mind you, that I've ever been pedantic about huge boobs and burgeoning bums, far from it. In fact, if anything, I have a leaning towards the greyhounds rather than the hippos. But, of course, in the final analysis it isn't, within reason, the packaging that counts, it's the girl inside that counts – and at that moment she was certainly counting – minutes – and getting madder with the passing of each.

Once again she glanced at her wrist watch, heaved a tight-lipped sigh, gave an irritable tut and scoured the room. And boy, did I know how she felt. Is the world *full* of unpunctual people?

Now, for a better view of the room, she stood up, and to my delighted I saw that the bottom half precisely complemented the top. She was greyhound all the way, wearing black velvet trousers and a white silk blouse the way those svelte creatures in *Vogue* wear them – perfectly.

Now she turned, reached for a short, grey fur jacket draped around the back of her chair, paused, glanced again at her watch, sighed dispiritedly and sat down again, obviously deciding to give him – or whoever – a couple more minutes, then that was it.

Well, Tobin, I thought, are you going to stand there gawping at her all night or are you going to do something about it? Time is getting mighty short. Any second now she'll up and away, and once she gets rolling nothing will stop her. In her mood she's liable to remove anything in her path with a wild swipe of her handbag and that'll be your lot. So . . .?

The task, I knew, would not be easy. It would have to be handled with the greatest delicacy, the utmost diplomacy, or disaster would swiftly ensue. In a mood like hers one is not easily distracted from it, yet I had to come up with something – and fast . . . no! even faster than that! By God, she'd had enough, she was making a move! She was getting up! . . . reaching for her coat! Don't just stand there, you chump, *do* something!

I did something. I was up there in six strides, came to a screeching halt . . . then just gaped at her, speechless.

She turned with a start, frowned at me, fiery-eyed, bewildered and suspicious, finally snorted, 'Yes?'

I gulped. 'Don't go . . .'

Her mouth dropped open. 'I beg your pardon?'

'Please . . . don't go. I want to talk to you.'

She winced, as if light was hurting her eyes. 'You're drunk . . . let me pass.'

'I'm not! I swear I'm not. Please . . .'

'Look, I don't know who you are or what you want, but if you don't get out of my way immediately . . .'

I did a swift side-step, unblocking her route. 'There . . .'

She made to move.

'Miss . . . for my mother's sake, don't go. *Please* give me a minute of your time . . . only *one* minute, not a second more.'

That got her.

She frowned at me, the beginnings of a smile tickling the corners of her wondrous mouth. 'For your *mother's* sake . . .?'

'Certainly. Heaven *knows* how badly she'll take the news that her son collapsed and died of a broken heart in the Flamingo casino . . . so very far from home.'

This time she laughed, and shook her head. 'Oh, brother, now I *have* heard everything.'

'You doubt it'll happen? All right, just go down those stairs and out of my life and you'll see what happens! I'll be a stone-cold gonner before you reach the first blackjack tables, I promise.'

She gave a little sigh. 'You know what I think?'

'Tell me what you think.'

'I think you're a nut.'

'Almost right – but plural, not singular. Nut*s*. I *am* nuts – about you.'

'Well, I'm sorry. I can't return the compliment, mister . . .'

'Tobin. Russ Tobin.'

'I wasn't inviting your name, I was just calling you mister . . .'

'Tobin. Russ Tobin.'

She snorted again, sort of irritably. 'Really, I . . .'

'Look. . . seriously,' I said seriously, 'I know my approach was . . . unusual, to say the least . . .'

'The very least.'

'. . . but I had to act quickly. It was an emergency. There was no time left . . .'

'For what?'

'Before *you* left. I could see you were blazing mad about him not turning up and . . .'

She exploded a laugh. 'Who *are* you, Mysto the Mind Reader?'

'No, just a fella who has already suffered tonight what you've just suffered. I recognized the symptoms immediately – dark anger, indecision, disbelief. You gave him until eleven fifteen, then one minute for luck, then that was it. You were so hopping mad you'd have killed anyone who got in your way between here and the Strip.'

'I still might,' she murmured threateningly.

'No, you won't – not now. Now it would have to be premeditated murder, not hot-blooded reaction. You've cooled down a lot now.'

'Oh, really . . .' she drawled, clasping her hands in front of her in an attitude of aggressive pursuit of the matter. My heart did a back-flip. She intended to stay at least a bit longer and put me in my place. 'And would you mind telling me just . . . *how* you know so much about me and what's going on in my mind? If you're not a mind-reader, what are you – a psychiatrist or something?'

I grinned. 'No. But you don't need a diploma on the wall to tell when a girl . . . a person has been stood up. They . . .'

'I have *not* been stood up!' she rapped.

'Oh. No, of course not . . .'

'There's been a mis . . .'

'. . . understanding,' I nodded. 'Of course.'

'He probably thought I said meet me at the . . . Frontier or . . .'

'An understandable mistake,' I agreed. 'Both hotels beginning with F.'

'Quite.' She became silent, lowered her eyes and inspected her shoes.

'Well,' I sighed, 'wherever he is, I certainly feel sorry for him, poor devil.'

Her eyes flashed. 'You feel sorry for *him*!'

'Certainly,' I grinned. 'Look what he's missing. I reckon he's having the lousiest New Year ever. Well, whoever he is, I'm very grateful to him . . . because he's giving me one of my best New Years ever.'

Now she smiled, really smiled, and it was a lovely sight. 'You're impossible, you know that?'

'How different you look from a few moments ago. Are you *sure* you won't have that drink now?'

'Well, I . . .' she pulled up sharp and frowned. 'Hey, *what* drink now? Boy, you really . . .'

I lifted my hands in surrender. 'All right, I'll re-phrase the invitation. Would you care to have a drink with me, Miss . . .'

She eyed me suspiciously. 'Well, I don't know, you're a pretty smooth character.'

'Not normally, cross my heart. The situation called for boldness just this once. Give me time and I'll revert to my normal, retiring, introvert self.'

'Ha!' she laughed.

'Truly!'

'You're about as retiring and introvert as Bluebeard the Pirate. They should have cast you for Gondorff in "The Sting".'

'I tried, but that pushy Paul Newman talked them into using him. You can't win against that sort of nerve. Well, *will* you have a drink with me, Miss . . . er . . .?'

With a sigh she capitulated, settled the coat back on the chair and sat down. 'But just one, mind.'

My heart sang, then burst into a high-key yodel as I sat next to her and caught a whiff of her scent.

I signalled the waitress who I knew had been watching us and was intrigued by the encounter. She came over smiling, as though happy with the outcome, took our orders and departed.

'Cigarette?'

She accepted it, placed it between her scrumptious lips, then did wondrous things while blowing out a long, thin stream of smoke.

'Firstly . . . I cannot go on calling you "miss" all night . . . I mean, I *could*, but . . .'

'It's Katt,' she smiled, anticipating my reaction. 'Pussy Katt.'

I turned in my seat, searched the bar. 'Where?'

'Idiot,' she laughed.

'You're putting me on.'

'I'm not. Well, the Pussy part is contrived, it's really Sandra, but the Katt part is mine. K-A-T-T.'

'I love it. It suits you, you move like a cat. You're built like one, too.'

'Big ears and sharp teeth?' she smiled, showing them to me.

'Well, no, I didn't really have those parts in mind . . .'

'You shouldn't have any parts in mind. I thought you just wanted to talk.'

'Oh, I do, I do.'

'Well, here I am . . . what do we talk about?'

'You – and we'll start with your name. What nationality is Katt?'

'German.'

'You speak it?'

'Fluently. How about you?'

'Not a word. So – tell me about the . . . "Pussy" part.' I was doing my best to keep all hint of sexual innuendo out of both eye and inflection, and, by God, she was looking for it, ready to pounce and annihilate at its first suggestion. 'Are you . . . inordinately fond of cats, perhaps . . . or is it just a natural nickname for a girl named Katt?'

'I like cats,' she allowed, turning her huge green feline orbs upon me, but with no hint of awareness of how devastating they were at this close range. Then they softened in a secret smile. 'You were closer on the second guess – it is just a nickname, though not quite.'

'Oh? Anything you can tell me about?'

She shrugged. 'Don't see why not – everybody who gambles at Circus Circus knows.'

I frowned. 'Circus . . . Circus . . . the hotel down the Strip?'

'Sure. I work there . . . up in the roof. Pussy Katt is my professional name. I'm a high-wire and trapeze artiste.'

'You're . . . Good God.'

She laughed. 'Don't you believe me?'

'Well, of course . . . Ha!, well blow me . . . Sorry, it's just that you're . . .'

'. . . the first high-wire and trapeze artiste you've ever met,' she nodded. 'Yes, they all say that.'

'Oh . . . black mark for triteness.'

'No,' she smiled. 'It's a natural reaction. We *are* a bit thin on the ground, I admit . . . and if you reply – yes, and you wouldn't be all that fat up in the roof, either, I will crown you with this ashtray.'

I held up two fingers. 'Scout's honour, the thought didn't cross my mind. Well, well . . . I *am* in rare company – in more than one respect. You'll have to give me a moment to recover, you kind of knocked me sideways.'

'Take your time – as long as you recover before I finish my drink.'

'Ah, now, you can't really mean that. I mean, you're not *really* going to hold me strictly to one drink, are you?'

'That's all I drink, anyway. Hangover and high-wires are not terribly compatible, as you might imagine.'

'Yes, I can appreciate that . . . but, you *could* go on to orange juice.'

'I could . . . but I'm not going to. I shall sit here and see the New Year in with you, kiss you once in traditional celebration . . .' my heart exploded, '. . . and for no *other* reason whatever,' she grinned, catching my soaring optimism, '. . . and then go home to bed – alone.'

I nodded, knowing I was licked. 'Of course. Right. Well, I shall be boundlessly happy with that arrangement, provided, of course, that in the meantime you don't expect any more coherence from me . . . because the prospect of kissing you or rather of being kissed *by* you in another . . . fifteen minutes has altogether scuttled my sanity and I have the vaguest suspicion that long before midnight I shall be violently ill from overexcitement.'

She sighed and asked, 'Does it tend to run in your family?'

'What?'

'This . . . occasional tendency to slight exaggeration?'

'Ah, you think I'm exaggerating. Dear Pussycat, at this very moment my stomach is tied in eight thousand granny knots, my heart is thundering as though I'd just run from L.A. carrying a dice table, and I can scarcely speak for the lump in my throat the size of a football.'

'I'll amend the question – this *frequent* tendency to *wild* imagination.'

'But it's true, it's true!'

'Well, in that case I simply can't kiss you. If this is what the mere prospect does to you, I hate to think what the actual act would cause. And I can't be responsible, it's far too risky.'

I slumped. 'Tell you what does run in my family . . . a big mouth.'

She laughed.

The drinks arrived. 'Everything all right, folks?' enquired the waitress, really quite concerned about the development of the affair.

'No,' I told her. 'I'm ill with despondency,' and received a kick on the shin from Pussycat.

'Sssshh.'

'I don't care. Anyway, it's only right the management *should* know of a pending suicide on their premises. I shall stick my head in that spinning wheel and roulette myself to death.'

'Is he *really* bad?' asked the waitress.

'No – only his acting,' sighed Pussycat.

'I know the type. I'm married to a guy who thinks he's Marlon Brando. Trouble is – he looks like Lon Chaney.'

She took the money and departed.

I offered her a toast. 'Here's to the sweetest, shortest love affair on record – about twenty-five minutes. After you leave, I shall go and quietly lie down on the Strip and allow the traffic to run over me.'

She grinned and sipped her drink. 'Despite all your faults – and you do have many – I'll give you credit for one thing, you sure saved my New Year's night. I was just about to lie down on the Strip myself when you arrived.'

'I'm very glad I did, it would have been a terrible waste. Was he something special?'

She shook her head. 'Nope, not really . . . the bum. How about yours?'

'Mine?' I grinned. 'Very interesting case. I only took her out once – last night. She obviously decided once was enough.'

'She just didn't show, huh?'

'Just didn't show. A dirty business.'

'I'll drink to that,' she said, doing so.

'Go easy with that, you've got to make it last a long time.'

'Oh? Just how long did you have in mind?'

'Until it evaporates.'

She laughed. 'You never stop trying, do you. Tell me, what are you doing in Vegas? You're English, aren't you?'

'Yes. I'm on my way to Australia. I should have landed in L.A. but the plane hit a spot of trouble over the Grand Canyon and we dropped into Vegas for a tune-up. I'll be flying out again tomorrow night.'

'A bird of passage,' she mused. 'Everyone in town's a bird of passage.'

'Everyone but you. How long have you been here?'

'Ten thousand years,' she smiled. 'Shouldn't complain, I suppose, the money's fabulous . . . but, God, this dreadful place. Siberia – without the good clean fun of the salt-mines.'

'It's really that bad, hm?'

'Much worse. The vulgarity is . . . quite breathtaking. I mean, can you *imagine* performing genuinely dangerous, death-defying acts on a high-wire above the heads of people much more interested in the result of two settling dice or the turn of a card?'

I shook my head. 'Doesn't your professional soul bleed every night?'

'It used to – but I learned to plug up the hole with money. Another year . . . , just one more year, and then . . .'

'Then you'll *buy* Circus Circus?'

'Then you won't find me within a thousand miles of Circus Circus . . . or Vegas. I shall be back with the family troupe, touring the country – but rich.'

'You seem to have life well organized.'

'I was lucky. I knew what I wanted to do when I was four years old. How about you? What do you do for a living – besides seducing strange women into drinking with you?'

I grinned. 'Nothing much else, really. Like you, I knew what I wanted to do when I was four, too. On my very first date with the blonde babe next door I said to myself, *this* is it. I shall dedicate my life to chatting up beautiful birds.'

'I believe you. How old was she at the time?'

'Going on three . . . but *very* sexy.'

She laughed, delightfully. 'I can see I'm not going to get much sense out of you tonight.'

'Well, I did warn you.' I looked at my watch. 'Five minutes to go. Maybe after I've been kissed I'll be more stable, but don't bank on it. I may even get worse. In fact, I think it's highly likely.' I looked around the casino, the bar, choked with people clutching drinks, waiting for midnight. 'What usually happens here when the gun goes off?'

'A curious phenomenon – everyone suddenly likes everyone else. They greet each other like long-lost lovers, spill their milk of human kindness over everyone in sight for, oh, all of an hour, then go back to detesting each other.'

'Very reassuring,' I nodded. 'It's nice to know I'm spending New Year in a completely normal place. Three minutes to go.'

Suddenly an announcement over the public address system cut the music that had been quietly playing and quelled the hubbub. A male American voice, rich in folksie bonhomie, cut through the furore with incisive charm. 'Ladies and gentlemen . . . patrons of the Fabulous Flamingo, may I have your attention, *please*! . . . we now have just a little more than two minutes to go before a brand, spankin' New Year comes in to replace the old . . . and the management and staff of the Flamingo would like to take this opportunity of thanking you, one and all, for your kind patronage during the fast-departing year, *and*, of course, we look forward to your *continuing* patronage during the year to come!'

A rousing, cynical cheer from the crowd.

'We-e-ell, we've all gotta make a crust, haven't we?' he laughed. 'But, seriously, folks . . .'

Pussycat laughed. 'He's trying to make out he was *kidding*?'

'. . . seriously, we do wish you and yours all that you wish yourselves during the coming year – health . . . happiness . . . wisdom and safe-keeping . . . and not forgetting, of course . . . the very best of GOOD FORTUNE!'

Another cheer, even more cynical.

'All . . . rightee . . . well, I'm tuned in here to our local radio station and they make the time precisely . . . *one minute to go!* . . . so fill your glasses . . . lubricate your vocal cords . . . and get ready for the countdown . . . !'

'Are *you* ready for the countdown?' smiled Pussycat, her eyes drifting meaningfully to my mouth.

I breathed in deeply to steady my pounding heart. 'I've been ready for twenty-five minutes.'

'How d'you want it – sitting down or standing up?'

'One of each.'

'Uh Uh – one only, that was the deal.'

'Then . . . standing up.'

'. . . ladies and gentlemen, we have *fifteen* seconds to go . . . now *four*teen . . . *thir*teen . . . *twelve* . . . all together now . . . *ten* . . . *nine* . . . !'

A thousand voices took up the chant, rattling the chandeliers.

'*Eight* . . . *seven* . . . *six* . . . !'

Pussycat narrow-eyed me. 'Be good, now – only one.'

'I was always a lousy counter.'

'Then I shall count for you.'

'*Four* . . . *three* . . . *two* . . . *ONE* . . . aaaannnnddddd HAAAAAPPPPYYYYYY NEEEEWWWW YEEEEAAAA-RRRR!'

The room erupted. Bells rang, music blared out Auld Lang Syne, people shouted, laughed, cried, kissed, hugged, shook hands, slapped shoulders and danced jigs. And in the middle of it all there was Pussycat, warm-eyed and faintly smiling, rising from her chair and waiting to be kissed.

I got to my feet and stood close to her, not daring to believe that all this loveliness was mine for at least the duration of a kiss.

'One,' she said determinedly.

'One,' I croaked . . . and took her face between my hands. 'Happy New Year, Pussycat.'

'And a happy one to you.'

I kissed her then, a gossamer touch, the merest, most delicate contact of lips, and remained there, quite still, for a small heart-thudding eternity. Her eyes opened, wonderingly, and, sustaining contact with my mouth, she murmured plaintively, 'You're cheating,' but while she was saying it her arms were sliding round my neck.

'It's all one kiss,' I whispered, nibbling her lips, now applying a little more pressure, stroking her face, her hair. 'I don't know any other way.'

'You're . . .' kiss . . . 'taking . . .' kiss . . . 'cruel . . . ' kiss . . . 'advantake of a . . .' kiss . . . 'technicality.'

'Did you know you have a mouth in a million?'

'You like my mouth?'

'I adore your mouth . . . it's so soft . . . and warm.'

'I like your mouth, too . . . it's very gentle.'

'Not always.'

'Keep it gentle . . . for now.'

My heart tripped. 'Of course . . . what time do you start work tomorrow?'

'Not until the afternoon.'

'Splendid.'

'Why?'

'Because you and I are going to have some fun. We're going dancing.'

'We are?' she whispered into my mouth.

'Yes . . . and we're also going to have a beautiful late supper . . . to start the New Year off right.'

She chuckled warmly against my lips. 'You're very persuasive.'

I frowned. 'You'll come?'

'Of course.'

'Wow.'

'Did you think I wouldn't? I was only waiting to be asked.'

'You . . .'

She laughed. 'Me what?'

'You . . . beautiful . . . you . . . kissable . . . you . . .'

'Don't you think we'd better sit down? Even for New Year this is getting a little drawn-out.'

I sighed. 'If we must.'

I sat down, aware of and excited by the change in her, knowing she'd given herself completely to the evening and that something wonderful would ensue.

We stayed there for another half-hour, drank our drinks and ordered another, not really needing to drink or needing to do anything but look at each other. Then we left and caught a cab downtown to a restaurant Pussycat often used, probably the only place we could have got into on this frantic New Year's night.

Greeted effusively by a flustered maître d' and settled at a small alcove table, Pussycat explained, 'I spend as little time as possible in the hotel and never eat there. After I finish a performance I have to get out.'

'Understandably. But do you live there?'

She smiled and shook her head. 'Nope. I have an apartment on the edge of town. It didn't take me long in Vegas to realize the only way to endure it was to have as much privacy and home comfort as possible. I'd have gone out of my mind living in the hotel . . . surrounded every minute of the day and night by the noise of those slot machines.'

'Do you ever get out of town – to Los Angeles, maybe?'

She gave a short laugh. 'I've had plenty of offers to go.'

'Oh? Oh, you mean from . . .'

'The punters,' she nodded smilingly. 'The dear punters . . . who believe that anything even *vaguely* attached to the hotel in which they are currently losing their money can be bought. I've had some incredible offers, believe me.'

'I do. Tell me about them.'

'Ohhhh . . . a new Cadillac in exchange for a week-end in San Francisco . . . an oil-well for a week in Oklahoma . . . *countless* offers of instant marriage by oilmen, cattlemen, hotel owners – even an Arab sheik.'

'How terribly romantic.'

'Ha! You should have *seen* the Arab sheik.'

'Were you ever tempted to accept?'

'We-e-ll, it's very difficult to say no when you realize you could accomplish in one short week what will otherwise take months, but so far I've managed to stay independent – though it was a pretty close call with one particular Texas oilman.'

I grinned. 'What happened?'

'Easier to tell you what *didn't* happen! He was quite mad, crazy . . . sent six dozen red roses to my dressing room *every single day* . . . I mean, *six dozen*! My dressing room is only seven feet by seven, I couldn't get in the door! And he pleaded his love in every conceivable way – by letter, cablegram, radio commercial, sky writing . . .'

I laughed. 'No!'

'Oh, sure. He had a plane write "Marry Me, Pussycat" right over Circus Circus. And he sent me the most *fabulous* presents, which needless to say I sent right back . . . diamond clips, bracelets, fur coats, perfume, a Cadillac, a Lincoln . . . oh, I can't remember what all. *And* in addition he promised to settle a quarter of a million dollars on me the moment we were married *and* build me a palatial house in Houston, and . . . so on and so on, the list is endless. No doubt about it, I'd have been a very rich lady.'

I frowned at her. 'And you turned all that down? Where was the catch?'

She sighed. 'He was the catch. He was a fire-breathing tyrant, rude, coarse, loud and vulgar *and* seventy-six years old. Oh, *why* do all these fabulously wealthy men have to be rude, coarse, loud and vulgar and seventy-six years old? Why can't they look like *you* and have a hundred million dollars?'

I laughed. 'I don't know, Pussycat, but thanks for the compliment. I think it deserves a dance. Should we risk life and limb trying to get onto the floor?'

We managed a tenuous foothold on the very edge and she came in close, disturbing me instantly with her scent and the warmth of her body. 'When there's a choice between this and money,' she chuckled in my ear, 'I'll take this every time.'

'Well,' I sighed, 'as a wise man once said, you can only eat one meal and wear one suit at a time. Who *needs* a hundred million dollars?'

'Which wise man said that?'

'Chap I knew named Harry Onions ... a scrap-metal tycoon, worth about ... oh, a hundred million, I should think.'

She laughed and snuggled closer. 'Y'know something ... I'm enjoying you.'

'Now, Pussycat, that sort of talk can only bring you a great deal of trouble. You may think high-wire walking is dangerous, but compared to that ...'

'Tobin ...'

'Yes, ma'm?'

'Kiss me.'

SEVEN

Three a.m.

She opened the door of her second-floor apartment and I followed her in, into a lovely room, neat, clean and comfortable, like Pussycat herself, the sort of room she would need to live in.

'Like a drink?' she asked, tossing her jacket onto the sofa.

'I'd love a coffee.'

'Come.'

We went into a small kitchen, Pussycat doing the chores while I sat on a stool at a peninsular counter and watched her, taking delight in the lithe, sure movement of her body.

'You're well-named, Pussycat,' I told her. 'You move like a spring-heeled cougar.'

'Ha! Your imagination, Tobin.'

'Well, you do. I could happily spend the rest of my life just sitting here watching you pad around the kitchen.'

'Well, you're not going to. You're going to drink this coffee and go, I've got to get some sleep or I'll fall off that wire tomorrow.'

'Yes, ma'm.'

'Yes, ma'm,' she mimicked. 'You say that with *deep* insincerity.'

'Yes, ma'm.'

She poured the coffee and brought it over, settling on a stool opposite me.

'Cigarette?' I offered.

'Tobin, you're getting me into some very bad habits ... smoking, drinking, staying up late ... you'll *have* to go.'

'I'm going. This time tomorrow I shall be . . . oh, in the air and on my way to Tahiti, I expect.'

'What on earth are you going to *do* in Tahiti? No, no need to answer that, I know *precisely* what you're going to do in Tahiti.'

I grinned. 'What?'

'From the look in your eye – the first available wahini or whatever they're called.'

'Madam, you wrong me. Quite to the contrary, I shall take this fleeting opportunity to study the flora and fauna of the island . . . its ancient customs, religious artefacts and . . .'

'Horsefeathers.'

'. . . and horsef . . . oh, do they have horses on Tahiti, I didn't know that.'

We both laughed, then I said, 'No, but seriously . . .'

'Ha!'

'Pussycat . . .'

'Pussycat, Pussycat . . . Tobin, stop! The only flora and fauna you'll be studying are "hay" and "birds" – and the problem of how quickly you can get the latter into the former.'

I clutched my heart. 'God forgive you for maligning so upright and spotless a character.'

'Upright, certainly,' she murmured mischievously. Then, suddenly, her mood changed. For a moment, in pensive silence, she regarded the glowing tip of her cigarette, then quickly ground it into the ashtray, held out her hand for mine, and whispered softly, 'Come.'

I knew where we were heading but couldn't believe it. I really had been prepared, in deference to her work, for an early departure, yet now it was happening I realized she had made up her mind it was going to happen quite a while back, possibly in the restaurant, maybe even before that.

There were no prolonged preliminaries; yet no feverish haste, either. She merely led me into her bedroom and there, in comfortable silence, we undressed. Then she was flying, naked, for the bed, ripping back the counterpane and plunging between the sheets.

'Quickly . . . it's cold!'

I leapt in beside her, thrilling to her body, and there for a long moment we lay, unmoving, welded like Siamese twins.

'I thought . . . that I . . . was being . . . kicked out. I thought

'. . . you had . . . to gets lots . . . of sleep. I thought . . . that you thought . . . that I thought . . .'

Punctuating each few words with tender kisses I worked my way from her lips to her breasts to her stomach, then back again to her mouth, while she chuckled and giggled and stroked my hair most lovingly.

'That's . . . gorgeous,' she whispered. 'You kiss so beautifully.'

'This is the last thing I thought would happen, Pussycat. I really did expect the imminent boot.'

'Just shows how little you know women. D'you think I'd spend the night alone in this big cold bed with a warm hunk of man on hand?'

I sighed despairingly. 'I do wish you gals would at least give a chap a *hint* that his luck was in. I could have been enjoying the prospect for hours.'

'That would've made you even more unmanageable than you've been. We have to keep men like you in their place, otherwise they get carried away with themselves . . . oh, that is *nice*.'

'You really like that, hm?'

'I really love that.'

'And . . . how about this?'

'I like that even more . . . Russ . . .?' she whispered.

'Yes, love?'

'I want you inside me.'

She spread wide and guided me in, gasping a long-drawn 'Ohhhhhhhhh', as I slid deep into her moist warmth.

'Don't move . . .' she whispered plaintively.

'No.'

'Just . . . lie there.'

'All right.'

'I just want to *feel* you in there . . . God, you're like iron.'

'Good, hm?'

'It's wonderful . . . and I think I'm coming.'

'Already?'

'Please . . . don't move!'

'No.'

'Oh, I . . . oh, my *God* . . . OHHHHHHHHH!'

It was all so incredibly simple, no great heaving, threshing holocaust, but nevertheless a deep internal cataclysm.

She relaxed beneath me. 'That was incredible . . . beautiful . . .

beautiful . . .' She opened her eyes and smiled, stroked my face. 'I used you, didn't I?'

I grinned. 'Shamelessly.'

'Do you mind?'

'Don't be daft.'

'You are awfully nice. I'm so very glad I met you.'

'And I you, Pussycat. You're the perfect start to a Happy New Year. I don't care now if the rest is lousy. I only wish I had more time to spend with you.'

'Yes . . . so do I. Russ . . .'

'Yes, love?'

'Fill me.'

I left her, most regretfully, at nine. We had slept like babes, cocooned in each other's warmth, detesting the shrill alarm that heralded the start of her working day. There was a lot she had to do . . . exercises, a costume to mend, and knowing I was a disconcerting intrusion I volunteered to leave.

'It seems indecent to say "thank you",' she smiled, holding me at the door. 'But thank you all the same. It was . . . very lovely.'

'Dear Pussycat, take care. Take great care. I'm worried you haven't had enough sleep.'

She laughed and hugged me. 'I've had plenty. I don't suppose it's likely you'll make Vegas again for a long time, but if you do . . .'

'Circus Circus will be my very first call, betcha life. And I do hope, at least for my sake, you're still there.'

'So do I,' she said earnestly, and kissed me.

I took a cab back to the Sahara, my mind tracing tender thoughts of Pussycat.

What, I wondered, *were* my chances of getting back to Vegas within the coming year? . . . this bright, new, brand New Year? What *does* it hold for you, Tobin, I pondered. Tahiti . . . Australia . . . and then where? And what *there*?

Rhetorical questions all.

I paid off the cab and entered the hotel, amazed, as always, to find the casino busy, a sight I knew I'd never completely get used to.

Along the corridor and into the elevator, my thoughts now turning with a grin and a surge of excitement to Buzz, wondering how the old bastard had made out. I hoped he was back. I was dying to hear all about it. I could imagine his face when I walked in, wreathed in a smug grin, lying, more than likely, on a bed ostentatiously smothered in ten-dollar bills. It was just the crazy sort of thing he'd do.

Well, he was back all right . . . and he was lying full-length on his bed, but there the similarity ended. The bed was not strewn with ten-dollar bills or any other kind of bills . . . and Buzz's face was not wreathed in a smug grin or any other kind of grin.

It was the picture of downright bleeding misery!

EIGHT

As I entered the room he turned his head towards me, muttered, 'Thank Christ,' and quickly swung his feet to the floor.

I came to a stunned halt, detecting terrible disaster. 'Buzz . . . man, what's the matter?'

He heaved a hugely despondent sigh and sank his face into his hands, rubbed at it wearily, then came up with the merest glimmer of a smile. 'Happy New Year, cock.'

I laughed unhumorously. 'And a Happy New Year to you, I don't think. It looks like it started with four funerals, three burglaries and a toothache for you.'

He gave me a twisted grin. 'Not quite, but you're on the right track.'

'Buzz . . .' I frowned, 'are you feeling all right? You don't look so great.'

'Still a bit whoozy but improving slowly . . . got a fag, mate, I'm out.'

'You're improving.'

I sat on the edge of my bed, facing him, gave him a cigarette and noticed the slight tremor in his hands as he lit it. This just wasn't Rockfist Malone at all!

I waited until he'd pulled down a good lungful, then said, 'Well, to say I'm *intrigued*, Malone, would be the understatement of the decade. Just . . .' I consulted my watch . . . 'thirteen hours ago I left you in the MGM Grand, leaping around like a two-year-old after winning all that lovely money, and now find you impersonating a bloke with yellow jaundice who has just *lost* all that . . . lovely . . . mon . . . hey, you didn't, did you?'

He lowered his head, in anguish, and absently flicked ash on the carpet.

'Buzz . . .' panic now, '*tell* me you didn't . . . Buzz, you couldn't! . . . you didn't . . . you haven't . . . !'

His voice was a despairing murmur. 'I could, . . . and did . . . and bloody have, mate.'

I gaped at him. 'Oh, you bloody nutter . . . *how*, for Godsake?'

He looked up at me, bewildered, shaking his head. 'It's a long, unbelievable story . . .'

'Just . . . tell it to me – from the top.'

'O.K. . . . but first you've got to promise to believe everything I tell you . . .'

'Well, of course, I'll believe you. It's . . . pretty unbelievable, hm?'

'It's bloody fantastic. I'm not sure I believe it myself now. I've been lying here since seven o'clock wondering whether it's all been real or a terrible nightmare.'

'Well, get on with it – right from the time I left you to get Angela . . .'

He frowned. 'Yeah . . . what in hell happened to you!'

Now it was my turn to sigh. 'Buddy, was *I* taken for a ride. You know I lent her two hundred dollars until she could get to the bank . . .'

'Yeh, sure.'

'Well, that was no loan, son – that was her fee! The sweet and oh-so-affable Angela was no mere secretary – she was one of those amateur, week-end hookers she was telling us about.'

His mouth dropped open. 'No!'

'Yes. I got to Caesar's Palace just after nine, as you know, and waited . . . and waited, you know how it is. How long d'you give them – ten . . . fifteen . . . twenty minutes? Believe me, I wanted to get back to you as fast as I could, but I didn't want to let her down. So I kept giving her another five minutes until suddenly I'd been there three quarters of an hour and the writing was on the wall. I jumped in a cab, intending to come back, but then I wondered if she could possibly be ill or something, so I changed course and went downtown to her motel. You can guess what I found.'

'The bird had flown.'

'She'd flown – and so had my two hundred bucks.'

'Oh, bloody hell . . .'

'Anyway, I shot back to the MGM and checked with the office who said you'd left, heading for the bar, so I checked with the waitress who told me you'd had one drink with Barney and the lads, then had got talking to a *very* classy bird, and had left about ten. So – that much I know.'

'The mere tip of the iceberg,' he intoned solemnly.

'Well, let's have the submerged bit.'

'O.K. . . . I went to the office and suffered a twenty-minute grilling – from the management, the Internal Revenue – Christ, you'd have thought I'd just tried to heist the casino! They wanted to know who I was, why I was there, where I was staying, for how long, where I'd come from, where I was going to . . . you've never heard such a bloody performance. Good job you don't have to go through all that when you're putting money *in* the fucking machine.'

'Did they hit you for tax?'

He grinned hugely. 'Not a cent. Whether it was because the tax bloke was an ardent pro-tennis fan or not, I don't know, but he actually *fed* me the suggestion that as you had been my partner, the money was therefore divisible between us and each share didn't constitute enough to be taxable.'

'Very decent of him.'

'Yeah, he was a nice old bloke. Then the management asked me how I wanted the loot and I said in hundreds and fifties. By God, mate, it felt wonderful, I can tell you . . . a great fat wad of . . .'

I could see the miseries were coming on him again, so I said, 'Don't dwell on it, Buzz, just get on with the story.'

'Well,' he sighed deeply, 'with a warning to be careful, that there were a lot of thieves, hookers and conmen around just waiting for a wad like mine, they pointed me in the direction of the casino and gave me a little shove, wishing me the best of luck *should* I intend to continue playing.'

I grinned. 'I'll bet.'

'Man, I tell you, it was breaking their hearts to see all that lovely money leave the office. I swear to God one of them had tears in his eyes as he opened the door for me.'

'*Were* you tempted to go on playing?'

'Nah, not likely. All I was thinking about was the terrific time we were going to have with the loot – not forgetting, of course, that half of it was yours.'

'Balls, I told you . . .'

'Nuts, Tobin, half of it was yours!' Black despair flickered again in his face. 'That's what makes it so bloody terrible . . .'

'Shut up, man, and go on.'

'Well, when I left the office Barney and his mates were there, waiting, I suspected, for their cut. Fine, I thought, Barney does deserve something, so I suggested we have a drink, intending to slip him a couple of hundred for doing his stuff. But, y'know, he wouldn't take anything . . .'

'He wouldn't?'

'Not a red cent. They let me buy them one drink and then they pushed off to meet their wives, real nice blokes.'

'Kind of restores your faith in human nature.'

'Well,' he said glumly, 'the way things turned out, I wish he'd insisted on a couple of *grand*, I'd feel a lot better knowing he was enjoying it instead of . . .'

He paused.

'Well, after they went, I sat there waiting for you, feeling four miles higher than the moon and planning a diabolical extra few days in Vegas. Tobin, you have no *idea* what I had lined up for us.'

'Oh, I think I have . . . penthouse in Caesar's Palace . . .?'

'The MGM, actually.'

'Wine . . . women . . . and one or two choruses of "Roll Me Over, Lay Me Down and Do It Again"?'

'With full string orchestra, mate. Dammit, I was even contemplating calling Aussie, cancelling the tennis thing and staying a bloomin' week!'

'I knew it, I knew it. Read your scheming, lecherous mind right down the line.'

'Well, hell, why not? But . . . there it is – all up the flamin' spout. Jesus, Tobin, if only you'd come back! I was in a right old spot there, not knowing what was happening. It got to half nine, then a quarter to ten . . . and about that time I figured you had something big going with Angela and weren't coming back.'

'Hell, Buzz, I'm sorry . . .'

'Nah, don't be daft, you were right up it yourself. Well, anyway, I was just sitting there, keeping an eye on the door, when suddenly into the bar walks this *gorgeous* piece of crumpet . . . I mean, a really knockout babe, well stacked, beautiful face, and wearing a fantastic grey-silk evening gown. This, son, was so *ritzy*, so far out of my class, I immediately slotted her into "totally unreachable" and was content to just sit there and stare.

'Well, she cased the joint, looking for a table, but didn't once look at me, then, blimey, she turned in my direction and sat at the very next table – not six feet away from me! And, Russ, old buddy, ashamed though I am to admit it, I'm afraid you did kind of slip from my mind there for a minute or two.'

'Rotten devil,' I laughed.

He shook his head. 'Oh, man, I'll tell you, even at six feet she turned me into a lump of quivering jelly. I kept getting whiffs of her perfume and thought I was going to pass out with delight. Everything about her was perfect . . . her soft, blonde, shiny hair, her skin, her hands . . .'

'Buzz, will you stop.'

'And the *diamonds* she was wearing! Christ, she had a ring on with a stone the size of a bleeding walnut! Talk about a million-dollar baby!'

'Buzz, I don't think I can stand the suspense – will you *please* get on with it!'

'I'm getting on with it, but you said you wanted every minute detail.'

'All right, all right, carry on – though I reckon I know what you're going to say.'

'What?'

'That she'd seen you hammering hell out of some poor jerk on the U.S. circuit and simply *adored* big, muscular pro-tennis players and . . .'

'Tobin, shut up, you're way out of court. No, she just sat there, regal as a queen, ordered a Bloody Mary and paid no attention to anyone, least of all to me. Not a rotten glance, though I was staring so hard at her she must have felt it.

'Five minutes passed and I was beginning to get the impression she was waiting for somebody. Every now and again she'd scan the room, look towards the main door, look at her watch, and one time gave an irritable tut like she was getting fed up waiting.'

I grinned. 'How well I know the symptoms. A couple of hours later I was watching a bird going through the same trauma in the Flamingo. It must have been stand-up night, maybe it's an epidemic.'

'Sorry to disappoint you, but this little act was not for real, only part of a . . . well, anyway, there she was, getting quietly hot and bothered, and there was I, suffering ten different kinds of torment and dreaming fantasies about me taking the place of the guy who should have been there but wasn't – and then it happened!

'She reached for her little silver-lamé evening bag that was lying on the table, got out a silver cigarette-case and lighter . . . then dropped the lot all over the floor, right at my feet! Everything shot all over the place – make-up, lipstick, keys, coins . . . *and* . . . the biggest bloody roll of bank notes you've ever laid eyes on! A fortune! Well, all I could see was the outside note, and, mate, that was a five-hundred-dollar job! So, you can bet your Aunt Fanny's feather boa she was carrying a minimum of ten . . . fifteen thousand semolians!'

'Wow! Must have made you feel like a kid with change from his piggy-bank.'

'Well, one thing it *did* instinctively make me feel was safe. I mean, displaying that sort of wealth, the last thing she'd be interested in was *our* little wad of pin-money. Not, mind you, that I'd even given the possibility a thought up to now, you wouldn't, would you?'

'Not the vaguest. Proceed.'

'There I was, then, up to my knees in her belongings, this thundering great roll of greenbacks actually resting against my foot and the other stuff strewn around like leaves in autumn. Quick as a wink I was on the floor, gathering it up and shoving it back in the bag, while Gorgeous Gussy up aloft was tutting and oh-ing and saying how very clumsy she was.'

'What sort of voice?'

'American . . . soft as blancmange.'

I sighed. 'Naturally. When these babes have it, they *really* have it.'

'In diamonds,' he agreed. 'Finally I got the stuff in but kept the wad of notes separate, got to my feet and handed it to her, then had a little joke as I gave her the money – you know, something instantly pithy and wildly witty like, "No, the dice tables are that way, miss." '

'Terrific. And she collapsed in hysterics.'

'She, son, gave me one of the most *devastating* smiles of gratitude it's ever been my joy to behold, a solid, forty-carat heart-stopper, very much akin to the two-hundred-mile-an-hour ace-serve I once stopped in the guts from Big Bernie Billowicz in Florida. Thwack! And I was her slave for life.

' "How very kind of you," she cooed, accidentally brushing my fingers as she took the wad and completely shattering what was left of my cool. "And how very clumsy of me." 'Entirely my fault, I assured her, I should've caught it before it hit the floor.'

I winced. 'Oh, Malone . . .'

'Well, you do say these damn silly things, don't you.'

'Always,' I admitted. 'So, naturally, you got to talking . . .'

'So, naturally, we got to talking . . .'

'And you told her about your big win on Big Bertha, just to put *her* at ease and let her know you weren't after *her* wad.'

He sighed and nodded. 'Right, chum, but not *totally* right. You see, I didn't have to tell her about my win, she already knew about it – as I found out to our bitter cost later.'

'Oh, Malone . . . I do believe you're about to ruin this beautiful story for me. Obviously she was not all she appeared to be.'

'One thing I've noticed about you, Tobin, is your tendency to understatement. However, after you've given me another fag I will proceed.'

I gave him one, lit one myself. 'Boy, I could do with a coffee. Shall we order one up?'

'Hang on a minute and we'll go down to the café. I need the air. Where was I . . .?'

'Shooting off your big mouth about the win.'

'Oh, yes. "Oh, really, how very nice for you," she said, quite off-hand, as though five thousand dollars was the tipping money she brought to Vegas.'

'She was from out of town?'

'Yes, L.A., but she gave me the impression she used Vegas like we use our garden at home – as much in it as out. Well, we chatted on for a while, me all nervous and unable to believe my luck, she all cool, calm, and casual, certainly friendly enough, though giving the impression she was just filling in time until Prince Charming arrived. Then, blow me, around ten o'clock I guess it would be, she suddenly looked at her watch, pulled a face, and asked me, sort of hesitantly, what I had planned for New Year's Eve!'

'Aye aye. And you replied, I'm supposed to be meeting a daft cunt named Tobin and doing the town but *he* hasn't turned up, either?'

He frowned. 'No, funnily enough I didn't get around to mentioning you, mate . . . sorry.'

'Go on,' I sneered.

'Tobin, you're hurt . . .'

'Cut to the flaming quick, if you want to know. Blimey, not even a mention. Now, if that had been me, Malone . . .'

'You'd have kept your trap shut, too.'

I laughed. 'White-hot irons would not have prised your name from my lips . . . get on with it.'

' "Me" I said, all innocent, "Why, nothing at all. As a matter of fact, I was just sitting here mulling over that particular problem." Then she gave me the eyes, so sad and appealing, and asked me whether, in the absence of the pig who hadn't turned up, I'd consider escorting her to a rather select party at which no lady would be welcome *without* an escort and on which she'd had her little heart set all year.'

'Oh, brother . . .'

'Precisely. My first reaction was, of course, that I couldn't possibly do her justice, that I wasn't dressed for the occasion . . . bla bla bla . . . to which she replied that not only was my gear eminently suitable for the occasion but that I, being a good six inches taller, fifty pounds heavier, and two thousand times handsomer than her intended escort, was *eminently* eminently suitable for the occasion, and that she was personally thrilled to bits that P.C. hadn't turned up!'

'Ace-serve, right down the line.'

'A winner all the way, mate. At which I did three back-somersaults, leapt to my feet and demanded why we were wasting so much precious time when we could be elsewhere.'

'And so you departed forthwith?'

'Well,' he frowned, 'not quite forthwith . . . and I reckon that was when the bitch set things rolling.'

'Oh? What things rolling?'

'The diabolical plot, cock. First, she said, she'd have to pay a quick visit to the Powder Room, and off she went . . .'

'Leaving you praying to Woden that I wouldn't pop through the front door right then?'

He grinned ashamedly. 'Well . . .'

'I forgive you, go on.'

'While she was gone all sorts of daft, panicky thoughts ran through my mind, like . . .'

'Like it was all a wild dream and she wouldn't come back – yes, I've been there.'

'But, by heck, she did come back, all smiles and looking eight times more desirable – *and*, mate, I suddenly got this sixth-sense feeling that she also might *just* be available, know what I mean?'

'Of course – I've been there, too . . . Paradise Island and the unbelievable Malinda.'

'So you told me – well, there you go. And there we went, out through the front door and . . .'

'Into a taxi.'

'Ha! You're kidding! No, buddy – into her own white, chauffeur-driven Cadillac convertible! Parked right outside, waiting for her.'

'Buzz . . . Buzz . . . Buzz,' I sighed. 'You're determined to ruin my day, aren't you?'

'Swear to God – a white Caddy convertible, black top, white leather seats, driven by this e-*normous* gorilla in uniform, giant of a bloke, made me feel like Twiggy . . . hands like dinner plates and muscles in his lips. So wide across the shoulders I couldn't see through the windscreen, so help me.'

I gave him the eyebrows. 'You . . . in the back with her . . . were worried about looking through the windscreen.'

'Hardly – but I couldn't help noticing. From the back he looked like an over-stuffed sofa.'

'What was her name, by the way?'

He grinned. 'It'll slay you.'

'So – slay me.'

'Felicia . . . DeCourcey-Holme.'

'Oh, boy . . . Christ, *right* out of the top drawer. How come we get lumbered with things like Tobin and Malone?'

'Steady on, son – as things turned out hers was probably Gladys Clutterbuck!'

'Buzz, don't . . . ! I beg you, do not destroy the beautiful illusion until you absolutely have to.'

'O.K., so it's still Felicia DeCourcey-Holme . . .'

'Anything happen between you while you were getting to where you were going?'

'Yes, but nothing obvious, she was playing it too classy for that – just little intimate smiles and the occasional flick of her eyes to my mouth while I was talking . . .'

I nodded. 'That'd be enough.'

'It was plenty. I was so balled up inside I wouldn't have known if we'd driven right out of town and into California.'

'Roger, know the feeling. And did you – drive out of town?'

He shook his head, bewilderedly. 'No, certainly not that far, but don't ask me where we got to. Next thing I knew we were pulling up outside a long, low, beautiful ranch-style house and she had me by the hand, saying, "Come on, don't be nervous, they're only ordinary people." '

'And were they?'

He nodded. 'Yup. There weren't as many as I'd expected – maybe twenty or so – but they were all letting their hair down, having fun, dancing, getting quietly drunk, making a lot of comforting noise. Felicia led me into a huge lounge, said hello to several people, left me alone for a second or two and came back with two enormous glasses of champagne, chinked glasses with me and told me how *very* grateful she was for what I'd done.'

'Yeah, some sacrifice,' I grinned. 'And you, of course, were totally preoccupied wondering just *how* grateful she would get, you randy swine.'

'Oh, I take it that your evening was entirely celibate, Tobin?'

I laughed. 'Never mind me, get back to you.'

'Of course that's what I was wondering. And when she asked me to dance, I was beginning to believe I knew the answer! So, swallowing two or three good belts of the champers to steady the nerves, away I went . . .' he groaned, 'oh, *man*, did she feel good . . .'

'I'm with you all the way.'

'And, by God, so was she . . . a little restrained at first, but after two or three numbers she decided to stop pretending she was a lady and came on strong. Jeezus, mate, I was in a hell of a mess – hard-on like the Town Hall flagpole – and she was loving it, moaning and groaning and rubbing herself against it, and then . . .' he paused, gulped, shook his head.

'Well, go on! And then . . .?'

'I suddenly felt sick . . .'

'You . . . *what*?'

'*Ill*, mate . . . diabolically nauseous. *God*, I felt bad . . . terrible! I broke out in a cold sweat . . . I felt weak, faint . . . so help me, I thought I was going to flake out on the spot.'

'Good God. Must have been quite a shock for her, too – a big, strong lump like you.'

'Oh, she played it beautifully – fluttered around, got me into another room, made me lie down on a sofa . . . then finally told me she was going to put me to bed and look after me until I recovered. Next thing I knew, Granite Gordon, the chauffeur, was hauling me off the couch as though I weighed ninety pounds stripped, and bundled me into the back of the Caddy. Then Felicia got in the back with me and told me she was taking me to her motel room and would call a doctor because she thought I had food poisoning.'

'Did *you* think you had food poisoning?'

'Mate, the way I was feeling I'd have believed cholera, leprosy – anything! I thought I was dying! Anyway, we arrived at this motel and as we were getting out, she whispered sort of urgently, "Look, this has got to look right or they won't let you in. We'll have to make it seem natural, sign you in as my husband who's just arrived, very much the worse for drink . . . we'll even put our money in a safety-deposit box as though we were retiring for the night, all right?" '

'Here,' I said, 'the rat begins to smell.'

'Spot on,' he nodded, 'though *you* are thinking with a clear and sober mind, not dying on your feet with beriberi. I was so damned anxious to get horizontal, I'd have crawled into that safety-deposit box and slammed the lid.'

'Yeah, I can imagine. So . . .'

'I managed to stay upright by the door while she was talking to the desk clerk, then she beckoned me over and I signed in, signed the safety-deposit card, put my wad next to hers in the box, saw it locked away in the safe, remember her stuffing one of the two keys the clerk had given us into my pocket, then teetered with her down a very long corridor to her room. Buddy, I *just* about made it. I reckon five more steps and I'd have been out cold.'

'Where was the chauffeur all this time?'

'Didn't see him. I suppose he stayed with the car.'

'O.K., go on . . . Jeezus, what an incredible story!'

'I did warn you it'd take some believing.'

'I believe . . . proceed.'

'There were two beds in the room and I hit one of them like a bag of wet cement. Felicia pulled my coat and shoes off, then started on my pants . . . and would you believe, Tobin, that even in my desperate condition, I . . .'

'Of course I believe it, you dirty pig. I reckon you'll be doing it after death!'

'Well, that's how desirable she was. Not that I got very far, she saw to that. All she was concerned about was getting me undressed and into bed and *asleep*! She even promised that if I'd make a big effort to get into bed, she'd get in with me to keep me warm! She really was very attentive, clucking around me like a mother hen, telling me there was nothing to worry about, and that if I hadn't improved by the time she came out of the bathroom, she'd call the doctor. Then she went into the bathroom. Got another ciggy, son?'

I waited impatiently until he'd lit up again, noting the trembling of his hands was subsiding. 'So – she went into the bathroom, what happened then?'

'I woke up at seven this morning.'

I gaped at him. 'You . . . oh, hell, you mean . . .?'

'Out like a proverbial light for seven solid hours. Don't remember a thing.'

'Oh, for Godsake, Malone . . .'

'And when I woke, she'd gone.'

'Eh?'

'Gone, vamoosed, scarpered . . . not a sign of her. No luggage, clothes, make-up, toothbrush. It was as though she'd never existed. Quite eerie, I can tell you, especially in my state of mind.'

'Which was?'

'Stupefied in the extreme. I felt lousy, dizzy, still nauseous, worse because she wasn't there. I called her, thinking she might be in the bathroom, then I noticed her bed hadn't been slept in.'

'But she said she was going to sleep with you.'

'Russell, as ill as I was, I'd sure as hell have known if that lovely creature had slept with me! Besides, there was no room for her, I was sprawled all over the bed. No, I'd been solo all night for certain.'

'What did you do then?'

'Staggered out of bed, searched the place, got very suspicious when I found nothing, then realized, though hating to admit it, that I'd been well and truly conned out of something or other.'

'The money. But it was locked in the safety-deposit box.'

He nodded. 'Yes, thank God. Then I remembered the key, made a dive for my coat, quite expecting the key to be gone, but there it was, and I felt a lot better – though extremely puzzled. Hell, if it wasn't the money she'd been after, what was the point in the whole damn game?'

'Not sex, that's for sure,' I grinned. 'Destry droops again.'

'Very funny, *you* should be so afflicted. Well, in a right old flummox, wondering where in Vegas I was and what had been the point of it all, I staggered down to the reception desk, showed the key and asked for the box. It was a new girl on duty, not the guy. She pulled out the box and slid it to me. I unlocked it and found . . .'

'Nothing.'

'Bare as a chimp's ass, son. Well, I started to give this bird hell but she shut me up instantly by showing me the card I'd signed the night before. "Don't yell at me, mister!" she said, "Your wife must have signed for the box sometime during the night and removed the contents. And it says right here that the management shall not be held responsible . . ." '

I slumped, gaping at him. 'Oh, mate . . .'

'Neat, hm?'

'Neat. *Jesus*, what a con trick . . . and Miss Felicia DeCourcey-Whatsername . . .'

'Could be anywhere by now and probably is. Come on, let's go down and get that coffee . . . we'll talk about what we should do down there.'

NINE

On the way down to the Caravan coffee shop we stopped at the TWA desk and picked up our air tickets, being reminded by the clerk to be at the airport by ten that night.

As we left the desk Buzz looked at his watch. 'Eleven hours left. I don't know whether I'll be glad or sorry to go. Great shame all this business had to spoil Vegas, I was having a great old time.'

'Well, it could be worse. Thank God you left all your other money in the safe here, we'd have been in a right old mess.'

'Yeah,' he laughed, brightening. 'At least we only lost what we'd just won. Sure would've like to have spent *some* of it though.'

The Caravan Room, with its entrance right in the foyer, is a very long room, having tables and chairs down its centre, the serving counters and cooking area on the left, and several window banquettes on the right, the windows looking out on the corridor we'd just walked along.

We chose a banquette and, with customary efficiency, a waitress was there almost before our trousers touched leather.

'*Good* morning, gentlemen, and what can we do for you this morning?'

'A gallon of scalding coffee and forty-two aspirins,' said Buzz.

'One regular New Year breakfast,' she cracked, scribbling '2 coffees' on a card. 'Really tied one on, huh?'

'No, no,' said Buzz. 'I was in bed by nine. Too much sleep always gives me a headache.'

She chuckled and departed.

'Well,' I said, offering him fag number ninety-seven, 'what are we going to do about it? Think we should go to the cops?'

He nodded. 'I've been thinking about it. People can't go around drugging other people with impunity. Apart from being bloody unpleasant and inconvenient, it could also be highly dangerous.'

'You reckon that's what happened, hm?'

'It must be, Russ. Heck, I hardly had anything to drink before I met Felicia and I was feeling marvellous before I drank that champagne. It *had* to be a mickey in the champers.'

I snorted a laugh. 'Sounds incredible, doesn't it? You accept these things so readily in fiction, but when it comes to the real thing – especially to a mate – it's hard to believe people have the nerve to do such things.'

'Trouble with us, Russ, is we're naive. We've never rubbed shoulders with the criminal element and actually seen these things happen. I've never seen anybody knifed or shot or mugged, and until I actually *do* witness it there'll always be that psychological credibility gap.'

'You know,' I said, 'what amazes me is that people, especially a bird as stupendous-looking as this Felicia, actually dedicate their lives to this sort of thing. Imagine asking her, "And what do you do for a living, miss?" "Oh, I'm a professional con-woman. I tour the casinos looking for a sucker with a big wad, take him to a motel room after slipping him a mickey, and when he's out cold, nip off with his bankroll." I mean, fancy doing it *all* the time, Buzz. The risk they take must be terrific!'

'Well, now, let's just think about that . . .'

The waitress returned with a glass flask of steaming coffee.

'There yuh go, boys, things'll be lookin' up in no time.' She poured two huge cups and departed.

'You were saying?' I prompted him, wincing as he ripped open six paper sugar sacs and tipped them in. 'I see you're cutting down.'

'I feel the need. Yeah, I was thinking about this risk thing. Why, I wondered, go to all the trouble of arranging the party, the motel, the safety-deposit box, when they could have mickeyed me out anytime, lifted my roll and dumped me by the roadside?'

'You got an answer?'

'I think so. That way they lay themselves open to charges of Christknowswhat – abduction, assault, robbery, something along those lines. But this way . . . well, imagine if we do go to the cops, what do I tell them? That I voluntarily booked into a motel with a good-looking girl and *registered* as Mister and Mrs. Malone, then signed a safety-deposit card as her husband, agreeing that *either* of us had the right to withdraw the contents, and . . .'

'Yeah,' I frowned. 'They're not going to give a damn that you weren't actually married. Hell, I reckon half the registered "Mister and Mrs." in town are phoney and . . . but, hey, hang *on*, Buzz. You said that Felicia had said "I'll take you to my motel and look after you . . ." '

'Yes, that's right.'

'But if she was already booked *into* a motel, she must have registered in her own name, surely? How, then, could she go back with you and tell them you were her husband, just arrived in town, the worse for drink? You signed in as "Malone", right?'

He was frowning, heavily. 'Yes, that's right.'

'And both you and Felicia signed the safety-deposit card as "Mister and Mrs. Malone", right?'

'Jeezus, yeah . . .'

'Now, how could that be?'

His face was twisted with bewilderment. 'Well . . . the only thing I can think of is . . . she hadn't booked into the motel at all . . . that she just took me to any old motel and . . .'

I was shaking my head. 'Impossible, son, the town is bulging. I reckon you'd be lucky to find a room in *any* motel or hotel on New Year's Eve, never mind in the first motel you just happened to pop into. No, there's got to be more to it than that. Listen, you said that just before you left the MGM with her, she went to the Powder Room, and you reckoned that was when she started the con ball rolling. What did you mean by that?'

He shrugged. 'Only that she must have phoned her chauffeur then, told him to meet us outside. He couldn't have been parked there all the time, it's a taxi route. He'd have had to park in the main lot, miles away . . .'

'Aha!' I exploded, making him jump and slop his coffee.

'Aha, what? Jeezus, you frightened the life out of me.'

'I think you've hit on something – the chauffeur. Tell me, by the time she went to the Powder Room, did she know your name?'

'Sure. I told her soon after I got talking to her.'

'Fine. Now – can you remember whether there was a phone in the car?'

'Yes, there was. It was built into the back of the front seat.'

'Great, I think we're getting somewhere. *She* phones the chauffeur, tells him she's got a big, fat, well-heeled fish on the hook named Malone, doing a solo, no friends or entanglements, nobody that'll come looking for him . . .' I grinned. 'See, if you'd told her you were waiting for me, all this wouldn't have happened!'

'Go on, rub salt in, you bastard.'

'Lovely, says the chauffeur, and whips round to the motel to book you in as Mister and Mrs. Mal . . .' my theory fizzled out. 'No, fuck it, we're back to the same conclusion – it simply wouldn't be that easy to whip round to any old motel and book you in . . .'

A sharp rap on the window behind us cut me short. We shot round, coming face-to-face with the grinning, cratered mush of Flush Foley, resplendent in green cowboy outfit piped in white and his battered old Stetson jammed on the back of his head.

He made a sign that he was coming in and a couple of minutes later came rolling up, thumbs stuck in his belt like a gun-slinger looking for trouble.

'Well, *howdy*, mah ole buddies . . . Happy Noo Year an' all that bananas. Mind if I join yuh for a bite?'

He slid into the banquette, looking eight thousand years old and as though he hadn't been to bed for any of them.

'How's the poker going, Flush?' I asked him.

'Well, now, no complaints in that department. As of this

moment Foley is up just about ten big ones an' things are gettin' better all the time. We're on a four-hour break right now for a shave, shampoo an' a bit a shut-eye and I'm so damn hungry Ah could swallow a Longhorn whole.'

The waitress arrived right on cue with her bottomless coffee flask, pouring us a couple of fresh ones while listening to Flush's recital.

'Well, now, ma'm, I'm gonna start off with a slice of ice-cold melon and a pint of tomato juice . . . then I'll have one dozen dollar-size pancakes, three strips o' streaky bacon, side-order of french fries, eight slices of toast, cawfee as fast as it comes . . . an' a big slice of apple-pie à la mode with three scoops of ice-cream – chocolate, strawberry 'n' vanilla. Let's start with that an' maybe we'll do it all over agin when I'm finished. Hey, you fellas eatin'? How 'bout the same for you out of mah winnings?'

It was a hard fight but we finally persuaded him we were happy with just coffee.

'Well,' he sighed, 'takes all sorts, though danged if Ah know how you fellas manage t'stay standin' up, eatin' as puny as that.'

'Flush,' I said, 'by "ten big ones" do you mean you're winning ten thousand dollars?'

He nodded. 'Give or take a sawbuck, yeh. Small-fry, yet, though. We won't be gettin' inta the real money until this evenin'. Well, now, what have you guys been up to? What d'you think of Vegas, great li'l town huh? Get anythin' good going for New Year's Eve?'

'Not bad,' grinned Buzz. 'We won a five-thousand-dollar jack-pot at the MGM . . .'

Flush gaped, then exploded with laughter and smote the table with his fist. 'Hot *damn*, yuh didn't! Well, Godamighty . . .'

'And then lost it,' Buzz added quietly, bringing Flush's hilarity to a pop-eyed halt.

He groaned miserably and shook his head. 'Aw, now fellas, whatya go an' do a damn-fool thing like that fur? How in hell's name did you lose it – craps, roulette . . .?'

'A bird,' said Buzz, grinning at Flush's expression of blank mystification.

'A . . . a *broad*!'

'Tell him from the beginning,' I said to Buzz. 'Maybe he can advise us what to do.'

'Yeh, shoot,' said Flush eagerly. 'Man, this has gotta be wild.'

Buzz started . . . and by the time he'd finished we'd each had three more cups of coffee and Flush was on his last bite of pie and ice-cream. All through the recital he'd hardly said a word, just frowned, groaned, shaken his head and grunted with dismay as though he already knew the story and its sad conclusion.

'So – here we are,' Buzz said finally, 'sitting here wondering whether to go to the cops or . . .'

Flush negatived the suggestion, tidied up his plate and shoved it away. 'Waste of time, boys,' he said regretfully. 'Bookin' into a motel as Mister and Mrs. did it for yuh, Buzz. Don't forget, this is a wild town an' the cops don't give a hoot whether a couple are churched or not when they bed down for the night. All they'll see is two names on a register and on the safety-deposit card, and that's all kosher.'

'That's what we thought,' said Buzz.

'And . . .' continued Flush, 'about bein' drugged, well, there's just no way of provin' that – not short of a physical examination, anyways, and even then you'd have one hell of a time provin' it was this Felicia dame that slipped it to yuh. No, sir, I reckon you're ass-up over a barrel on this one.'

I said, 'You didn't seem too surprised by the story, Flush, have you heard it before?'

'Yeh, I heard it,' he said, getting out his cigarettes. 'I reckon ten new con tricks hit Vegas every single week o' the year – it's just gotta be with all this dough lyin' around loose. Hell, it's a conman's paradise. I ran across this particular one coupla years back, happened to a good buddy of mine, only they took him *real* good – close on thirty thousand.'

We gaped. 'Thirty thousand!'

Flush grinned sympathetically. 'Don't mean to diminish th' importance of your loss, fellas, I know five grand is quite a piece of change to you guys, but compared to some rolls bein' toted around this town, it's cab fare. Yessir, there's real big money to be picked up by dames like Felicia DeWhatsit Thingummybob – an' I'd lay odds Buzz's roll was one of the smaller wads she picked up last night.'

Buzz frowned, shocked. 'You mean . . . she'd do that more than once a night?'

Flush laughed. 'Christ, sure. This is a big operation, Buzz, with overheads. They need to collect! Five grand wouldn't go far between that bunch.'

'Bunch?' muttered Buzz. 'But there were only two of them . . .
weren't there?'

'Hell, no! What about all those people at the party? They'd
want their cut.'

Buzz's mouth dropped open. 'You mean . . . *they* were all in
on it?'

Flush nodded emphatically. 'Two bits to a boot in the ass, they
were. Heck, I don't reckon you guys realize what a sophisticated
operation this was you got tangled in. Yuh just can't drug a guy
in the middle of a private party and hope to get away with it.
Hell, there mighta bin a doctor there, or a cop . . . who knows
who anybody is at a party? No, sir, that sorta thing has to be
kept under strict control. So – the logical answer is to organize
your own party, fill the room with your own people, get it?'

We got it.

'My God,' laughed Buzz, 'I'm beginning to feel highly
honoured.'

'Flush,' I said, 'there are a couple of things we can't work out,
maybe you can supply the answers.'

'Shoot.'

'Well, for one thing we know that accommodation is very
scarce in Vegas this time of year . . .'

'Right,' he nodded. 'Scarcer than bibles in a Biloxi brothel.'

'Well, we've been trying to work out how, once they'd got
Buzz's name, they could've found a motel room so easily.'

'That's no problem, Russ. The gang does a lot of preparatory
work before they move inta town – maybe weeks before. First
they rent a house where they can throw the "parties" and mickey
the suckers, then they book maybe a dozen or more rooms in
different motels – always motels because they're easier to get into
and out of than hotels – an' they book them in the name of some
fictitious company or other and pay for them in advance. That
way the motels don't give a damn about there bein' no baggage,
right?

'O.K., now, you know how it is when a big convention hits
town? The company holdin' the convention books maybe a hundred rooms in *its* name, not in the name of the employees who're
gonna stay there, then, when the employee arrives he just signs in
in his own name – simple.'

I glanced at Buzz. 'Sure – so this gang would have already
booked the room as a company room, and when Felicia arrived

with you all she had to do was flash some phoney company card and say Mister and Mrs. Malone are booking in.'

Flush nodded. 'Four bits to a cow feather that's the way it happened.'

'Jeezuschrist,' gasped Buzz. 'And you reckon I wasn't the only sucker taken last night, Flush?'

'I'd be mighty surprised if you were. Hell, you were out cold an' nicely tucked away by . . . what? – midnight? This old girl woulda had time to bed down a couple more before dawn. An' who's to say you were the *first* last night? And, furthermore, who's to say she was the only shill workin' for the gang! There mighta bin *six* broads like her . . . think about it.'

'I'm thinking,' groaned Buzz. 'But . . . don't they leave a lot to chance, Flush? I mean, they've got to find a sucker with the big wad in the first place, that can't be too easy.'

Flush swallowed his sixth cup of coffee and signalled the waitress for more. 'Well, now, Buzz, you're right, but ask yourself how she knew *you* had a big fat wad in your pocket.'

Buzz frowned. 'Yes, I've been wondering about that. I didn't see her around Big Bertha when I won the jackpot . . .'

'Highly unlikely she'd *be* around, buddy . . . but somebody was, hm?'

Buzz laughed. 'Yeah, about two hundred somebodys! We collected quite a crowd.'

'Sure, you did – an' so does *every* big winner, whether it's at craps or roulette or anything else. A punter on a big winning streak makes a lot of noise, creates a lot of excitement, pulls the crowds . . . and *in* that crowd . . .'

'Are spies,' Buzz finished for him, then he sighed. 'I was shopped.'

Flush nodded. 'You were fingered, baby . . .'

'By a member of the gang?' I asked.

Flush shrugged. 'Who knows . . . maybe a hotel employee earnin' a little extra bread – a waitress, change girl, croupier . . . Christ, it coulda bin anybody. A quick phone call . . . Felicia arrives . . . a nod in the right direction, and you, old buddy, were target for tonight.'

'Wow,' breathed Buzz. 'By God, you live and learn.' He looked at me and gave me a woeful grin. 'Not bad going, son, for a couple of much-travelled know-alls – both of us taken to the cleaners inside forty-eight hours.'

Flush nearly spilled his coffee. 'Christ, Russ, were you hit, *too*?'

I grinned sheepishly. 'Two hundred dollars. Nice girl . . . just wanted a small loan until she could get to the bank. That's why Buzz was alone for so long in the MGM. I was over at Caesar's Palace waiting for her. She . . . didn't show.'

Flush groaned like a dying steer. 'Oh, boy, did this town see *you* two coming. You know, fellas, the crooks hereabouts get down on their knees every night and *pray* guys like you get off the plane. But, hell, I'm sorry t'hear it . . . look, how're you fixed for dough? I know you've got a long ways to go . . .' his hand was already moving inside his shirt, '. . . an' I would deem it a *big* personal favour if you'd let me smooth the way a bit with a . . .' he yanked out a leather wallet stuffed to bursting point with bills, '. . . a small loan . . .'

'No,' we chorused.

'Thanks all the same, Flush,' said Buzz, 'it's damn good of you, but we're all right, really.'

He narrow-eyed Buzz. 'Truly?'

'Honest to God. Thank Christ I locked all my carrying money in the safe here . . . we've got plenty, believe me.'

'Well, if you're sure. Jeez, I've got more damn bread than I know what t'do with. Sure wish you'd take a thousand, get this bulge down a bit.'

'Change it into big ones,' grinned Buzz.

'Hell, they *are* big ones!' Flush scowled, pulling out a couple of five hundreds. 'And they sure spoil the cut of mah shirt.'

I laughed. 'Me – I'd be happy walking around like Quasimodo if the hump was stuffed with those.'

'Well, if you won't . . .' sighed Flush, stowing the wallet away again. 'So, what are you guys plannin' to do between now and ten o'clock tonight – gonna take on Big Bertha again?'

'Sure,' grinned Buzz, then became serious. 'I don't know, Flush . . . I was wondering . . . what are the chances of finding that Felicia again.'

I glanced at him but he was deep in thought.

Flush shrugged. 'She could still be in town – most likely is. New Year ain't half over and there's too many rich pickin's to quit yet. Trouble is, she most likely won't start operatin' until dark around five, and there are a hell of a lotta places to cover in five hours. The odds ain't exac'ly in your favour, old buddy.'

'No, I know,' Buzz said pensively. 'Still, I feel I ought to have a crack at it . . . what do you think, Russ?'

'Me! Hell, I'm all for it. Pity I don't know what she looks like, otherwise we could split up, take one side of the Strip each and halve the time. But I'm certainly willing to have a go.'

'Er,' went Flush thoughtfully, 'what about this house you went to? Any idea at *all* where it was?'

Buzz shook his head. 'Not a clue. I've been giving it a lot of thought, but it's hopeless. It could be anywhere.'

'Pretty swanky place, hm? Ranch style, you said . . . long driveway?'

'Yeah, beautiful place, but that's all I saw. I didn't see any name or house number on a gate or anything.'

'Would you remember the house if you saw it again?'

Buzz nodded. 'Possibly . . . but of course it'd look different in the daylight. Aw, but I wouldn't know where to start looking, Flush . . . it could be anywhere within a radius of five . . . ten miles from the MGM.'

'Mmm . . . well, I'll tell yuh, Buzz, there ain't *too* many real swank houses around Vegas. Most of the rich folks here are hotel people and they usually live on the premises in a penthouse suite or a house in the grounds, know what I mean? So that kinda limits the number of big fancy houses in town. Take away the houses set in a big acreage – the ranches – and I reckon you could cover the real swank settlements hereabouts in a couple of hours by car.'

'Really?' said Buzz, warming to the idea. 'How about a cab?'

Flush shook his head. 'I wouldn't do it that way – too expensive and you won't have the freedom of movement you need. If it was me, I'd hire a jalopy for a few hours, cost yuh next to nothin' *and* it'd save you the cab fare to the airport tonight. Just leave the car there, they'll collect it.'

'Sounds good,' said Buzz, turning to me. 'What about it, mate?'

'I'm all for it.'

'Well, best of luck, fellas,' said Flush, sliding out of the banquette. 'Sure would like to join you, but I've just gotta get some shut-eye before the big session tonight.' He held out a gnarled hand. 'Best of luck, Buzz . . . sure has been nice meetin' yuh, Russ. Sure hope you find that dame. Me – I'd walk right up to her, snatch her pocketbook out of her hand and help myself to that fat wad she's carryin' – and I don't reckon you'd get a peep outta her. And who knows,' he grinned, 'maybe I'd even come out a few bucks ahead! She sounded loaded. Well, so long, fellas . . .'

We watched him go, turning at the cash-desk for a final wave, then disappearing into the casino.

'Well,' I said, 'time is a-wastin', Malone, let's hit the trail.'

'You really want to do it, Russ?'

'Of course I want to do it!'

'But it's such a hell of a long shot – either finding Felicia or the house.'

'Maybe – but I still think it's worth a try. Come on, we'll ask about hiring a car at Reception and get a map of Vegas. Maybe Max will mark out the likely areas for us.'

He brightened determinedly. 'You're a good man. Boy, what I'd give to run smack into that bitch in one of the casinos. I'd do a bloody sight more than snatch her purse, I'll tell you.'

'Oh, what *would* you do, Malone?'

He grinned obscenely. 'When I'd finished with Lady Felicia DeCourcey-Holme, buddy, her gait would resemble that of a ninety-year-old jockey with rickets! Mind you,' he added, sliding out of the banquette, 'if I got the chance to do that, I could happily forget the money. Come on, let's find Max.'

TEN

Ever-helpful, Max not only arranged the hired car in double-quick time but also provided a detailed map of Vegas and ringed the areas of possible interest. There weren't many, four in all, which gave us fresh hope and encouragement to start.

'One thing about Vegas,' he explained, 'its suburbs don't straggle out for miles. It's a pretty compact town and when you reach the end, that's it – the rest is desert. Have a nice day now.'

Nowadays, with a fuel crisis, the 'in' thing in the States is to drive a small car and many of the car-hire firms are pushing Minis and Volkswagens, so, as much as we'd have liked to flounce around town in an eight-block-long Chrysler or Buick, we settled for a Volks and by two o'clock were on our way.

'I don't suppose it'd be any good going back to the MGM and trying to reconstruct the route by instinct?' I suggested to Buzz, who was driving.

'Not unless I could sit in the back with Felicia while you drove,' he grinned. 'Nah, I haven't a clue, son. I vaguely remember turning onto the Strip after we left the MGM, but my interest in geography kinda waned at that point because Felicia put her hand on my knee while I lit her cigarette. After that, I don't recall consciously looking out of the window once.'

'O.K. . . .' I spread the map on my knee. 'Well, it's anybody's choice . . . how about tackling them in anti-clockwise order – up to the North East first? Straight up Las Vegas Boulevard and turn right on Fremont Street.'

'Roger, Navigator. Hey, zippy little fellas, these Volks, wouldn't mind a couple myself.'

'A couple?'

'One for each foot.'

'Don't forget to drive on the right, hm?'

'Who – me? Tobin, you are talking to a truly international driver. Why, I've driven . . .'

A raucous blast of horn shattered us from behind.

'Now, what's the matter with that silly bugger . . . ?'

'I believe he wants to pass, Malone. You happen to be crawling in the fast lane. Move over.'

'Oh . . . well, bloody ridiculous law, anyway, why can't they drive on the left like civilized countries?'

The true size of Vegas becomes very apparent when you're embarked on a project like ours – and it really is quite small. Nevertheless, once we had quickly reached a search area we discovered an appreciable maze of criss-crossing streets, most of them looking promising, and so the actual inspection of the houses, often set well back from the road behind shrubbery and trees, became a slow process, and the early evening was soon upon us.

'How about this one?' I asked, nodding to the right at a lovely ranch-style bungalow half-screened by trees.

He screwed up his eyes and pondered, as he'd done fifty times in the past two hours, but shook his head again. 'No, that's not it – too close to the road. I don't know, mate, there's something *missing* and I'm damned if I know what it is.'

'Something like what? – a formation of trees . . . a bend in the road?'

'I'm *fucked* if I know!' he said, beginning to sound desperate.

'Can you remember which way you turned into the driveway – left or right?'

'Erm . . . I think it was left. Yes, it *was* left . . . I remember swaying against Felicia who was sitting on my right. Why?'

I shrugged. 'Not much . . . but you should bear it in mind when you're looking at these houses, might make a difference. Driving this way, the house would be on your left. But if the house happened to pop up on our right, you'd be approaching it from the wrong direction and it might look different.'

'Oh, Christ, that means we should cover all these streets *twice* – up and down. There just isn't time, Russ, it's getting dusk now. We'll be lucky to cover that last place before dark. What's it called?'

'Rancho Circle. Over on the west side.'

'Yeah, well by the time we get there . . . hey!'

He gave a sudden start, jammed his boot on the brake, and stared hard at a long, low job on the left side of the road, set well back beyond a long, tarmac-ed drive. 'By Jesus, Russ, that could be it.'

I gulped. 'You're sure?'

'Well, it's got a wrought-iron gate and a long drive . . . certainly looks big enough . . . hey, I remember now – it had a white front door!'

'Oh, my God, that's certainly white.'

'*And* it had a wrought-iron lamp on the wall by the door!'

'I thought you said you couldn't remember anything!'

'It comes back to me when I *see* these things . . . now, let me think . . . we drove up the driveway . . . turned left in front of the door . . . got out . . . approached the front door and Felicia rang a *bell* on the *right* side of the door . . . !'

'It's there . . . It's there!'

'. . . and while we waited, the chauffeur backed the car into a *turn-round space* . . . in front of a double garage . . . !'

'It's there! It's bloody there!'

Buzz had gone quite pale. 'Oh, Jesus . . .'

'What are we going to do? Call the cops?'

'And say what? That the whole thing is a set-up for drugging unsuspecting victims? That there's a bird in there with my five thousand dollars? No, mate, we have no proof of anything, and besides we haven't got time! We've got to be at the airport at ten.'

'Well, what, then?'

'First off, we've got to make absolutely sure it *is* the right house. It's pointless sitting here if it isn't. And the only way to do that is to get a look at that lounge, it's the only room I remember.'

'You mean . . . look through the windows?'

'Yeah.'

'Oh.'

For a moment or two Buzz continued to stare at the house. 'Looks empty, doesn't it? No lights . . . no movement.'

'It's too early for them to start the party, maybe . . . or they could all be at the back of the house.'

'Yeah,' he said thoughtfully, then, suddenly galvanized into action, flung open the door. 'Come on!'

With clattering heart I followed him, across the quiet road to the closed iron gates. Here a pause, then quietly Buzz raised the securing bar and pushed the gate open.

'So – if it's the wrong house, we're just asking the way to Rancho Circle,' he said, desperately trying to calm his nervousness. 'No law against asking directions, is there?'

'Who're you trying to convince – me or you?'

He gave me a sickly grin.

'And if it *is* the right house?' I pursued.

'I'll ask if Felicia is at home, get her to the door . . .' he shrugged, 'and see what happens.'

'And what if Neanderthal Ned, the chauffeur, answers the door?'

Buzz gulped. 'The bigger they are, the harder they fall, mate. Any rough stuff and he'll feel the full force of your fury.'

'*My* fury!'

'Sure – half the money's yours, isn't it?'

'Positively not – at least not until you've wiped the floor with him. Then I might consider . . .'

'Tobin, you're chicken.'

'Cheep cheep.'

Gingerly, gazing furtively about us, we proceeded up the drive and reached the front door.

'Well,' sighed Buzz, 'here we are.'

'Yes.' Pause. 'Well, go on, ring the bell.'

'I've . . . been thinking.'

'About running? So have I.'

'No, about that lounge . . . I think it was at the *back* of the house. I remember following Felicia down a corridor . . . yes, I'm sure it's at the back.'

'Have a look through the letter-box, maybe . . .' The suggestion petered out. The letter-box was at the bottom of the door, six inches off the ground. 'Well, how about those windows?' I pointed off left.

'Yeah, come on.'

Like thieves in the night, we crept along the house, pausing at each of four windows while Buzz cupped his hands to his eyes and took a squint.

He came away from each, shaking his head. 'Nah, it's a corridor with doors, probably bedrooms. I'm sure I'm right – the living quarters are at the back.'

'So – let's go.'

Now, for strangers to approach a house and knock on the door is one thing, perfectly acceptable if they're making genuine enquiries, but to go skulking round the back without even having knocked or rung the bell is quite another, and the demarcation line between the acceptable and the forbidden seems to me to be the corner of the house. Once you pass it and start down the side of the house, then you're in for a heapin' helpin' of trouble.

So it's hardly surprising what did happen, did happen.

With Buzz in the lead and me riding his coat-tail, we crept down the path of crazy paving and reached the rear corner of the building, and there, hugging the wall, we stopped for a reconnoitre. The gardens, running to half an acre or more, were beautiful. A verdant lawn, sculptured with flower beds and exotic shrubbery, extended from a large sun patio immediately behind the house down to a thickly-wooded area three hundred feet away, now indistinct in the quickly gathering dusk.

Over on the right, designed as an integral part of the patio, sprawled a magnificent swimming pool, and beyond it – a line of four cabañas, changing rooms, and a small roofed bar. All very luxurious, but eerily deserted.

'It's like a morgue,' I whispered, patently unnerved. 'Too damn quiet, mate.'

'Yeah,' he murmured, convinced.

'Well, get on with it! Nip round and have a look!'

'O.K., here we go.'

He made it sound as though he was going to break into a

sprint. Instead he flattened himself to the wall and slid round the corner like he was glued to it, edged most furtively along the solid brick section and came to a halt at the beginning of an enormous picture window. I, of course, was still right behind him.

'Ready?' he whispered.

'For what?'

'For a bloody fast retreat if there's anybody in there!'

'I've been ready since we came through the gate!'

'O.K. . . . here goes!'

Slowly, inch by inch, he poked his nose round the window frame . . . a pause . . . an uncertain frown . . . a squint . . . hands up to his eyes . . . two more steps along the window . . . then a gasp. 'Russ . . .!'

'What!?'

'It's the . . .'

That was all he was able to get out before the eerie silence was shattered by the terrifying, death-rattling, throat-growling, boom-bark of an enormous dog and in the next instant he was hurtling round the corner of the cabañas and heading straight for us, at nine hundred miles an hour, the wickedest, savagest-looking Alsatian it has ever been my misfortune to encounter, and believe me I have encountered one or two heart-stoppers in my time.

'Ohhhhhhhhhh . . .!' was all Buzz could manage, gaping with horror as he plastered himself to the window, petrified.

I couldn't even manage that much. I just cringed against the glass, my blood turned to ice, and waited numbly for the worst. I couldn't think, I couldn't move. It was all over. With the fatalism of a plummeting sky-diver whose parachute cord has just come away in his hand, I shut my eyes and awaited death, imminently anticipating the pile-driver impact of this four-hundred-pound canine maniac and the crunch of its four-inch teeth in my throat. Goodbye, mother . . . dad . . . what a stupid way to go – chewed to bits like a tin of Chunky.

God, the noise was deafening, awful, so close . . . the vicious, barrel-chested rattling, see-saw growl of absolute menace. It was there, only inches away, but I daren't look. But why wasn't it attacking . . .! Was he feeding off Buzz first? Did he have him on the ground, ripping out his windpipe, chewing off his ear?

Then, wiping away my gruesome reverie – a thin, piercing

command from the direction of the cabañas. 'Stay right where you are, you varmints! Don't move a goddamn muscle or he'll tear your legs off!'

I opened my eyes . . . and nearly passed out with fright. Bonzo's huge snarling head, big as a bucket, was right there, not three inches from Herc! Oh, the horror of it . . . one lightning bite and . . . *please*, not there, not with Tahiti coming up . . . take a leg, a hand, *anything* . . .

I glanced up at the old guy trundling across the patio, bayonet-charging us with a rusty old garden fork, a grizzled old soul in crumpled gardening clothes, a shock of grey hair standing on end like an Afro in a high wind.

'Now, then . . . now . . .' he gasped, spluttering toothlessly like Gabby Hayes and dribbling spit down his unshaven chin, just as nervous as we were – almost. '*Gotcha*, ain't we, yuh thievin' skunks. Well, now, you move so much as an eyelash and Emperor will have the two of you. One word from me . . . *one* word, mind, and yuh blood'll be gushin' over this patio like Niagara in high flood . . .'

'M . . . mister,' stammered Buzz, still plastered against the window, arms outstretched, one eye on Gabby and the other staring horror-stricken at the dog, '. . .y . . .you've got it wrong. We're not thieves, we . . .'

'Ho, no, you're not thieves,' mimicked Gabby, brandishing the fork as though about to run Buzz through the gut. 'So how come yuh came creepin' round the back of the house like a coupla scavengin' weasels! Honest folk don't behave thataway, they ring decent – at the front door!'

'W . . . we tried the door bell, but . . .'

'Lies!' rapped Gabby. 'I got me an extension bell in that cabaña over there, an' it hasn't rung all day. O.K., now you two just keep yuh hands pointin' at that roof while I call the cops . . .'

Buzz and I chorused, 'No!'

'. . . and don't worry your thievin' heads about gettin' away while I'm gone. The phone's over there in the cabaña an' I'll be watchin' yuh all the time – and one word from me and Emperor'll have yuh for supper – bones an' all. Emperor . . . guard!'

The dog, who had so far not moved one eighth of an inch from its quivering, slavering stance, reaffirmed its evil-hearted dedication to duty with a sudden yelp and dropped into an even lower crouch, drawing back its lips so far they almost met over the top. Jesus, I've never seen such fangs – except maybe on lions in the African bush. And the bastard looked not only ready and able but exceedingly willing to use them . . . and I knew precisely what he had his eye on as hors d'oeuvres!

'Mister, listen . . .' Buzz pleaded, 'before you call the police, will you give us a minute to explain?'

'Explain it t'them, they gotta knack of knowin' whether you're tellin' the truth. Besides, I want you offa this property fast.'

'Oh, we'll go fast, believe me.'

'That you will – soon as the patrol car gits here.'

'Aw, come on, what difference will another minute make? We can't get away with this thing guarding us.'

The old guy chuckled. 'At least that bit's the truth. Mister, d'you know *why* we've gotta hound like him on this property? – because this is the *seventh* attempted robbery we've had in the last year an' the owner was beginnin' t'git just a *mite* fed up havin' his house bust inta and his things pinched.'

'But we weren't *trying* to break in, swear to God!' pleaded Buzz. 'Look, at least hear me out and then call the cops, if you must. But it's only going to waste everybody's time and we haven't got it to spare. We're catching a plane to L.A. at eleven o'clock and . . .'

'Ah, that's where yuh fence the stuff, huh – L.A. Anyways, what kinda punks are you two . . . English?'

Buzz sniffed, affronted. 'Certainly not – I'm Australian. He's English.'

'How d'you do,' I nodded.

'I'm Buzz Malone . . . he's Russ Tobin.'

'Them your real names or aliases?'

Buzz snorted, getting fed up with this. The silly old coot had been reading too much Mickey Spillane. 'They're our real names. Check with the Sahara Hotel, we're staying there.'

'Yeah, sure, and so are fifty folks named Smith an' Jones, but it don't mean . . .'

Buzz sighed. 'Look, we're foreigners – we had to show our passports when we booked in! Check with Max on the desk, he'll verify us.'

The old guy shrugged, seeming to thaw just a touch. 'Well . . . maybe y're Malone an' Turban . . .'

'Tobin,' I said. 'T-o-b . . .'

'That don't make yuh any less suspicious, creepin' round folks' houses like that an' peerin' through their windows. Thought the place was empty, didn't yuh? . . . just about t'break in when I stopped you?'

'No, we were not!' insisted Buzz, getting mad now. 'We were looking to see if this was the house I was at last night . . . the one I came to for a party . . .'

'Ha!' Gabby exploded, making even the dog jump. 'Mean t'tell me yuh don't know which house you wus at from the front . . . yuh had to come sneakin' round the back an' look through the window! Well, now I *know* you're ly . . .'

'Yes, I *do* mean to tell you that!' rapped Buzz. 'It was dark . . . I don't know the district . . . and this house *looks* like the one from the front but I had to make sure by looking in the lounge . . .'

'Then why didn't you ring the door bell!' spluttered Gabby, dribbling down his shirt, '. . . and ask outright! I coulda told yuh this wasn't the house yuh wus lookin' for, straight off – there ain't bin a party here for six months! There ain't bin *anythin'* here for six months 'cos the owner's in Florida! There's just me an' Emperor here, guardin' the place, an', by golly, we do a damn good job of it.'

'Oh,' I sighed, slumping.

'Yeah,' said Buzz, 'that was what I was about to tell you, mate – it's not the house.' He turned back to Gabby. 'Will you listen to me a minute . . .'

'Sure, I'll listen – soon as the cops git here. Now, don't you fellas move a goddamn hair till I git back or there'll be nuthin' left for the cops to question. That dawg is a killer!'

And then, secure in this belief, which we unquestioningly shared, he about-turned and headed back towards the cabaña.

Now, realizing the full weight of his responsibility, a new and even more terrifying light seemed to enter Emperor's eyes. Staring at us alternately, daring, almost begging, us to make the smallest move, he slowly backed up three or four feet, positioning himself precisely between us, then sank into a low crouch, ready for instant take-off.

'Oh, bloody mother,' moaned Buzz, his voice quavery with despair. 'Of all the fucking houses we could've looked at, we had to pick the one with this evil swine.'

As though in protest, Emperor emitted a sickening belly-growl and wiggled his lips in a snarl.

'Careful,' I muttered, 'he understands every bleeding word. And I wouldn't put it past him to ignore that old cunt and attack out of pure pleasure.'

'We've *got* to get away, mate!' Buzz whispered hoarsely. 'We can't afford to spend a couple of hours down at the cop shop! We'll miss the damn plane! . . . and, brother, I *want* to be on that plane!'

'O.K., tell you what I'll do, Buzz – I'll go over and tickle Emperor's belly for a while, then take him for walkies round the garden. In the meantime, you nip off and get the car and . . .'

'Russ . . . look!'

'Mm?'

He jerked his head to the right. 'That back door . . . it's open!'

I slid a glance past him, the merest movement of my head bringing fresh growls from Fang. By God, he was right! A small, glass-paned door, which probably led into the kitchen, had been pushed to but not properly closed. Judging the distance, I calculated it to be no further than twelve feet away, but with the dog watching our every breath, it may as well have been twelve miles.

'Great,' I muttered. 'So what are we waiting for?'

'We've got to distract that bloody thing! Two . . . three seconds, that's all we need – then we race through the house and out of the front door.'

'While he's racing around the house to meet us?'

He shook his head. 'No, I don't think so. It'd take the stupid oaf a few seconds to work it out, he'd be too busy trying to bite through the back door.'

'I hear he thinks highly of you, too. In any case, he looks more than capable *of* biting through the back door.'

'Maybe – but not until we're long gone out of the front door and into the car. Mate, we've got to try it.'

I nodded solemnly. 'I know . . . but how?'

'Get him used to a little sideways movement.'

'Sideways movement! Hell, he gets nasty when we blink!'

'It's got to be something . . . natural.'

'How about a Buffalo Shuffle – the step the old comedians used to get off the stage?'

'How about shutting up and letting me think? It's got to be something a dog does too, so he'll sympathize.'

'Like . . . peeing up the drainpipe?'

'Not bad, but a trifle extreme. Anyway, I don't need to go. Hey . . . I've got it . . . !'

'What?'

'A sneeze!'

'A what?'

'A *sneeze*, man – dogs do it all the time! He'd recognize a sneeze when he saw one.'

'You're joking!'

'I'm bloody not. Bet you he takes no notice of it.'

'Well,' I sighed, 'in the absence of any alternative suggestion, let's give it a try. Who goes first?'

'I'll do it.'

'Malone, your courage is exceeded only by your . . .'

'By my desperate need to get the hell out of here. O.K., here goes . . . aah . . . aaah . . . tchooooooo!'

He did a beaut, covering his face with his hands, the impetus of the explosion driving him backwards about two feet, towards the door.

The dog's head shot up, cocked quizzically at Buzz to the accompaniment of an automatic, half-hearted sort of growl, then, satisfied that it was only a sneeze, he settled down again.

'By God it worked!' I gasped. 'You smart old bastard.'

'I know dogs,' he said cunningly. 'They hate things up their noses and they don't like sneezing. One summer I had hayfever and a spaniel of mine used to whine in sympathy when I got going on a big sneezing session.'

'Great. Right, now I've got to get over to you. Here goes . . . aaah . . . aaaah . . . mamaha . . . aaaaattcchhooooooo!'

I staggered forward, driving Buzz back another foot or two.

'Good lad,' he murmured, watching the dog. 'But don't overdo it, he might get suspicious.'

Oh, he was suspicious all right. He'd even eased across to his left to compensate for our movement, but he hadn't growled. I glanced at the door, now only eight feet away; so near and yet still so far.

'How much further?' muttered Buzz.

'About three more should do it.'

'O.K., fire two . . . aaaaaaaaahhhhh . . . tchooooooooo!'

Doubled over, he staggered back a good three feet, but this time evoking a nervous shifting and a growl from Emperor.

'He's getting up-tight,' I warned Buzz. 'It's upsetting him.'

'Fuck him, it's me that's got the cold. Come on, over you come!'

'Weyhey . . . wahooo . . . ahhaaaa . . . aaaahhhh . . . tchooooo!'

Blindly I staggered forward, collided with Buzz, this time bringing Emperor to his feet with a fearsome growl, head low, lip curled, ready to attack.

'Christ, we've overdone it!' gasped Buzz. 'Freeze!'

I froze. God, how I froze.

Growling hideously, the dog crept sideways, glaring at us murderously, great strings of saliva dripping from its yellow fangs like glistening stalactites and plopping onto the patio.

And there he stayed, unmoving, a growl of unbelievable threat rumbling in his Samsonian chest.

'Steady, boy,' muttered Buzz. 'Steady, lad, we're not going anywhere.'

You're fucking right, mate, the dog said with his eyes. And I'm on to your little sneezing game, so you can pack *that* in.

'How . . . far is the door?' murmured Buzz, afraid to move his lips.

'So close you could reach out and touch it – about three feet, that's all.'

'What do we do now? We've got to get that thing distracted – for only a second or two, that would do it.'

I searched around. Apart from the summer furniture, stripped of its cushioning, the patio was as clean as a hound's tooth. I mean, there wasn't a thing we could throw at the dog or use as a shield to defend ourselves for that vital second or so.

'Oh, Jeezus, so close . . .' groaned Buzz.

'Hey . . .'

'What?'

'You reckon dogs are dogs are dogs, hm?'

'Sure they are – unless they've been specially trained to ignore their instincts – like guide dogs for the blind . . .'

I grinned. 'O.K. – get ready to hit that door.'

'Why . . . what . . .?'

'Just get ready.'

I turned to face the dog but ignored him and looked beyond him, way down the garden, paused there with a puzzled frown . . . then shot out my arm and hissed, 'Caaaaaatttttsssss! Get 'em, boy!'

Before he had time to think, the bloody thing leapt three feet in the air, did a mid-air turn and shot off down the lawn like a shell from a bazooka.

'Go!' I shouted at Buzz, giving him a thump in the back, and, by God, he went, yanked open the door and was out of the kitchen before I'd even got the door closed.

THUD! Wooooff! Wooooofffff! Woooooffffff!

We'd made it by a billionth of a second.

'Ah, shut up!' I yelled and raced after Buzz, out of the kitchen, into a corridor, turned right, and ran into him running back.

'Wrong way! That way!'

He turned me round and gave me a shove, trod on my heel and ripped off my shoe. No time to fix it . . . hobble . . . hobble . . . into a dining room, across it, out into the lounge, across it . . . opened a door . . . found myself back in the dining room . . . back into the lounge . . . took another door. It was the hall!

'BUZZ, where are you?!'

A door slammed behind me. 'Three doors in a dining room, bloody ridiculous! Come on!'

I hobbled after him, trying to get my shoe on, reached the front door, yanked it open, peered out, hearing Emperor's furious barking from the rear.

'Let's go!' urged Buzz.

Down the long driveway . . . hop . . . hop . . . hop, still trying to get my shoe on.

'Tobin, for Chrissake . . . !'

'You nearly pulled the bloody thing off!'

'Well, pull it right off – run in your sock! Oh, Jesus, here comes the dog!'

I didn't turn to look, just took off as fast as my legs would work. Clang! Buzz hit the gate, pulled it open.

Woooff! Wooofff! Wooofff! The bastard was roaring down the drive like a motorbike.

'Tobin, come on . . . come on!'

The last six strides were a headlong, teetering plummet, and as I crossed the threshold I could hold it no longer, pitched forward, arms flailing like windmill sails, crashed into the grass verge, rolled over three times and fell in the gutter.

CRASH! The gate slammed shut, right in old Ugly's face, but he'd been coming so fast his head and neck shot through the bars and there he was, stuck, going berserk, barking and snarling something awful, mostly with frustration that he couldn't get through to dismember us.

Buzz yanked me to my feet and half-carried, half-dragged me across the road to the car.

'In!'

'Buzz . . .! The old bloke . . . he's opening the gate!'

'Ohhhhhhhhhh . . .!'

Abandoning me, he leapt round the car, ripped open the driver's door and threw himself in, slamming the door as the dog was in the air.

Bang!

You've never heard such a racket. It went barmy, scratching at the window, snapping at Buzz, its teeth smashing against the glass and its spit flying all over the car.

And now the old bloke was about to join in. Across the road he charged, wielding the garden fork as though intending to smash it through the windscreen or drive it into a tyre.

'Stop . . .! Stop . . .! The cops are comin' . . .! You can't get away!'

'We're going to have a bleeding good try, dad,' muttered Buzz, turning the ignition key.

I have never heard a sweeter sound in my life than the roar of that beautiful engine.

Baaazzzoooommmm!

We were away.

Clonk! The car reverberated to a mighty crash from the garden fork, but, by God, we were away.

The dog kept us company to the next intersection, leaping up at us, snapping at the wheels, then suddenly it gave up and slunk back to the old man, consumed with frustration.

Buzz heaved a huge sigh and held out a trembling hand. 'Fag, mate, for the love of pity.'

I got two roaring away and gave him one.

'Woooow!' he gasped.

'Yeah,' I sighed.

And that's all either of us said until we reached Rancho Circle.

ELEVEN

'Recognize anything?'

Buzz shook his head. 'Could be Hong Kong for all I know.'

It was full night now, a little after five o'clock, though the road we were driving along was well lit.

I consulted the map again. 'One of the entrances to Rancho Circle should be coming up on the right any time now.'

He slowed. 'There it is. Where's the other entrance?'

'Round the corner.'

He turned right into a dark, tree-lined road and immediately we started encountering houses of substance, long rambling jobs with big gardens, some conventional, others way out – including one designed like a miniature English castle.

'Wild,' grinned Buzz. 'What's the betting they imported it stone by stone from Northumberland or som . . . ouch!'

We weren't moving fast, maybe only twenty-five miles an hour, but when we hit the tarmac ramp in the road it was fast enough to shoot us headfirst into the roof.

'Yike!' I grimaced, rubbing my nut. 'What a daft place to . . .'

'Russ . . .!'

'Mm?'

'That was it! That's the thing I couldn't remember – the ramp! I was lighting a fag when we hit it and I damn-near stuck the flame up my nose! This is the place! There's a ramp like that every few yards to slow the traffic . . . mate, this is the place!'

'Good man! So . . . the house should be on our left?'

'Well, not necessarily – we may have come in through the other entrance.'

'Anyway, there can't be all that number of houses in here, it looks like a very exclusive park.'

'It sure does . . . boy, look at that place over there. Must be worth half a million. Well, we'll just take it nice and easy and cover every inch of the place. It's got to be in here somewhere.'

I suppose we'd gone about half a mile, stopping every now and then to take a good look at some of the beauties almost hidden from the road by trees and shrubs, when suddenly, out of no-where, a cop car swung past us, its red roof-light flashing, and screeched to a halt a few yards in front of us, barring our way.

My blood froze.

Buzz slammed on the brakes. 'Oh, Christ, they've got us. That old bloke . . .'

'Oh, blimey . . .'

Aghast, we watched a burly cop get out of the car, open the rear door and haul out another bloody enormous Alsatian.

'Oh, no . . .' groaned Buzz, dropping his head to the wheel.

With the easy gait of bullying authority, primed for fun and games with a couple of helpless, trembling victims, the cop approached, the dog loping at his side, eager and hungry.

Buzz wound down his window, managed a quivery smile that came out too much like a sneer, and in a thin voice said too damned heartily, 'Good evening, officer, lovely night. Nice looking dog you've . . . got . . . there.'

The cop lowered his face to the window, a hell of a face, veteran of a thousand criminal encounters and victim of most, judging by the amount of scar tissue he'd collected.

'O.K., you guys,' he drawled cynically, 'let's have some I.D.'

'Erm . . .I.D.?' enquired Buzz.

'Yeah, like a driving licence, maybe. You do *have* a driving licence, I take it?'

'Oh, c . . . certainly, certainly.'

' 'Kay, let me have it.'

Buzz dug out his wallet and produced his International Licence, handed it through. With a torch the cop inspected it minutely, flicked the beam from it to Buzz's face to compare it with the photograph.

'Australian, huh?'

'Yes, sir, yes, that's right, Australian. You ever been there, officer?'

'This a hired car?'

'Yes . . . yes, it is. Nice little job, too, never driven a Volks before, really ver . . .'

'Papers?'

'Erm . . . oh, yes, certainly . . .'

Buzz pulled them out from under the dash.

The cop inspected them. 'You're stayin' at the Sahara, right?'

'Right!' laughed Buzz, on the verge of collapse. 'Lovely hotel, the Sahara . . . you ever stayed at the S . . .'

'See here you only hired this ve-hicle for one day. You plannin' on leavin' Vegas soon?'

'Er, *yes*, as a matter of fact we're leaving tonight! We're catching the eleven o'clock flight to L.A.'

'Both of yuh, huh?' He blinded me with the torch. 'You leavin', too? What's your name, son?'

'Yes, I am. My name's Russ Robin ... Tobin ... Russ Tobin.'

'You don't seem one hundred percent sure 'bout that. You got any I.D.?'

'Y ... yes ... I've got an International licence, too.'

''Kay, let's have it.'

'Erm ... I'm afraid it's back at the hotel ... with my passport ... in the hotel safe.'

'Sure,' he nodded. 'Why not? O.K., fellas, just slip out for a minute, will yuh, this won't take long.'

I glanced at Buzz. He was as pale as I felt. Well, this was it ... on with the cuffs ... into the back of the paddy-wagon and straight back to Gabby Hayes for identification. And then ... I gave up wondering, it was making me sick.

'You first,' he said to me. 'Get out and come round here where Cannonball can keep an eye on yuh.'

Oh, Christ ... Cannonball! Twice as fast as the real thing and just as lethal. This one made Emperor seem like a lap-fed Chihuahua!

I scrambled out and weak-kneed it round the front of the car, deliriously relieved that Cannonball was not a snarling, growling, dribbling psycho, merely watchful.

'O.K., hands up on the car, legs spread wide,' ordered the cop.

How bloody ridiculous, they actually *said* those things!

His hands flashed all over me, patted here, there and everywhere. 'O-kay, just step aside there and try not to move too much. Cannonball don't like too much movement. Now you, mister ...'

Buzz got out and suffered the same routine. Then, leaving an almost sleepy-looking Cannonball to watch over us, the cop went quickly through the car, under the dash, the seats, then the engine compartment, finally the boot.

''Kay, you're clean, in you get.'

In we got.

'Here on vacation, fellas?' he asked, his tone infinitely more friendly now.

'We were forced down by engine trouble,' explained Buzz, 'but we decided to stay an extra day for New Year and see the town.'

'Great little town – long as you can hold onta your shirt. But, you know, one thing kinda puzzles me . . . most young fellas your age would be where all the action is – the Strip and downtown, not drivin' around residential parks like this at this time of night. Mind tellin' me what you're doin' in Rancho Circle?'

Buzz coughed. 'Well, you see . . . Russ, here, is very interested in architecture, aren't you, Russ . . .'

'Mm . . .? Oh, yes, very . . .'

'He's planning to get married soon and build his own house . . .'

'That's right, officer.'

'And he very much favours the American ranch-style of house, so he likes to look round parks like this, see what ideas he can pick up, isn't that right, Russell?'

'Oh, in . . . dubitably.'

'I see,' said the cop, smiling pleasantly. 'Well, that's understandable . . . 'cept it's so damned dark in here 'bout all you'd see are the front gates. Like to try again, fellas?'

'No, really!' protested Buzz, hauling out our road map. 'See . . . we've ringed four areas of expensive, ranch-style houses and we've been round the other three. Rancho Circle just happened to be the last on the list . . . look, you can check with Max on Reception at the Sahara, he ringed them for us.'

'Yeah?' drawled the cop, still innately suspicious. The incredible thing was he still hadn't made any reference to the trouble with Gabby Hayes! Was it possible he didn't know about it? . . . that Gabby hadn't got around to calling the cops? Why, then, had we been stopped? It wasn't a private estate or anything.

'Well, now, maybe I'll just do that li'l thing. You guys sit tight, gimme your car keys. An' I'll leave old Cannonball here to keep yuh from gettin' lonely.'

He took the keys from Buzz, spoke a command to the dog who immediately sat down in front of the car, and strolled back to the squad car to make the call.

Buzz blew out a sigh wearily. 'You know, son, I will *never* understand how two completely innocent guys can get into so much goddamn trouble in so short a time. Fine – if we really *were* on the make, or associated with criminal types . . . or even *looked* like a couple of heavies, I could understand it. But being two clean-cut, straight-limbed, radiantly healthy-looking specimens ...'

'Eh?' I frowned. 'Have you had a good close look at yourself lately, Malone? You've got bags under your eyes like black puddings, eyes like stop-lights ...'

'Yeah, well, these are exceptional circumstances. Normally I ...' He stopped, stared, his mouth dropped open, hands gripped the wheel. 'Jeezuschrist ... it's them!'

I followed his gaze, past the cop car and into the darkness beyond, seeing a white, black-topped convertible sliding out of a gateway fifty yards down the road, and turning away from us.

'Russ, it's them ... I swear! Just caught a glimpse of the big bastard driving it. It's Felicia's Caddy!'

'Did you see her?'

'No, she'd be tucked well back.'

'Buzz, white Caddys aren't rare, you know – and this is the sort of place to find them.'

'I know – but that was George the Giant driving that one, I'd stake my life on it. Oh, come *on*, copper, let's get going.'

'We're going to follow them?'

'Of course – if that stupid sod gets back here in time. Anyway, we know where they're heading, don't we?'

'Where – the MGM?'

He shook his head. 'I doubt it. She knows I'm still in town. I told her I was flying at eleven, so she'll know I'm a potential danger until ten. I reckon she'll keep away from the MGM. Why should she use the same place when there are twenty other hotels on the Strip?'

'True, true. Well, we'd better not lose them.'

'It's up to this dozey cunt. What the hell's he doing – calling my mother in Sydney?'

'You think he's a regular patrol in the park?'

'Yeah, I'd say so. There's more money around here than in Saudi Arabia. I should think he's permanent – which is probably why he doesn't know of the little fracas back there with the gardener ... oh, come on ... come *on*!'

It was a two-minute eternity before the cop finally hung up his radio mike and strolled back to us, poked his head in Buzz's window and handed back his papers and licence.

'Well, now, seems like you guys were tellin' the truth. Sorry for the inconvenience, but we gotta be careful in a place like this. Got some mighty wealthy folk livin' here who pay a lotta taxes for protection. Just wouldn't do to let every Tom, Dick or Buzz and Russ wander round pokin' their noses into people's private property, now, would it?'

'Must be a difficult job at night, though,' said Buzz, starting the engine. 'Being so dark, I mean.'

The cop grinned. 'Daylight or dark, makes no never mind to me. I had you on closed-circuit T.V. the moment you set fender over the park boundary. Not even a fieldmouse gets in here uninvited.'

'Oh,' gulped Buzz. 'Well, are we free to go now?'

'As birds. Nice talkin' to yuh. Drive careful, now – and watch out for the ramps. Guess you'll be headin' straight back to the Strip, hm?'

'As fast as we can get,' grinned Buzz, moving off. 'Goodbye.'

Out of earshot he thumped the wheel and cursed. 'Fuck it, we've lost them. They'll be in town by now.'

'Don't suppose you managed to get the licence number or anything last night, did you?' I asked.

He withered me with a look.

'No, of course you didn't. You were so gone on Felicia's it's remarkable you even knew it was a white Cadillac convertible. Wonder where they're heading?'

He shrugged. 'All I know is that time is galloping. We've got to pack, pay the hotel account, and get out to the airport, all by ten o'clock. What time is it now?'

'Nearly six.'

'Blimey, four hours. Knock an hour off for packing and getting out to the airport . . . three hours to find them and get the money back. What you might call cutting it fine, mate.'

'Yes, but we'll feel better if we at least try.'

'Oh, we'll *try* all right,' he said vehemently, ramming the gear shift into third. 'And God help her *and* her bleeding chauffeur if we do find them. I'm beginning to feel very pissed off with Felicia Whatsit Whatsit. Any interference from Musclehead and he'll get a scrotumful of size eleven boot, straight off.'

'That's fighting talk, laddie. You handle him, I'll take on Felicia. We'll show them who's boss.'

He turned and grinned, his anger gone. 'How can a guy fail when he has a mate like you at his side to share his burden?'

'With . . . consummate ease?' I suggested.

'Yeah, something like that.'

TWELVE

We rejoined the Strip at Sahara Avenue, turned south onto it and began a slow, watchful cruise, Buzz, seated on my left, scanning the hotels on the far side of the Strip and me hawk-eyeing the ones on the right.

It was not an easy job, some of the hotels and their parking lots being set so far back from the Strip as to be almost out of sight. Then again, many of the hotels accommodated cars at the rear and at the sides of the buildings, but these we had to ignore for the moment.

The plan we had devised was to first make one down and one up run on the Strip, down as far as the Tropicana and back again to the Sahara, covering the parking areas that could be easily seen from the road. Then, failing any result, we would begin a more comprehensive investigation, driving right into each parking lot and inspecting every single line of cars.

A gigantic task, you might think, but thank God it was a white Cadillac convertible we were looking for and not a blue Ford or Plymouth, of which a dozen could be seen at any given moment.

A further clue to help us was, of course, the telephone aerial, an extra long, extra thick job easily distinguishable from a normal radio aerial. So, unless they'd removed it, which was highly un-likely, we could safely dismiss any white Caddy convertible that wasn't sporting one.

Incredibly how, once you start looking for a particular make of car, they appear in vast numbers. We spotted five white Caddy convertibles before we reached the Tropicana, each one giving us a jolt of excitement until we diagnosed their aerials as ordinary radio and our hopes subsided.

We made a U-turn at the Tropicana and started back up the Strip, passed the Aladdin, the ill-fated MGM Grand, the Flam-ingo with its happy memories of Pussycat, on to the Holiday Inn and then the Sands . . . which was when Buzz smashed his foot down so hard on the brake I almost carried on to the Desert Inn all by myself.

'Russ . . . there!'

I got my head out of the glove compartment and followed his pointing finger. Sure enough, parked under the awning covering the entrance to the Sands was a white Cadillac convertible, sporting not only a telephone aerial but also a ten-foot chauffeur who was just about to climb back in the car, having, presumably, just opened the door for the lady who, presumably, had just disappeared into the hotel.

'Got you, you bastard,' grinned Buzz. 'Son, our luck's in. Another second or two and he'd have been gone. Keep an eye on him while I park in front.'

Buzz turned into the forecourt and parked with his tail to the Strip, ready for a quick getaway.

'See him?'

'Yes, he's turned down the side of the hotel.'

'Right . . .' he cut the engine, sighed with relief and borrowed another fag. 'What's the time?'

'Nearly half six.'

'Damn . . .'

'Look, Buzz, I've been thinking . . . you can't just storm into a swish place like this, snatch her handbag and run. Christ, the security lads would be on you like a caved-in roof before you could blink . . .'

'I know. I've been thinking about that, too.'

'So what are you going to do?'

His answer began with a secretive, lop-sided grin which broadened as the humour took him, erupted into a contained snort, and, finally, in response to my narrow-eyed suspicion, exploded into a full-blooded laugh. 'Tobin . . . I have a plan.'

'Oh, my God . . .'

'A plan of such poignant genius, it almost frightens me.'

'Then it'll scare the living daylights out of *me*. No, Malone, the answer is no . . .!'

'Don't you *want* to recover your half of five thousand bucks?'

'I keep telling you, it never was mine.'

'It is!'

' 'Tisn't! It was your stake, so it's your winnings. You've done enough for me.'

'Bollocks! Now, listen, we haven't got a moment to lose . . .'

'You sound like Dick Barton, Special Agent.'

'Tobin, will you listen . . .'

'O.K., I'm listening.'

'She . . . that cat . . . Felicia . . . is sitting in there right now, all dolled up to the nines, waiting to pounce on another poor sucker, right?'

'Presumably, yes.'

'Well, in a minute we're going to make sure, we're going in to have a look. Anyway, let us assume she's in there. One thing we can count on is that these people stick as close to the nightly routine as possible – otherwise too many things could go wrong. That's why the chauffeur is tucked just round the corner right now, waiting for her phone call with news of a new sucker. Tell me, Tobin . . . how's your acting?'

I frowned. 'My what?'

'Your acting . . . your Thespian talent?'

'Terrific. I once played a stunning Hiawatha in a school play – had to shoot another guy, who was playing a deer, in the backside with a cane bow-and-arrow. I missed him, hit the teacher in the balls, brought the house down – and my trousers. He gave me six of the best with my own arrow.'

'Anything else?'

'No, that's it.'

'Well, no matter . . . this part is right up your street . . .'

'Malone . . .'

'. . . the seduction of a *very* gorgeous piece of crumpet . . .'

'Malone . . . no!'

'Russ, man, there's nothing to it! All you've got to do is act natural – do what you've done a thousand times before – chat her up! She'll do the rest – believe me!'

'In other words, you want *me* to go through exactly the same routine you went through last night – get drugged, sick to the verge of death . . .'

'No, no! Hell, that would ruin everything. The object of the exercise, son, is to reverse the rolls – instead of her pinching your wad, you pinch hers! Don't you see . . .'

'Oh, now, h-a-n-g on a minute, Malone, I think you're getting carried away a bit here. For starters we haven't *got* another wad . . .'

He grinned. 'Sure we have.'

'Mm?'

'I've got a wad, mate, don't worry about that.'

'Buzz, you're mad! You're not going to risk what money you've got left chasing . . .'

He was shaking his head. 'No, I am not – just a few dollars of it.'

'How few?'

'Five hundred.'

'Five hun . . . !'

'To catch maybe . . . ten thousand?'

That stopped me. 'Her roll was really that big, hm?'

'Minimum.'

'Well . . . go on, then.'

'Interested?'

'I said go on. I'll agree to listen, no more.'

'O.K., this is what we do. She doesn't know you, has never seen you. We nip back to the hotel, get you all sharped up in your best bib and tucker, load you with a great fat wad of seemingly big dollar bills – a couple of hundreds on the outside and inside but *singles* in the centre – then give you a gentle shove in her direction and Bob's your uncle.'

'No, sorry, Buzz, he's not. I need pictures . . . draw me pictures.'

'Jesus, some imagination. No wonder you didn't graduate from Hiawatha. O.K., you roll up to the bar or wherever she is – and I do mean roll. You're cut, squiffed, happy-happy, because you've just taken the . . . oh, the Thunderbird for ten thousand. I'll leave it to you how you play it – either flash the roll accidentally or drop it . . . don't worry, when she sees it she'll start talking to you and you'll get the same pitch she gave me – and from there on it's a cake-walk.'

'Really.'

'Why shouldn't it be? Everything will happen as it happened to me – except you *won't* drink the bubbly, and when she nips into the bathroom in the motel, you nip along to the Reception and empty the safety deposit box of her wad as well as ours. It's easy!'

'Sublimely,' I agreed, already feeling sick to my stomach. 'Malone, you're mad, barmy, bananas . . .'

'*Why?*'

'Because you are looking at one of the unluckiest blokes born. Nothing . . . absolutely *nothing* would happen as you described it. That may well be her M.O. for 364 days a year, but you can bet your tennis balls that tonight, just for the hell of it, they'll do something entirely different. There'll be no party . . . no motel . . . she'll slip me a mickey right there in the bar and they'll lay me to rest on a building site or something . . .'

He was shaking his head again. 'No, no, no – you heard what Flush Foley said – they daren't do a thing like that. That'd be robbery with assault. No, mate, you can take it as gospel they'll follow the routine *exactly* as it happened to me.'

'Well, I don't know . . .'

'What time is it?'

'Getting on for seven.'

'We've got three hours, that's all. In four hours' time we could climb aboard that jet broke – or with a small fortune, most of which is rightly ours. Think about it . . . think of the high old time we could have in Tahiti with . . . ten . . . thousand . . . dollars . . . !'

'I'm thinking . . .'

'Ten . . . *thousand* . . . dollars, . . . Tobin !'

'Malone, shut up, I'm thinking!'

'What about?'

'The worst that could happen . . . I mean, if anything *did* go wrong.'

'And . . . ?'

I shrugged. 'I can't think of anything that bad.'

His eyes popped. 'You'll do it?'

I grinned at him. 'Why not? Any time the going looks like getting rough I can always run for it.'

'Good man, good man . . .'

'*But* . . .'

'Yes, what?'

'We've only got three hours to get an awful lot done – so you've got to be packed, paid-up and ready to move the second I hit the Sahara.'

He saluted. 'Roger.'

'Right – let's go.'

We were back at the Sahara in minutes. At the reception desk Buzz emptied the safety deposit box, then went down to the cashier's cage and cashed some travellers' cheques into five one-hundred-dollar bills and one hundred singles, returned to the

Reception and settled the bill for the extra day we'd had, then we went up to the room.

While I was changing into my midnight-blue creation, pale blue silk shirt and dark tie, Buzz was making up the wad, facing and backing the one hundred singles with a couple of the C-notes, then he rolled them tightly and secured them with a thick elastic band.

'There y'are, cock,' he grinned, throwing it in the air. 'Ten thousand of the very best.'

'If only, if only.'

'Well, you play your part right and we'll be flying off with a real ten Gs.'

I emerged from the bathroom, slapping on a final touch of 'Swoon' aftershave. 'How do I look?'

'Terrific. I almost fancy you myself. Ready?'

I nodded. 'As I'll ever be.'

'Now, don't worry about a thing, it'll be a doddle. Come on.'

On the return journey to the Sands, Buzz asked, 'Any idea how you're going to play it? . . . straight or what?'

'I've been thinking about it . . . thought maybe I'd put on a bit of "top drawer silly ass" act, nicely pissed. We're running desperately short of time, only two and a half hours left. If she thinks I'm an easy take, she'll probably get things moving faster.'

He nodded. 'Good idea. We've got to be away from the Sahara nine thirty sharp – not a second later. I'll have the bags all packed – you just get there . . . and for God's sake *don't* drink any of that champagne.'

'She hit you with the first drink, hm?'

'The only drink. They don't waste time.'

'Right, I'll have to find a convenient plant pot.'

'Now, you've got everything . . . fags, lighter, money – besides the roll, I mean?'

'Yes, I've got a hundred or so.'

'Whatever you do, don't open that wad. If she sees the singles you're a dead duck.'

'Don't worry . . .'

'And keep an eye on it. You don't want your pocket picked before she has a chance to have a go at it.'

'Buzz, don't worry . . .'

'Feeling O.K.?'

'Yes, fine.'

'Then why's your hand shaking like that?'

'Because I'm scared stupid, that's why.'

'Too late to back out now, we're here.'

He swung into the forecourt of the Sands and stopped short of the main entrance, then held out his hand with a grin. 'Best of luck, cock. Bring home the bacon and we'll have a time in Tahiti like you can't imagine.'

'By God, I'll need it. O.K., son, see you back at the hotel. Keep praying.'

'You're a brave man, Tobin, you deserve a medal – even posthumously.'

I replied with two very rude words and got out of the car, almost fell down with nervous weakness, took three steps towards the door, then turned and came back.

'Just one very minor point of practically no importance whatever, Malone . . . I don't even know what the bird looks like, you berk!'

'Oh, Christ . . .'

Into the hotel we went, Buzz in the lead, cautiously sweeping the foyer, then stopping so suddenly I ran into him.

'Ummph!'

'She's there!' he whispered. 'Sitting at the bar!'

I moved to one side, followed his pointing thumb. At the far end of the Sands' foyer and in its centre is a round, sunken bar, a low structure with tiny stools, the serving area set well below floor level, so that from where I stood the barmen looked three feet tall.

Although most of the stools were occupied, there was no mistaking Felicia DeCourcey-Holme, and at first sight of her, even knowing what she was, the old ticker broke into triple time. She was a corker, a blonde goddess in a pale green silk gown, her hair a curtain of shimmering gold.

'Oh, Buzz . . .'

'Really something, hm? Do you wonder I got hooked?'

'Oh, man . . . Buzz, I don't think I can go through with it. I want to rush over there and *give* her the money!'

'Steady, Tobin, think of Tahiti.'

'I'm trying, I'm trying! But Tahiti's so far away and she's so close.'

'Think of her as Rosa Klebb – with a razor in her boot.'

'Don't be ridiculous. God, she's beautiful.'

'And all yours – I'm off before she spots me. Best of luck – and keep your pecker up.'

'Yeah . . . not even that to look forward to.'

'Keep thinking about Tahiti!' he grinned . . . and then he was gone.

Oh, Gawd.

Suddenly alone, the scheme became insane. I felt like the office boy who'd geared himself up over a period of months to tell the boss exactly what he thought of him, and now, having knocked on the door, was suddenly appalled at what he'd done.

I wanted to turn and run but knew I couldn't, so I stood there for a lot of shuffling seconds, staring down the room at this formidably beautiful and frighteningly chic bird, terrified at the prospect of even talking to her, never mind acting out a nerve-racking two-hour charade.

It wouldn't work, I knew it, felt it. Something would go diabolically wrong. The moment I reached her she'd get up and walk off, having already got another sucker lined up, something . . . anything . . .

Well, you can't just stand there for two hours, you chump. At least go over, sit next to her and order a drink, see what happens after that. In any case you *need* a drink. Go on – move!

I moved.

Suddenly, half-way down the room, the need for decision overwhelmed me. If I was going to pretend to be a drunken idiot, I'd have to get into the part right there and then, it'd be too late once I'd sat down.

Now, believe me, this sort of extrovertism doesn't come easily to me. If anything I'm more inclined to be the other way – not the shrinking violet, exactly, but not the sort to take my trousers off at a party, either – at least not in public!

And yet I suppose in most of us there's the ability to act a part when the need arises – even if it's only putting over a sob story to the Inland Revenue – and the closer I got to the bar so the natural ham in me began to rise to the surface.

Tahiti, I thought . . . Buzz's five thousand dollars, I thought . . . she's a witch, a bitch, a low-down thieving conwoman. Damn it, Tobin, you've *got* to do it! Sock it to her, man, get that money back! You are no longer Tobin the Penniless, you are the Right Hon. Russell Tobin Esquire, Idiot Son of a top-drawer Idiot

Family – vague, clumsy, gormless and naive . . . and the ripest mark she's come across all year.

Now . . . do it!

'I say . . . excuse me . . . b . . . but is this seat taken?'

She turned her head, bewildered, the incisive English accent causing as much consternation as the unfamiliarity of the enquiry. In America, nobody ever asks whether an empty barstool is taken, they just take it.

Dammit, even though I'd steeled myself against it, the startling beauty of her soft green eyes and the lushness of her perfect mouth almost undid me. In the drift of her perfume I felt my resolve slipping. I was going . . . going . . . Buzz . . . Tahiti . . . help me . . . heeelllppp . . . !

Her cool sarcasm saved the day. With a glance down at the stool, then up at me, the smile faded from her eyes as she slotted me neatly into 'Cunt' category, then she drawled, 'Somebody tried . . . it's bolted to the floor.'

I guffawed. 'Ha, ha! Now I *like* that. One thing I do appreciate is a wry sense of humour.' I slid onto the stool, knocking over a holder of toothpicks and scattering them all over the bar. 'Oops, oh, I say, how damn clumsy of me.'

'Yes,' she sighed, picking some out of her lap and throwing them down in front of me.

'I'm frightfully sorry. Not a very ausp . . . auspishus beginning, is it?'

'To what?'

'Well . . . to our conversation.'

'Oh, we're about to have a conversation?'

She sounded as delighted at the prospect as being buried alive in a coffin full of spiders.

'Well, seeing that you're s . . . sitting here all alone . . . and I'm sitting here all al . . . lone . . . hic! pardon . . . I thought at least we might pass the time of day.'

She shrugged. 'O.K., I make it seven thirty two – end of conversation.'

'Ha, ha!' I chortled. 'I *do* like your sense of humour. There *is* a d . . . difference you know – between British and American humour. Yours is far more . . . far more . . .'

'Oh, you're British,' she sighed. 'I'd *never* have guessed.'

'*Really?* Oh, but surely . . . ah, you're pulling my leg!'

'Believe me, I wouldn't touch your leg.'

'Oh, no! I didn't mean . . . literar . . . *lit*rerar . . . *actually* pulling my leg, it's just an expression we use. It means joking . . . I mean, you can *tell* I'm British, can't you?'

'In spades,' she muttered.

The barman arrived, Edward G. Robinson to a T. 'Yeah, what'll it be?'

'*Ah*, now let me see . . . do you have any champagne, my good man?'

He winced, threw a glance at Felicia, wondering if she was with me and if so why.

'Yeah, we got champagne.'

'On ice?'

'No, we're different, we keep ours in the boiler room. Sure it's on ice.'

'And what labels do you stock?'

'Mostly paper ones.'

'Ha!' I exploded, turning to Felicia. 'See what I mean . . . delightfully wry sense of humour.'

'Sir, would you mind, I'm busy . . .'

'Oh, sorry. Erm . . . how about Moet Chandon?'

He nodded. 'We got Moet.'

'Ah, but do you have a '59 Moet?' I turned again to Felicia. 'S . . . splendid year for champagne – '59. '52, '53, '55, '59 and '61 – all absolutely top-hole years for vintage champers.'

And in case you're wondering how I knew all this, I learned it off a card I picked up at my local bottle store in the Edgware Road.

'Do tell,' she yawned.

'No, I ain't gotta '59,' growled Edward G. 'Neither do I have a '52, a '53, a '55 or a '61 – but I'll tell yuh what I *do* have, mister – I gotta whole barful of customers waitin' to be soived, so if you'd kindly make up your mind . . .'

'Oh,' I said disappointedly. 'In that case I'll have a v . . . vodka and tonic.'

'Vodka tonic,' he nodded, looking enquiringly at Felicia's empty glass. 'Miss?'

'Same again – campari soda.'

He departed.

'Ah, very refreshing, too, campari soda,' I allowed, fishing in my pockets for my cigarettes. 'Great favourite of mater's on warm summer evenings.'

She frowned. 'Whose?'

'M . . . mater's . . . my mother's.' I grinned apologetically. 'Sorry, of course you don't use the term over here, do you . . . mater . . . pater . . . silly, I suppose. Hangover from public school days, referring to one's parents in Latin terminology. Difficult habit to b . . . break. Would you care for a cigarette?'

'No, thank you, I'll smoke my own.'

From her lap she brought up the infamous little silver-lamé evening bag, and now, seeing it for the first time, the reality of all Buzz had told me suddenly struck home. Surreptitiously I watched her open it. She did so guardedly, opening it just wide enough to extract her silver cigarette-case, and yet, careful though she was, I managed to catch a glimpse of a roll of bills. That, plus the bulge it created, told me she was fully loaded for stag and on the hunt.

I offered her a light which she took without comment.

'Have you . . . ever been to England?' I asked casually.

'No.'

'Have you any d . . . desire to visit England?'

'No.'

'Oh.'

I tried again.

'It, er, r . . . really is the most beautiful country, you know . . .'

'Really.'

'Indeed, yes . . . the Cotswolds in high summer . . . the Lake District in autumn . . .'

I'd lost her.

Edward G. returned, gently placing her campari soda in front of her and slamming my vodka and a small bottle of tonic in front of me. 'There yuh go, sir . . . sorry we're outta '59 tonic, but I'm sure you'll find this '74 most palatable. That'll be two dollars.'

'And the lady's?'

She rounded on me. 'I'll buy my own.'

'No, really . . .'

'I *said* I'll buy my own.'

I shrugged, hurt. 'No offence int . . . tended, madam, I assure you. I merely . . .'

I dug into my pocket and pulled out the loose hundred-dollar bill.

'Yuh got nuthin' smaller?' grumbled Edward G.

'No, frightfully sorry.'

The exchange was not missed by Felicia. She shot a glance at me, then quickly looked away and fumbled for some small money in her bag.

'Frightfully witty fellow,' I remarked as the barman departed, picking up the tonic and preparing to tip some into the vodka. ' "Sorry, we're all out of '59 tonic, but you'll find this '74 most palatable!" . . . ha, ha ha! . . . *ha!* . . . *ha!* . . . *ha!*'

Overdoing the joviality to a ridiculous degree, I overshot the glass and slopped tonic all over the bar, some of it dribbling over the lip and threatening Felicia's gown.

With a cry she swung away.

'Oh, my God . . .!' I gasped, diving in my pocket for my hanky, taking a firm grip on my roll of notes and yanking them both out together, then lunging for the pool of tonic and sending the wad rolling down the bar. 'Oh, I'm most *frightfully* s . . . sorry . . . how *wretchedly* clumsy of me. D . . . did it catch your dress . . .? Oh, Lord, I do wish I wasn't so damnably accident-prone . . . runs in the f . . . family, you know . . . pater has the most *appalling* accident propensity . . . fell off the lower battlements last summer, fortunately, thank heaven, straight into the moat, otherwise . . . look, are you sure it didn't catch your lovely g . . . gown? I say, Miss . . .'

'Mm . . .? Oh, no, don't worry about it, didn't catch a drop.'

Miss Felicia DeCourcey-Holme wouldn't have known if she'd been smeared from head to foot in tomato ketchup right then, because her full and total concentration was centred upon a wrist-thick bundle of one-hundred-dollar greenbacks languishing against the napkin box.

'Oh,' I said, grinning foolishly, 'would you be so kind. I must have pulled it out with my hanky.'

'Yes . . .' she murmured quietly. 'You did.'

She reached for it, peering intently at it, doing her damndest to X-ray it, then, with a slight catch of breath, handed it back to me. But how different her reaction to me now. Gone was the hard protective shell, the bored indifference, the sneering cynicism. Here was womanhood at its softest, gentlest, and most alluring . . . the smiling, slightly censorious eyes, the teasing curve of mouth she knew could drive men potty with desire.

'You . . . really should be more careful with it. It seems an awful lot of money to be carrying around.'

'Well, yes, I suppose it is a fair bit of change,' I said lightly, stuffing the roll carelessly back in my pocket. 'Now, are you absolutely p . . . positive I didn't catch your gown. It's so beautiful, I'd never forgive myself . . .'

Her hand reached out to mine, as though to stop me dabbing further at the spilled tonic. 'Honestly . . . look, see for yourself, not a single spot. And never mind the counter, the barman will see to that. It's very sweet of you to be so concerned, though.'

I shrugged, bashfully. 'Well, dash it all, I . . .'

'Do you have enough tonic left? We'll get some more . . .'

'No, no, really, there's plenty here, thanks all the same.'

She smiled, teasingly. 'Perhaps I'd better pour it.'

'Well, that's . . . thanks awfully . . .'

She did so, elegantly, and even passed me the glass, then picked up hers. 'Don't feel badly about it, accidents do happen. There's no harm done . . . except to my cigarette,' she laughed, dumping the soggy butt in the ashtray.

Hurriedly I put down my drink. 'Look . . . d . . . do have one of mine.'

'Thanks, but I think I'll stick to mine, they're extra mild. You try one.'

'Well, that's very kind . . .'

Up came the bag again, but this time she opened it wide, gave a few tugs at the cigarette-case, making it appear as though it was caught in the lining, then out it came with a rush – together with her lighter, lipstick, make-up . . . and, of course, that great fat juicy roll of notes – not far, just enough to make sure I got a good eyeful.

'Oh!' she laughed, quickly stuffing the bits and pieces back in. 'There, you see, you're not the only one who's accident prone. It's this darned cigarette-case, it's too big for the purse . . . always gets caught in the lining.'

She offered me a cigarette and as I lit hers I gave her a teasing grin to let her know I wasn't as big a fool as she'd taken me for.

'Now it's my turn to w . . . warn you, I think.'

'Mm . . .?' she went, contriving innocence.

'I couldn't help noticing . . . you're carrying a fair p . . . piece of change yourself.'

Her eyes crinkled. 'You're very observant.'

'One could hardly *fail* to notice.'

She laughed. 'Well, one doesn't come to Vegas without a little spending money, does one?'

'Of course not. Ten thousand doesn't go far in this iniquitous burg.'

'Have you . . . had any luck?'

I shrugged. 'Oh, a little, here and there. I'm afraid I'm a bit of an idiot where money's concerned. I was here in August and managed to leave enough behind to *completely* refurnish Caesar's Palace . . .' She laughed gaily, as though everybody did it from time to time. 'But this trip . . .' I patted my pocket, 'I managed to get a little of it back. Not much, but even ten thousand's better than a sock on the jolly old jaw, what?'

'Yes, even a measly ten,' she agreed, her eyes lighting up like a pinball machine and the wheels going round in her pretty head like cogs in an overwound clock. 'Tell me . . .' she paused nonchalantly to sip her drink, making little of the question, '. . . do you intend gambling here tonight?'

'Here – in the Sands? Well, hadn't given it a thought, really . . . pretty much at a loose end, doncha know. Had a little flutter at Caesar's P. earlier on, then strolled over to the Flamingo for a throw or two, then thought I'd pop in here and take the weight off my feet for a while. Damn hard on the feet, all this gambling, what?'

'Right,' she smiled. 'And you've been doing all this . . . solo?'

'Mm . . .? Oh, yes, rather . . . yes, I . . .' here a touching little smile, '. . . I'm not the sort of chap girls fall over themselves to get at, somehow. Bit clumsy at it, I suppose . . . always putting my foot in it – like knocking over bottles of tonic and things.'

Her voice was a feathery caress. 'I am surprised – about the girls, I mean.'

'Well, that's . . . very decent of you . . .'

'No, I mean it. You're a very good-looking man . . . you have impeccable manners. I'd have thought you'd have been inundated.'

I grinned bashfully. 'Well, thanks awfully, but I'm afraid not. It's probably the English public school system to blame, y'know. From prep school at eight right through public school to eighteen we see neither hide nor hair of the fairer sex. We have a f . . . *frightful* amount of catching up to do. I must be at least ten years behind the average chap when it comes to . . . well, romance.'

'So, you're here all on your own?'

'Quite on my tod, as we say in England.' I laughed bravely. 'Still, never mind . . .'

'And . . . how long are you staying?'

'In Vegas? Oh, off tomorrow, back to jolly old Frisco. I'm staying with an aunt there. Dear old soul. I try to get to see her a couple of times a year but when I do she always insists I pop over to Vegas for a little fun. Feel frightfully sorry for her . . . living in that *enormous* house all alone . . .'

'What's your name?'

I looked at her, stunned by the incredible softness of her voice. 'M . . . my name? T . . . Tobin . . . Russell Tobin. May I know yours?'

'It's Felicia . . .'

'Yes, I knew it had to be s . . . something extraordinarily beautiful.'

She laughed. 'Why?'

'B . . . because you are extraordinarily beautiful.'

'Well . . . thank you.'

'What's your surname?'

'DeCourcey-Holme.'

'De . . .' I gaped at her. 'DeCourcey-Holme . . . spelled H-o-l-m-e?'

'Yes,' she laughed. 'Why?'

'Good Lord, you couldn't possibly be related to the Winchester DeCourcey-Holmes?'

She shook her head regretfully. 'I don't think so. As far as I *know* I have no English relatives.'

'Oh. But how incredible . . . *very* great friend of the family's, the DeCourcey-Holmes. Had a villa next to ours in Nice . . . went to Charterhouse with their youngest son, Aubrey. Bit of an ass but a *marvellous* opening bat. Well, what an incredible co-incidence. I say, I . . . wonder if you'd care for another drink? That one must be cold by now.'

She laughed politely and looked at her watch. 'Well . . .'

My face fell. 'Oh, you're waiting for someone. Of course, you must be.'

'Why "must be"?'

'Well . . . if you'll forgive the familiarity, a girl as beautiful as you is never unescorted without good reason. *Are* you waiting for someone?'

She gave me a tight smile. 'Yes, I am . . . and I'm afraid he's putting me in a *very* embarrassing position.'

'Oh? Oh, how perfectly rotten for you.'

'We were supposed to be going to a party – a rather exclusive little gathering that one doesn't attend unescorted, I'm sure you understand.'

'Oh, absolutely – not the done thing, what?'

'Quite. Oh, I know the people, and I'm quite sure under the circumstances they'd understand, but . . . well, being the odd girl out . . .'

'Oh, how perfectly hideous for you. Er . . . *would* you care for another drink?'

'Well, yes, thank you. I'll give him another ten minutes and then . . .'

She let it hang, so I let it hang and signalled Edward G. who gave a wince and trundled over. 'What'll it be this time – a Château-bottled Coke or Sauterne-on-a-Stick?'

'Ha, ha! You're absolutely priceless.'

I ordered the drinks and then she got working on me, subtly fingering her rings so that the reflection from the diamonds brought tears to my eyes. 'You like Nice?' she asked casually.

'Adore it. Frightfully fond of the whole of the Côte d'Azur, though I do think St. Trop is getting a *teensy* bit tacky these days, don't you agree?'

'Do you ski?' she asked, skilfully avoiding the question.

I grinned modestly. 'I manage.'

'I'll bet you're very good.'

'Well . . .'

'You're far too self-effacing, you know. What else do you do?'

Birds like you for a start, love, I thought, wondering if there was the slightest chance of picking up that little bonus in addition to her bankroll. She really was a corking bit of crumpet.

'What . . . in the sports line, you mean? Oh . . . a little polo, water skiing, squash, tennis, golf . . . the usual things.'

Her eyes melted me. 'You must be very fit.'

I laughed. 'Not bad, I supp . . .'

'Do you like dancing?'

'Dancing! I adore it . . . but I . . . don't seem to get the chance to do much of it, somehow. Trouble with dancing is you generally need a girl to do it with, what, ha ha. Do, er, you like dancing?'

'It's one of my great passions in life.'

'Oh? And . . . what are the others?' I pursued daringly.

She responded with a naughty smile but didn't answer. Things were coming along nicely.

The barman was back with the drinks. 'Shall *I* pour it over the lady or will you, sir?'

I hooted with laughter. 'You know, you missed your calling – you should be on the stage.' The Wells Fargo, I thought – heading for Texas.

'What sort of house do you live in in England?' she asked cozily.

'Oldish,' I said. 'Though some parts of it have been modernized since William lived there.'

'William?'

'Yes, the . . . The Conqueror. The garden's the biggest problem, though, you just can't get the labour nowadays.'

'How much garden do you have?'

'About six thousand acres. How about you, where's your home?'

'Oh, we have several . . .'

'Naturally.'

'Los Angeles . . . New York . . . Paris . . .'

'What fun.'

Again she looked at her watch and sighed a little sigh.

'He's not going to show, is he?' I suggested.

'No, it doesn't look like it. Mind you, he did say he might not be able to. He has a *very* important meeting tonight . . . he's considering buying the Tropicana Hotel . . .'

'Ah, well, that would explain it. Rotten shame, though – about your party.'

'Yes, I . . .' For a moment she wrestled with indecision, twirled her glass thoughtfully, then turned to me with a wan little smile. 'Russell . . . you don't mind me calling you Russell, do you . . .?'

'Gosh, no, not in the least.'

'I was wondering . . . as you're "at a bit of a loose end" as you put it, would you care to . . . take his place?'

I gaped at her.

'I realize it's a terrible imposition,' she continued hurriedly, 'and, believe me, it's not the sort of thing I'd normally *dream* of doing, but I feel you would be so right for this party, and . . . well, if you'd consider escorting me, I'd be *very* grateful.'

I stared at her, gulped nervously. 'Well, I . . . gosh, yes, I'd *love* to!'

'Oh, would you . . . ?'

'Well, of course I would. Heavens, a chap would have to be off his chump to pass up an opportunity like this. My word, what an incredible . . .'

Her hand reached for mine. 'Thank you, you are kind. Look, I'll have to make a quick telephone call – let them know you're coming instead of George – and also call my chauffeur.'

I grinned delightedly. 'You have a chauffeur? How incredibly civilized.'

'I won't be long.'

She disappeared in the direction of the casino, a vision of elegant loveliness, capturing the attention of every male eye in the room. I smiled to myself, imagining the conversation that would ensue. 'Baby, have we got a *ripe* one! An aristocratic English lunatic with a wad as thick as a toilet roll and all C-notes! Must be at least ten grand. His name is Tobin. Get the party rolling and pick us up in five minutes.'

Back she came, a light flush of excitement colouring her cheeks.

'Fine . . . everything's just fine. They said they'd be delighted to meet you.'

'Well, this is frightfully kind of you, Felicia . . .'

'Nonsense! You're doing me the favour . . . and in return I'll see you have a very interesting evening.'

I'll bet!

I smiled bashfully. 'Perhaps we might do a little dancing?'

'Oh, we'll dance, I promise you. And I wouldn't be at all surprised if there wasn't some *very* special champagne there.'

'Oh, I say, how super.'

As she looked at her watch, I looked at mine. Hell's bells, it was almost eight! Only two hours left to do everything in – including getting out to the airport.

'Time to go?' I asked.

'Yes, Kohlman should be outside by now.'

'Then . . . shall we go?'

She laughed at my impatience. 'You really *are* fond of dancing, aren't you?'

'With you, yes . . . I must admit the prospect leaves me . . . quite breathless.'

She laughed. 'Come on, then.'

Well, so far so good. Up to now it had been a piece of cake, simply doing what came naturally – chatting up a marvellous-looking bird. But the moment we emerged from the hotel it all suddenly became frighteningly earnest, the sight of Kohlman turning my blood to ice-water.

He was even bigger than I'd reckoned – six foot seven in his socks and rock-hard muscle every inch of the way.

As we appeared, he snapped a smart salute and bent almost double to open the rear door for Felicia, turning his glass-cold eyes on me with a small welcoming nod.

'Good evening, sir,' rumbled up from a ninety-six-inch chest.

'Good evening,' I chortled. 'How frightfully kind.'

I settled into the luxurious leather upholstery beside Felicia, gazing around admiringly. 'How perfectly splendid. Rather tempted to buy one myself as a change from the DBS and the Rolls . . .'

'You . . . have a Rolls-Royce?'

'Yes – California Sage Corniche . . . natty little job. Did Europe in it last year, ran like a dream.'

Kohlman got in, tilting the Cadillac twenty degrees to port with his monstrous weight, and we were away.

'Telephone, too,' I remarked. 'Frightfully handy, aren't they?'

'Wouldn't be without it,' she smiled, and I caught Kohlman's responding grin in the mirror.

'Where are we going for the party, may I ask?'

'Oh, not too far, just on the edge of town. I . . . don't suppose you're too familiar with the residential parts of Vegas? Most people aren't.'

'No, I haven't seen any of it besides the Strip and downtown. I imagine there must be some frightfully nice houses on the out-skirts?'

She laughed. 'Yes, but nothing like your castle with six thou-sand acres, I'm afraid.'

'I should hope not. Draughty holes, castles, really not all they're cracked up to be at all. Frightfully picturesque and all that, but highly impractical. We t . . . tend to huddle together in the East Wing in, oh, just twenty or thirty rooms. Bit of a squeeze but much more cozy.'

Oh, mother, I thought, forgive me. Not only didn't we have

room to *swing* a cat at home, we didn't even have room for the bleeding cat!

We were now passing the Sahara and my thoughts flew to Buzz, up there in the room, furiously packing, checking his watch every three minutes, wondering how I was getting on, whether I'd make it in time, whether I'd make it at all and if he'd ever see me again, a question, here in Kohlman's bulging presence, that had crossed my mind more than once since I'd climbed in the car.

These people were professionals. One mistake on my part, one threat to their operation, and by God I wouldn't put it past them to resort to extreme self-protective measures. There was an awful lot of sand out there just beyond the town, as many a Mafia victim had discovered. A deep hole, a quick push, and Tobin's disappearance from the face of the earth would be the great unsolved mystery of the century.

Her hand on my knee made me jump. 'Penny for them,' she smiled.

'Er, oh, I was just . . .'

'Nervous about the party – about the people you're going to meet?'

'Ha, you must be a mind-reader. Yes, I was rather . . .'

A comforting, reassuring squeeze. 'Don't be. They're very nice. When I said an exclusive little party, I didn't mean to imply "stuffy". They're all great fun . . . but very rich, that's what I meant by exclusive. They wouldn't want just anybody crashing in and lowering the tone, you know what I mean?'

'Oh, absolutely . . .'

'That's why I consider myself doubly fortunate to have met someone like you tonight. You'll fit in just beautifully.'

'I do hope so.'

She smiled archly. 'In any case, I have no intention of letting you out of my sight. I found you and you're mine, so there.'

'Well, that's . . .'

'You shall dance with me all evening, how's that?'

I shook my head. 'That's . . . just beautiful. I can't believe my luck.'

Oh, Buzz, I thought, if this is the treatment you got, lad, no wonder you fell for it hook, line and hard-on. Even though I had both eyes wide open to what she was, I was having a terrible time fighting the urge. Her hand had now crept another six inches up my thigh and had come to rest just below Herc's lower extremity, and the vision of it moving north just that extra inch brought me out in a hot flush.

'Wh . . .' I coughed. 'Er, where do you stay when you come to Vegas? In one of the Strip hotels I suppose?'

A whimsical smile. 'As a matter of fact, no, I don't. I find them far too . . . restricting. I like to come and go as I please, out of the gaze of prying eyes. Unfortunately one can become too well-known in a small town like this – especially when one's father is a man of . . . shall we say "of certain distinction".'

I raised a dutiful brow. 'I see.'

'He's very well known around town, so naturally one has to be . . . cautious in one's private arrangements.'

'Oh, yes, rather . . . yes, of course.'

'So . . . I prefer the freedom of the less well-known motels to the comfort of the Strip hotels, if you see what I mean.'

'Oh, ind . . . dubitably.' I grinned knowingly. 'Jolly sound scheme. So, you're booked into a motel now, I take it?'

Her smile deepened, reading my lecherous intentions and letting me know it. 'Oh, the device is much more devious than that. I have a room booked, but not in my name. You see, my father does so much business entertaining in Vegas, invites so many out-of-town associates here, that he has a dozen or so rooms reserved in the company's name all year round. Then when his associates arrive, they simply sign in in their own names. So . . .'

I gave a laugh, as though the import of what she was implying had just sunk in. 'So . . . *you* have the choice of any of these rooms . . . and can book in in any name you like!'

She answered with a tight, jubilant smile. 'Provided I pay the bill, yes . . . my father never gets to know about it.'

'Ha! How absolutely spiffing!'

'A little devious, I agree, but with a father as strict as mine . . .'

'Needs must when the devil drives,' I chortled. 'Well, I take my hat off to you. Golly, I sympathize, too – had the same trouble myself until I reached the age of consent . . .'

Her smile slipped. 'With girls? But I thought you said . . .'

'Oh . . . oh, *no*, gosh, no . . .' God, nearly put my foot in it. I'd make a lousy spy. 'I, er . . . well, my escapades ran to nothing as exciting as secret assignations with the opposite sex, I'm afraid. Mine were terribly t . . . timid by comparison – just a f . . . few f . . . furtive pints in the local hostelry.'

'Pints?' she frowned.

'Yes, beer, old thing. Used to sneak out and sink a few at the pub with the local farmers . . . my father's tenants, actually, that's what he objected to. Frightful snob, pater. Didn't mind me wetting my whistle at home, but not with the peasants. Damn silly, really, but there you are. Well, good for you, delighted you've managed to work something out to escape the tyranny of paternal oppression.'

'Yes,' she smiled, 'so am I . . . very delighted.'

It was subtly done, but I caught the glance she sent Kohlman in the mirror and saw his eyes crinkle.

Go on – laugh while you can, you bloody great lump. By nine thirty you'll be chuckling on the other side of that road accident you call a face!

All the same, I was unnerved by the bloomer I'd just made. Watch it, son, or a few months from now a six-foot-long clump of lush green grass will inexplicably bloom out there in the desert . . . and the cause won't be I.C.I. Growmore!

THIRTEEN

It was an eerie experience turning again into the dark, tree-lined avenues of Rancho Circle, this time in such very different circumstances.

'Pity it isn't daylight,' said Felicia. 'There are some lovely houses here. I believe the famous and mysterious Howard Hughes himself once lived here.'

'Really?' I gave a laugh. 'Perhaps I could induce my aunt to move here from San Francisco . . . it would save me a lot of commuting.'

We turned left into the already familiar driveway and now my heart really began thudding. Suddenly I was scared. Up to now it had been relatively easy, but in a few minutes I was going to have to put on an act for a dozen strangers, conmen and women all, cute buggers who knew all the tricks, who'd be watching me like hawks. I only prayed I hadn't over-done my part with Felicia and maybe come face-to-face with some smart-ass who'd actually *been* to Charterhouse, or had intimately studied English castles, or . . . highly unlikely, maybe, but there are a billion blacksheep Englishmen knocking around the world, picking up an easy dollar here and there rather than do a day's work, and one thing I've learned on my travels is that you meet the most unlikely people in the most unlikely places.

Still, there was nothing I could do about it now. If I did come face-to-face with some awkward sod I'd just have to bluff it out, play snooty, or shy, hide behind Felicia's protection and pretend to get sick as quickly as possible.

The Cadillac soughed to a halt in front of a long, low and very beautiful house, the features of which I already knew by heart.

Kohlman climbed out and opened the door for Felicia.

'Thank you, Kohlman, I won't be needing you for several hours, but don't leave the premises. You'll find coffee in the kitchen.'

'Thank you, madam.'

As we approached the front door, Kohlman was backing the Caddy into the turn-round space in front of the garages and preparing to park the car alongside half a dozen others in a parking area, just as Buzz had described it. Up to now everything had gone just as Buzz had described it and I sent up a prayer that it'd stay that way.

The door was opened by a dark, handsome young bloke in a very expensive suit and three hundred beautiful teeth.

'Felicia, angel . . .!' he gushed, waving a huge glass of champers at her. 'Come in . . . come in.' He flashed me a look, smiled, then returned to her. 'Sorry to hear about George, hear he's been incarcerated in the boardroom for eight hours on this Tropicana thing. Still, delighted you've brought a friend . . .'

'This is Russell Tobin . . . from England. Russell, say hello to our host, Paul Raggoni.'

'How d'you do. F . . . frightfully nice of you to invite me.'

'My pleasure, my pleasure . . . come in and meet the others and have a drink, I'm sure you need one. After New Year's night *everybody* needs one!'

'Big night last night, Paul?' Felicia enquired archly.

He smiled at her, their eyes exchanging triumphant secrets. 'One of the biggest, pet.'

Yeah, I'll bet, you bastard. Buzz and who else passed through these portals and left a few minutes later, sick to death. I wondered what their total haul had been. Must have been a fortune.

Raggoni led the way into a large, superbly-furnished lounge at the back of the house, occupied by about twenty people. The atmosphere was boisterous and relaxed, everybody chatting or dancing or doing both and enjoying themselves.

As we entered, several people waved hello to Felicia but made no attempt to come over, for which I was very thankful.

'Right,' said Raggoni, 'let's get you both primed. You like champagne, Russell . . .?'

'He *adores* champagne,' laughed Felicia. 'He's just had a hard time trying to find a Moet '59 in the Sands, he's quite an expert. I told him you were bound to have something very special here.'

'Well . . .' Raggoni said doubtfully, 'I can't *swear* I've got any '59 left, but I have got some excellent . . .' he paused, glanced at Felicia. 'Look, why don't you pop downstairs and have a look . . .'

'No, really!' I protested. 'Heavens, I'm not insistent on Moet . . . anything will do, honestly!'

Felicia lowered a placatory hand to my arm. 'It won't take a moment to look. And if I can't find any, I'll make sure you get something really nice in its place.'

'Good girl,' said Raggoni. 'Open anything you like the look of – it's all for blow, not for show. I'll introduce Russell to a few people while you're gone.'

Oh, blimey.

He took my arm. 'So – you're something of a wine expert, heh – then you must certainly meet Karl Renner and exchange some views – if you can get a word in!'

Oh, my Gawd . . .

'Karl is a living, breathing encyclopaedia on the grape, I'm sure you'll find it a most interesting discussion.'

'Yes,' I gulped. 'I'm sure.'

He led me (as in lamb to the slaughter) to a group of five people clustered around a grand piano which they were using as a table for their enormous, sawn-off brandy balloons of champagne.

There were three men and two women, one of whom, a blonde, looked delightfully dizzy and three-quarters smashed. She appeared to be arguing with a tall, distinguished-looking man in thick spectacles and a small goatee beard, instinct telling me that this was Renner, the living, breathing encyclopaedia on the grape and my imminent downfall.

The blonde was prodding him amicably in the chest, obviously refuting something he'd just said, and looked, if he side-stepped, as if she'd fall flat on her face.

'. . . and *I* think it's all a lotta chi-chi nonsense, Karl . . . I mean, who're *they* to tell *me* wha' kinda wine I have to drink with what cheese? Jesus, is there no liberty left in the world . . . even t' drinkin' what you like with a lousy piece of cheese?'

'Lucinda, darling, that is *not* the point,' retorted Renner, seemingly not too happy either with the pokes in the chest or her drunkenness. 'Of course you're at liberty to drink *diesel oil* with your cheese, if you so wish. I am merely pointing out that in, shall we say, more *enlightened* societies in which people do *care* what they pour down their gullets, certain wines are known to complement the flavour and texture of certain cheeses more appetizingly than others, and therefore . . .'

Raggoni broke in, saying laughingly to me, 'There, what did I tell you? Karl, I'm going to make your evening for you . . . let me introduce Russell Tobin from England, a man who professes to know more about the grape than anyone this side of Bordeaux.'

Oh, the rotten bastard.

'Oh, *no* . . .' I protested, very loudly, and to absolutely no avail.

Renner's eyes lit up, his hand shot out and took mine with a grip like a navvy. 'My God, at last . . . a connoisseur in a land of gastronomic Philistines! Tobin, I am de-lighted to make your acquaintance.'

Raggoni quickly introduced me to the others, whose names I didn't even hear because my mind was locked in a thick blue funk. Hell, I didn't know an Anjou from an aniseed ball!

'Tobin, my dear fellow . . .' Renner was saying, chuffing me round the shoulder like a long-lost school chum. 'I was just trying to impress upon *dear* Lucinda the merits of selecting the correct wine for different types of cheese.'

'And I was trying to impress upon *him* that it's all a lotta chi-chi nonsense . . .' said Lucinda, pausing momentarily to throw another large champers down her throat. 'Karl Renner is a wine snob . . . and if you tell me you're another one, I shall simply *refuse* to dance with you.'

Wow, what a break. I smiled at her, as disarmingly as I could muster. 'Lucinda, in the face of such a s . . . serious threat, I disdain all knowledge of wine . . .'

She giggled victoriously . . . but Renner wasn't having any. 'Oh, no you don't, Tobin. I haven't languished in this cultural wilderness all these hours to be thwarted now! I *must* hear your views on the merits of a *Chassagne-Montrachet* as opposed to a *Gewürztraminer* or a *Mersault* with a blue-veined cheese! Come now – your particular preference and why?'

'Well, I . . . well, it sort of depends, doesn't it . . .?'

'On the cheese?'

'Well, it does . . . make a difference . . .'

'Yes, of course, but . . . *ah!*, perhaps you're more inclined towards a *Sauterne* or a *Barsac*?'

'Well, there again . . .'

'Aha! a *Condrieu* . . .?'

'Certainly . . . I mean, why not a jolly old . . .'

'Why not indeed! Not forgetting, of course, our old friend the *Jura* yellow!'

I laughed easily, sick to my stomach. 'How could we possibly forget him?'

Lucinda, bless her, saved the day. Slamming down her glass, she wailed, 'Oh, for Godsake, Karl, can it, will yuh? Russell, come and dance with me!'

I had no choice in the matter. She was into my arms before Renner could open his mouth to object.

'Never mind, I'll talk to you later, Tobin!'

'Yes, c . . . certainly . . .'

'You don't really want to, do you,' chuckled Lucinda, smiling up at me mischievously. 'I could tell you were bored. You'd much rather be doing this, wouldn't you?'

'Of course,' I grinned.

Now, something about all this struck me as being very odd. If, as Flush Foley had conjectured, this was a highly-sophisticated con set-up and all these people merely 'plants' to lure the sucker, was it likely they'd let a bird like Lucinda get smashed? She'd be a potential danger, surely, in case she let something out of the bag?

Then another thought struck me – say I wasn't the only sucker in the room! Maybe Lucinda had been hooked by Renner or one of the other men!

I had to find out.

'Have you known these people long?' I asked nonchalantly.

She looked about her, got them in focus, then giggled confidentially. 'Karl Renner has bin borin' me with his damn wine as long as I can remember . . . years and years and years.'

'I . . . suppose you know everybody here?'

'Oh, sure. I guess you're feelin' a little bit strange, hm? Well, you'll be feelin' a whole lot more relaxed when you've had a li'l drink . . . here comes Felicia with a couple now. Take a tip from an old campaigner – get the first one down fast! After that, you won't have a nerve in your body, I promise.'

I'll bloody bet!

So dear Lucinda wasn't a victim after all, just another shill to colour the scene and get me drinking. They certainly didn't waste any time, but then why should they? One sucker at a time, in and out fast . . . quicker turn-over, bigger profits.

'Come on, let's go get you a tranquillizer,' she laughed, taking my arm and leading me to Felicia. 'Here – I just saved him from a vintage death at the hands of Karl Renner. Take good care of him, he's a nice guy . . . dances up a storm, too.'

Felicia smiled at me enigmatically, sending me secret signals of forthcoming attractions. 'Oh, I'll take care of him, Lucinda . . . thanks for keeping an eye on him.'

'My pleasure . . . see you later. Have a ball, hm?'

But I wasn't listening to this. I was concentrating on the bowl of champagne Felicia was holding out to me, my mind racing, wondering how I was going to avoid having to drink it.

I recalled what Buzz had said . . . that he'd only taken three or four gulps before he started dancing with Felicia but that had been enough to do the dirty trick. So . . . somehow or other I had to lower the level of that glass without drinking it, one hell of a job with her standing so close and obviously watching me like a vulture to see I *did* drink it.

Well, here it came! I took the glass from her . . . she raised hers, smiled at me over the rim. 'Paul was right, he is out of Moet . . . but I'm sure you'll like this. Try it – see if you can guess the vintage.'

Oh, Gawd . . .

I raised it to my nose, sniffed it, lifted it ostentatiously to the light, peered into it, swirled it in the glass . . . and now the moment of truth was upon me! What could I *do*! She was standing so close, her eyes consuming me, pensive, poised, expectant . . . I just *had* to drink some!

And then, from behind me . . . a miracle!

Lucinda, supposedly smashed, let out a shriek of laughter. 'Oh, Karl, *really* . . . ! *Goat* cheese, for Chrissake . . . !'

It was the distraction I needed. I shot round, using the impetus of the movement to slop a good quarter inch of champagne onto the thick, curly carpet while my back was to Felicia, then, before turning to her again, I raised the glass to my mouth and pretended a couple of good swallows, bringing the glass down as I turned to face her.

'Lucinda ap . . . pears to find this champagne as irresistible as I do,' I grinned, wiping my mouth. 'It really is delightful.'

Her smile was one of genuine relief. 'I'm glad you like it.'

'Exceedingly smooth . . . beautifully dry. Now, how about that dance?'

'I'm all yours.'

I looked around for a place to deposit my glass, spotted a small table and strolled over to it. Again, with my back to Felicia, I contrived a couple of hefty swallows, then, as I bent down, tipped another good dollop of champagne onto the carpet as I put down the glass.

'Really is excellent,' I smiled, smacking my lips. 'Oh, I'm frightfully sorry, your glass . . .'

I held out my hand for it but she wasn't having any. She was going to make damn sure our glasses didn't get mixed up. Instead, she took my hand and led me to the small area cleared for dancing, placing her glass on another table as we passed.

Then she was in my arms, wasting no time, obviously starting a mental countdown to the start of Russell's demise.

About ten minutes, Buzz had said. I sneaked a glance at my watch. Good God, it was eight thirty! It was going to be a *very* tight thing. Ten minutes before I could start feeling poorly . . . another five to get into the death-throes . . . at least another fifteen before we reached the motel! Heck, it was going to be nine o'clock before we got going on the booking-in bit! Then there'd be the getting-into-bed bit . . . her retiring to the bathroom . . . my creeping out of the room and collecting the money from the safety deposit box . . . the race back to the Sahara. My God, I only had half an hour to do the lot!

Well, there was only one thing for it – I'd have to hasten the process.

'Comfy?' she whispered, snuggling closer.

Goddamn it, she felt so wonderful . . . I might at least have got a *bit* of pleasure out of this in exchange for all the risk.

'F . . . fantastically,' I stammered. 'I c . . . could stay right here all night.'

She chuckled. 'Then stay. I'm not going anywhere . . . at least not for a while.'

'And th . . then where?'

She looked up at me, her eyes languid, smilingly suggestive. 'Well, a girl's got to go to bed sometime, hasn't she?'

'Y . . . yes, I suppose . . .'

'Has any girl ever told you you're a very attractive man, Russell?'

I gulped. 'No . . .'

'Perhaps you haven't given them the chance? *I* think you are . . . terribly attractive.'

'Y . . . you do?'

'Huh huh. You have a . . .' she smiled, 'a certain naive charm that I find totally disarming. You're gentle . . . and you also have a *very* good body.'

'Oh, I say . . .'

She squeezed me tightly, enjoying my embarrassment. 'In fact, I think you're altogether *very* yummy.'

Well, damn it to hell, what a turn up . . . my arms full of supple, silky, sensuous crumpet and I couldn't do a thing about it. I shot another glance at my watch, appalled to find another five minutes had gone already. Oh . . . buggerit, all this going on and it was time to start! If only we'd booked on a later plane – even an hour later – I'd have made damn sure I got more for my money than just money!

Well, Olivier, hang on to your laurels – here we go with a performance that'll make your Hamlet seem like amateur night on Southend Pier.

First . . . a falter, almost a stumble.

'Oh . . .'

She looked up at me, alarmed by my tone. 'What . . . what's the matter? Are you feeling all right?'

'Yes . . . yes, perfectly . . . just a . . .' I brought my hand to my forehead.

'Russell, what *is* it?'

I gave a short, puzzled laugh. 'Nothing . . . really . . . just a strange . . . sorry, Felicia, but for a moment there . . . it's probably the champagne, probably drank it too quickly. My word, it's frightfully warm in here, isn't it?'

'Well, no I . . . Russell, are you *sure* you're all right? I must say you do look a bit . . .'

I staggered against her, clutched at her for support. 'Oh, my God . . .'

'Russell, darling, there *is* something the matter. Perhaps you'd better sit down.'

'Well, I . . . hate to cause a fuss, Felicia, but perhaps . . . you're right.'

She took my hand, led me quickly into the entrance hall and sat me on a small couch. 'Oh, Russell, I am sorry . . .'

'Now, don't you worry about a thing . . .' I murmured weakly, passing a shaking hand over my brow. 'It's . . . a little cooler out here and . . .' Suddenly I fell forward, my face buried in my hands. 'Oh, my God, this is ridiculous . . .'

Deep concern, almost panic from Felicia. 'What . . .? What is it?'

I shook my head. 'I . . . I feel quite dreadful. It's almost like . . .'

'Like what? Oh, Russell . . .'

'Had . . . food poisoning once . . . oysters . . . damn-near died.'

'Have you eaten any tonight?'

'No . . . nothing. Perhaps that's it . . . champers on an empty stomach.'

'Russell, I must get a doctor for you!'

'No, no, please . . . I'll be all right, really . . . perhaps if I could . . . just lie down for a while.'

'Yes, I think you ought to.'

Suddenly the hallway was filled with people, all very concerned about my condition, acting it up a treat.

Lucinda: 'Aw, honey, what's the matter with you?'

Felicia: 'He just felt a little faint, that's all. He's had nothing to eat all day.'

Renner: 'Anything we can do? I know a splendid recipe . . .'

Felicia: 'No, thank you, I think he's better left alone. Now, please, all of you go back and enjoy yourselves, he just wants to be left alone.'

Muttering between themselves, they wandered back into the lounge and closed the door, and I'd have given anything to see their faces right then. There'd be winks and grins and a lot of rubbing of hands over the prospect of another ten grand in the kitty.

Felicia, bless her, was now kneeling at my side and stroking my head. 'Russell, I have an idea . . .'

'Ohhhhhh,' I moaned, shivering beautifully. 'God, it's so cold now . . .'

'We've got to get you to bed and let a doctor examine you. If it *is* food poisoning, it can be very serious. Tell you what I'm going to do. I'm going to get Kohlman in to help you into the car, then we're going to drive to my motel. We'll put you to bed there, all right?'

I nodded feverishly, my face still buried in my hands. 'Yes . . . please . . .'

'Good . . . I'll call Kohlman.'

She left me but returned almost immediately with Stonehenge Stan. 'Be very careful with him, Kohlman, he's very poorly. Get him to the motel as fast as you can.'

'Yes, ma'm. Up you come, sir . . .'

Up I went, sir, light as a hydrogen balloon . . . and out I went, sir – into the back of the Cadillac, Felicia slipping in beside me to hold my hand as I rested my feverish forehead against the cold side window and shivered and groaned and wondered why I'd never taken up acting as a full-time career.

'You poor, poor man,' she cooed broken-heartedly. 'What a terrible thing to happen. Never mind, we'll soon have you tucked up in a nice warm bed . . .'

'It's . . . t . . . terribly kind of you to d . . . do all this for me,' I croaked, teeth chattering like castanets.

'Nonsense, it's the very least I can do. I feel responsible for it happening. If it hadn't been for that champagne . . .'

'Oh, no . . . no . . . no . . . m . . . must be a ch . . . chill . . . always f . . . frightfully prone to ch . . . chills as a ch . . . child.'

'Well, some of us are stronger than others. And this desert air can be very deceiving this time of year. But never mind, you can stay in the motel as long as you like – and I'll be there to take care of you.'

'Felicia, this is frightfully kind of you . . .'

'Not at all. Who knows – maybe there'll be some way in which you can pay me back someday.'

Like in two hours' time, you scheming witch. I wasn't in a position to see her face right then, but I'd have bet Buzz's bankroll she and Kohlman were grinning themselves silly.

A few minutes more and we were turning off the Strip into the forecourt of a big single-storey motel built in the shape of a three-sided square, its open side facing the Strip.

Kohlman drew up outside the office, situated at the front of the left-hand wing, and cut the motor. At this point I started a fresh bout of anguished moaning to move things along a bit faster. Felicia got out while Kohlman helped me out and got me reasonably vertical, then she came to my side, oozing compassion. 'Oh, you poor, poor man . . . never mind, we'll have you in bed in no time at all. Oh, but there's just one thing . . . Russell, are you listening?'

'Yes,' I groaned, then slumped against the car, face buried in my hands.

'Russell, listen . . . we'll *have* to book in as Mister and Mrs. Tobin . . . I explained about my father's company . . .'

'Yes, of course, anything . . .'

'Good . . . now, let's do *everything* naturally, just like a man and wife booking in for a few days. We'll even deposit our money in a safety deposit box, it's what everybody does . . .'

'Felicia . . . let me lie down . . . *please* . . . !'

'Yes, of course, come on . . . Kohlman, park the car, we won't be needing you now.'

'Yes, ma'm . . . goodnight, ma'm . . . goodnight, sir. I trust you'll be feeling better in the morning.'

I could only manage a nod.

Felicia hooked an arm round my waist and helped me into the office, dumped me into a suitable chair and went to the desk.

I couldn't catch all the conversation, but from the snippets I did get I gathered she was explaining we were Mister and Mrs. Tobin here on convention with the Ragner Corporation (Raggoni-Renner?), that we'd lost our luggage on the flight from Baltimore but that it would be delivered the following morning. Then, leaning closer, Felicia murmured sotto-voce, woman-to-woman, causing the girl to shoot an amused smile in my direction and offer Felicia a sympathetic 'ain't that like men – every convention an excuse for a big drunk' shrug.

Smiling in response, Felicia left the counter and came over to help me up. 'Come on, Charlton Heston, on your feet . . . all we need from you is one little signature, then it's beddy-byes.'

Hardly able to contain her smirk, the receptionist held out the pen to me and pointed at the registration card. 'Right there, sir, please.'

'No, not on her finger, darling,' sighed Felicia, hanging on grimly in case I fell down and ruined everything. 'Oh . . . yes . . .' she said to the girl, as an after-thought. 'I think we'd better have a safety deposit box.'

'Certainly, madam.'

The girl turned away, unlocked a safe door, pulled out one of the oblong steel boxes and gave it to us, then took a white card from a shelf and filled in our details.

'Either or both to withdraw?' she asked Felicia.

'Er . . . either. I'll want to do some shopping tomorrow while Sleeping Beauty here is still in the Land of Nod.'

I just stood there weaving about, pretending I didn't understand what was going on.

Felicia then opened her bag and took out the roll of notes, the sight of it setting my pulse racing. Then, with the off-handedness of a wife used to picking her husband's pockets, she plunged her hand into mine, pulled out my roll and casually tossed them both into the box.

I made to move away, clutching my stomach, my head. 'Felicia . . .'

'Oho, hang on, lover, don't you want your key?'

'Mm . . .? Oh . . .'

She sighed in despair at the receptionist who grinned and handed her two keys. 'Take good care of them. If you lose one, a new lock will cost you twenty-five dollars.'

'You hear that?' Felicia asked me jokingly. 'Look, I'm putting your key in your top pocket . . . see . . . there . . . in there!'

'Yes . . .' I muttered, weaving away. 'Felicia, will you *please* . . .'

'Yes, yes, all right.' She caught me round the waist. 'Come on, Romeo, let's get you tucked away and out of trouble.'

'Sleep well,' smiled the receptionist.

'You'll be lucky to see him this side of noon,' laughed Felicia.

And that's no lie, I thought. Well, by golly, I had to hand it to them – a really slick, painless operation – well, painless for them! I was supposed to be grovelling in agony.

'Oh, God, Felicia, I feel absolutely *dreadful*! I really think you better had call a doctor.'

'Of course – as soon as we get you into bed. Just a few more yards . . . try and hold on.'

We started down a long, long corridor, windowed on the right, that ran the length of the motel.

Out in the centre courtyard a score of cars were parked facing the three wings, and as we reached the end of the first wing and turned into the second, I saw Kohlman swing the Cadillac into an empty space facing the third wing!

My heart sank. He'd presumably parked right outside our room!

Now I saw that the line of picture windows on our right was interrupted every now and again by a french door leading out to the parking lot, and suddenly I realized that Kohlman had parked there to give Felicia her quickest line of escape once I was out for the count. She'd nip out of the room, into the car, over to the office, clean out the safety deposit box, and they'd be on their way before you could say spit!

But in the process he'd completely scuttled my own plan!

How was I going to get out of the room with Kohlman sitting right outside there, smack in front of the window through which he could clearly see our bedroom door!

I suddenly felt really sick. God, to have got so far only to be thwarted in the closing seconds! And the seconds were closing mighty fast. It was almost nine! It was too late! I couldn't go through with it! If I turned and ran now, I'd only just get back to the Sahara in time! Oh . . . fuck it, fuck it and double fuck it!

What could I *do* – clock Felicia on the jaw and make a dash for the Reception? I glanced down at her sweet chin, the curved perfection of her mouth and knew I couldn't sock her for all the money in the world. Bogart, maybe . . . Lee Marvin without a second thought . . . and Mike Hammer could put a .45 slug through her navel while picking his teeth and laying another broad, but not Tobin. It hurts my feelings to swat flies.

No, I had to wait until I got in the room and work it out some other way.

'Here we go, honey, just another few doors.'

We swung into the third wing, fast closing on Kohlman, but then . . . a break! She stopped short of Kohlman by two doors and about twenty feet, and fitted the key in the lock.

Inwardly I sighed with relief. Maybe . . . just maybe! The picture windows didn't reach the floor. There was a partition, about three feet high, that carried the central heating rads. If I could get out of the room on my hands and knees and crawl part-way back along the corridor . . . !

'Come on, in you go.'

Remembering Buzz's reaction, I made a bee-line for the right-hand bed and flung myself on it, clutching my stomach, groaning horribly.

'There . . . there,' she cooed. 'You'll feel much better once you're in bed.'

'The doctor . . .'

'Yes, of course . . . try and relax . . . straighten out your legs and I'll take your shoes off. You'll feel a whole lot better un-dressed and tucked between nice cool sheets . . .'

'But I'm freezing!'

'Then we'll make them nice *warm* sheets. Tell you what, let me undress you and get you into bed, then I'll get in with you and keep you warm, how does that sound?'

I smiled weakly. 'Wonderful. Felicia . . . come and lie down with me now.'

'Er . . . well, not for a moment . . .'

'God, I suddenly feel so . . . so tired.'

'That's the best thing for you – sleep.'

I stifled a huge yawn. '*Please* come and lie down with me, Felicia . . .'

'In a moment. I've . . . just got to go to the bathroom. Come on, now, how about getting undressed?'

'I will . . . I will . . .' I slurred sleepily. 'You . . . do what you have to . . . in the bathroom.'

She patted my hand. 'All right, then, but don't you dare go to sleep on me before I come back.'

My eyes drifted closed and I fought them open again. 'You think I'd . . . do a thing like that . . . to a lady?'

'No, of course not. You just rest your eyes . . . that's it, close your eyes . . . and start counting. And before you reach a hundred I'll be back. All right?'

I nodded stupidly. 'F . . . ine.'

'Right, start counting . . . one . . . two . . . three . . .'

In a doleful tone, heavy-laden with sleep, I began. '. . . four . . . five . . . sis . . . seben . . . eigh . . . ni . . .'

She got off the bed and stood looking down at me, then the rustle of her gown told me she was slowly backing away towards the bathroom. Then, silence . . . as she paused at the door.

On I droned, becoming less and less coherent. '. . . ten . . . eleben . . . twel . . . firteen . . .' I allowed one arm to flop from my chest to the bed. '. . . sist . . . seben . . .' then I stopped counting for a couple of beats and picked it up again at nine. '. . . ten . . . eleben . . .'

That convinced her.

A rustle of clothing . . . then the soft click of the bathroom door . . . and a moment later the reassuring sound, for my benefit, of the shower spray.

That was it!

I shot up in bed, checked the time. Jesus wept . . . ten past nine! Buzz would have a hernia!

With thundering heart I nipped off the bed and over to the door on tip-toe, thankful for the heavy carpet. I eased the door open a sliver and peered out, spotting Kohlman at the wheel of the Caddy, not twenty feet away and looking straight at me!

I hung on, not daring to close the door again. *Could* he see me? The corridor was lit up like a Christmas tree but there was no telling how much reflection he was getting from the lights in the parking lot.

For a moment longer he held his gaze, then looked down, at his knees. Maybe he was reading a paper or something. Should I take a chance and nip out now? I'd give it a count of three, then slip out on my hands and knees, closing the door behind me.

Right, here goes . . . one . . . two . . . th . . . Christ, he looked up again, straight at me.

Well, that was going to be the pattern. Obviously expecting Felicia to emerge at any moment, he was on the alert – a glance up every few seconds. O.K., in that case I had about three seconds after his next glance to get out of the door and get it closed again.

With an ear on what Felicia was up to in the bathroom and both eyes glued on Kohlman, I waited, sick with apprehension, conscious of every racing second.

It was now . . . nine fifteen!

Come on, Kohlman – get back to your comics!

He rubbed his eye, picked his nose, scratched his ear . . . and lowered his head! This was it!

I dropped to my knees, squeezed through the door, reached up and silently closed the door . . . and then I was off down the corridor as fast as my knees would carry me.

Left . . . right . . . left . . . right . . . corner coming up fast . . . another six or seven yards to go and I'd be into the second wing and out of Kohlman's sight!

And then . . . 'Hey!'

A shout from behind!

I froze. It had to be Kohlman! I shot round . . . almost fainting with relief at the sight of a little fat guy in janitor's uniform, a cigar butt stuck in his mouth, a crumpled white cap perched on the back of his head.

'Hey, you lost sumthin'?'

'Er . . . oh, yes! Yes . . . my . . . wife . . . she, erm, lost a stone out of her ring . . . thinks it may be around here somewhere.'

'Gee, dat's too bad.' He waddled up, his bucket clanking. 'Valu'ble, was it?'

'Well, fairly . . .'

He stopped behind me, set down the bucket and mop and went into a crouch, peering into the pile of the brown carpeting.

'Women are always losin' things . . . what colour is it?'

'Er . . . sort of brownish. It's a topaz.'

'Couldn' be woise. Now, if it wus an emerald or a diamond . . .'

'No, it was a topaz.'

'How big . . . bigger'n a penny?'

'Erm . . . yes, about that.'

'Shouldn't be too hard t' find. I'll give you a hand.'

'No, no really . . .'

Oh, brother, this was all I needed! Another look at my watch . . . nine nineteen! I groaned in anguish.

'Yeh, I know how it is,' he commiserated. 'My old lady once lost her weddin' ring . . .' he dropped to his knees and began thumping the carpet, searching the gaps at the wall. 'Couldn' find it nowhere . . . took the house apart . . . searched high 'n' low, from basement t' attic, but not a sign of it. Then yuh know what, damndest thing . . . she's fond of goin' to dese fortune tellers – yuh know, dey read yuh palm for half-a-dollar . . . well, it musta bin three weeks later she went ta see one of dese old boids and told her about the weddin' ring. Quit worryin', de old crow tells her, you go straight home an' you'll find it. But we already tore the house apart lookin' for it, says Agnes. Never you mind, lady, just do as I tell yuh, you'll find it! So Agnes slips her half-a-dollar and runs all the way home and yuh know what . . .?'

'No, what?' I grimaced, watching the minute hand race to twenty-two minutes past nine.

'We took the damned house apart again – I mean *really* gave it the woiks dis time, pulled the carpets up . . . emptied the sink traps . . . did everythin' but peel the paper offa the walls . . . an' yuh know where we finally found it?'

'No, where?'

'Un'er the goddam bed-sheet! She'd bin lyin on it all dat time an' complainin' a mattress-button was stickin' in her ass! Women . . .'

Sweating profusely, I checked the time again. Nine twenty-three! Now there was no choice, I *had* to go!

'Look . . . thanks all the same, but I've got to leave it. I'm in a terrible hurry . . .'

At that moment a young girl came round the corner, a room-maid I guessed from her uniform. She came to a halt at the sight of us crawling along on our hands and knees and giggled.

'Watcha doin', Charlie, havin' a race?'

'No, we ain't havin' a race, Miss Smart Pants, we're tryin' to find dis gentleman's wife's ring stone. She reckon she lost it along here somewheres.'

'Wow, what was it – a diamond?'

'No a topaz – big as a one-cent piece.'

'I'll help you look.'

'No, no,' I protested. 'Really, I'm in a terrible hurry . . .'

'That's O.K.,' said Charlie, 'you go ahead, we'll look. What room yuh stayin' in?'

'Er . . . well, perhaps you could just . . . leave it at the Reception, I'll pick it up there.'

'Sure thing. Come on, Lou, down on your honkers.'

'Well, that's very kind of you.' I hated doing it to them, but there was no other way.

'Think nuthin' of it,' said Charlie. 'If it's here, we'll find it. Off you go, now.'

Off I went, breaking into a gallop as soon as I turned the corner into the first wing and racing down to the Reception.

The girl looked up, blanching at the sight of me. 'Oh, it's you! My, you've recovered quickly.'

'Had . . . a cold shower,' I gasped. 'Pulled me round a treat. My wife . . . and I decided to go out after all. I wonder if I could . . .' I produced the key '. . . get a few dollars out?'

'Yes, sure.'

With a slowness that bordered on paraplegia, she crossed to the safe, unlocked the outer door, pulled out our box and came back with it. And as she passed it to me . . . a commotion broke out way down the corridor. I could hear Felicia's penetrating demand . . . and Charlie's reply. I ran to the mouth of the corridor, caught a glimpse of Felicia in the second wing, bending over him, extremely agitated.

I ran back to the desk, inserted the key in the box.

'You'll have to sign the card, sir,' insisted the girl. 'What's happening down there?'

'Somebody having an argument,' I croaked, wiping my signature across the 'withdrawal' column. Then I was attacking the box, fumbling with the lock, each hand having suddenly sprouted ten more fingers and three thumbs. Finally I got the lid open, groaned with relief to find the two rolls of notes still there. I grabbed them both, stuffed one in each pocket, shoved the box back to her.

'What *is* going on down there?'

What was going on was Felicia charging towards me like a thousand-pound bomb was just about to explode behind her, her eyes twin saucers of horrified disbelief. 'You . . .! You . . .! Stop . . .!'

At that moment the french door to the courtyard swung inwards and in came Kohlman, almost colliding with Felicia. They dodged, side-stepped . . . and that was the cue for Tobin's exit! I was off like a rocket, out of the front door, as Felicia screamed at Kohlman, 'Get the car! Get the car!'

Out across the paved courtyard, through a clump of bushes, a zig-zag slalom between a plantation of palm trees and onto the pavement. A panicky glance behind me and there was Kohlman, beating all track records across the courtyard to the Cadillac, Felicia galloping after him.

God, they were coming after me . . . would be on me in seconds!

I broke into demented flight along the crowded pavement,

swerving and weaving, leaving behind me a wake of gaping citizens, and as I ran I threw desperate glances over my shoulder, expecting the Caddy to appear at any moment.

Dammit . . . eight million cabs in Las Vegas and not one in sight. On I ran, gasping for breath, my heart banging like crazy and my throat dry as the Nevada desert. Oh, Buzz . . . Buzz . . . if only we'd planned for you to follow me . . . to be waiting outside the motel! What idiots! We could have been on our way to the airport by now.

Another glance . . . still no cab in sight . . . eighty thousand going south on the far carriageway but not a sod going north.

On and on . . . risking death at each intersection, dodging between honking cars . . . and where the hell *was* I? Good God, I was only at the Desert Inn! I still had more than a mile to go!

Yet another glance . . . and, Christ, they were there! . . . stopped at a red light at the last intersection! I was too late! I was done for! Another few seconds and they'd be on me . . . a quick karate chop on the back of the neck and I'd be . . .

Where the cab came from God only knows but I reckon He must have sent it. I suppose it must have turned onto the Strip from the Desert Inn road and hadn't had time to get into more than second gear when it reached me. All I know is that it was there and I was leaping up and down and waving my arms like a lunatic and all but jumped on the bonnet to stop it.

The driver hit the brakes and stopped on a dime.

I yanked open the rear.

'Were you by any chance tryin' to attract my attention?' he drawled.

'Sahara . . . and fast!' I gasped. 'Gotta . . . plane to catch.'

'Oh, they're flyin' 'em from the Sahara now?'

'Hurry . . . please! I've got to pick up my luggage . . . be at the airport by ten.'

He glanced at his watch. 'Oh, you've got plenty of time – all of twenty minutes. Provided you do a hundred and ninety all the way, you may even have time to check your bags in.'

Give him one thing – while he was yacking he was driving. He put his foot to the floor, throwing me back into the seat. I hauled myself out of the upholstery and peered through the rear window. Jesus, there they were . . . four cars behind and sticking like glue. I couldn't see their faces for the reflection in the windscreen, but it was them all right.

I checked the meter, calculated what the fare would be, added a good tip and got the money ready. Within a couple of minutes we were swirling into the Sahara forecourt and squealing to a halt at the front door.

'You're a genius,' I said, thrusting the money at him. 'Happy New Year.'

I was into the hotel before he could reply. A fast run-walk through the foyer and into the long corridor, then a hectic sprint for the elevators, hitting both buttons.

'Come on . . . come on!'

The right elevator crawled down with agonizing slowness, stopped at the floor above, then slid to ground. The doors opened . . . it was bulging. Out they crawled, old birds in blue rinses, men with cigars. It was an eternity before it emptied, then I was in.

Bang! I flattened the button and danced a psychotic jig while it crawled up to our floor.

At last! The doors opened . . . and there, bless his sweaty old tennis socks, was Buzz, surrounded by our luggage, looking quite demented and so relieved to see me he damn-near burst into tears.

'Christalmighty . . . !'

'Buzz! Terrific! Thank God . . . quick, get those cases in here!'

'Man d'you know what *time* it is! I've been waiting here half a bloody hour!'

'I know, I know . . . good man . . . quick, get in! Buzz, they're after us . . . me. They're downstairs! You just don't know what I've been through . . .'

He punched the lobby button. '*Who's* downstairs – the chauffeur?'

'Kohlman, yes – and Felicia. I had to make a run for it! She caught me with my mitt in the till . . . chased me down the Strip in the Caddy . . . thank God for a cruising cab . . . but they'll be waiting out there for us!'

'Out front?'

'Or in the foyer . . . *or* at the elevators. I reckon they came in and checked my room number, it's what I'd do.'

'In which case, they'll know we're sharing . . . that we're working together! Oh, blimey . . .' His eyes darted around like Bingo balls. 'O.K. . . .' He moved to the control panel, put his thumb on the 'Close Doors' button. 'If they're waiting down here for us, we hit this and shoot back up . . . take the stairs. If they're not down here, we don't go out through the foyer – we take the side entrance.'

'Roger.'

'And flex your muscles, son, you've got a two-hundred-yard dash with fifty pounds of luggage.'

'Mate, with Kohlman waiting for me, I'd do a two-hundred-yard dash with *two hundred* pounds of luggage.'

'Well . . .' he smiled grimly, 'did you *get* it?'

I patted both pockets. 'I got it – both of them – and hers is a beaut.'

'What – ten grand?'

'At least. It's as fat as an elephant's dick.'

'Whee hee!'

'Look out . . . here we are.'

Poised for flight, we watched the indicator light hit ground. The doors opened . . . revealing, to our immense relief, an empty lobby.

Buzz stuck his head out, looked left . . . right . . . then grabbed his cases.

'Come on!'

We were out of there like a couple of Olympic sprinters, a quick turn to the left and out through the side entrance of the hotel.

Waddling comically under the weight of our cases, we heel-toe-ed it fast down the prodigious length of the hotel, Buzz way out in front, me straggling behind, wishing I was fifty pounds heavier and as strong as the big lummox in front.

'Come on, Tobin . . . it's ten to bleeding ten!'

'I'm coming as fast as I can, you pillock!'

'That's what you get for doin' all that screwing! You ought to live a good, clean, celibate life like me!'

God, would this road *never* end.

'Tell you one thing, Malone . . . If I ever get . . . out of this alive . . . I'm going into strict training . . . no more booze . . . and no more birds.'

'Yeah,' he laughed, 'and I hear the Pope's going to marry the Happy Hooker, too. Come on . . . there's the car . . . only another fifty yards.'

I staggered on, lungs bursting and arm muscles screaming,

and finally collapsed over the Volks hood. 'Oh, my God, I'm dying . . .'

'You will be if Kohlman catches you.'

I recovered fast, scanned the car lot. 'You can see them? !'

He nodded towards the entrance of the hotel. 'There's a white thing over there . . . it'll be them.'

Revitalized by blatant funk, I opened the front boot and threw in my cases while Buzz was stowing his away inside the car.

'Right,' he said, looking at his watch, 'we have precisely . . . eight minutes to make the airport. Get in and hold tight to that luggage.'

Bang . . . bang . . .baaarrroooommmmm!

We were away, swerving insanely between the rows of parked cars, then zooming past the front of the hotel, out across the dual-carriageway and into the south lane to a storm of honking abuse from on-coming drivers.

'Did you see them?' he asked.

'There was something white there, all right, but I couldn't see clearly for the line of cabs.'

'Keep watching . . . and hold on, we're going to make a little time.'

Jesus, he really took off . . . flashed past Circus Circus, jumped the lights at the Stardust, had to slow for another set at the Silver Slipper but judged them beautifully and was into second as they hit green.

'Any sign?'

I nodded. 'Yes, I reckon they're on to us. There's something white with a black top about six cars back.'

'Yeah,' he muttered grimly. 'Well, if they went to all that trouble to get our five grand, they'll go to a hell of a lot more trouble to get back their own ten! Hang on . . .'

Zoooooom! He threw the little Volks into the slow lane, whipped past a scarlet Buick that was hogging the fast lane, then flung us back into the fast track, flashed through the lights at the Frontier, belted past the Castaways and came to a squealing halt on a red at Caesar's Palace.

'Come on . . . come on!' he cursed, revving the engine in desperation.

'They're still back there, mate . . . just biding their time.'

'Because they think they've got us,' he nodded. 'I told Felicia I was catching the eleven o'clock flight to L.A., so they know where we're heading . . . and they know damn well they can catch us before we even get the bags out of the car. Well, at least they *think* they can catch us before we get the bags out of the car . . . hang on!'

He slammed his foot to the floor and all but hurled me into the back seat with the luggage. Across the intersection we shot, hitting sixty before we reached the Dunes, then, on the less-congested airport road, really opened her up.

'Just pray that the cops are nursing hangovers,' he growled, jaw set grimly, hunched over the wheel, his bulk filling the cab.

Well, I reckon if Buzz ever felt like a change from tennis he could always take up motor racing, because he produced a performance from that little roller skate that even the manufacturers wouldn't have believed. He went up and down the gears like he was playing a xylophone, whipped in and out of traffic with the balletic grace of a terrified cat, took corners on the door handles, and was vulcanizing the gutter outside the main airport entrance with eight seconds to spare.

'Christalmighty!' I gasped, collapsing against the door. 'Buzz, we've *got* to go back to the Tropicana intersection.'

'Eh? What for?'

'My stomach, you maniac.'

'Ha! Well, I got you here, didn't I?'

'Not all of me . . . there's a heart missing . . . and a couple of kidneys . . .'

'Tobin . . . move!'

Abandoning the car, we yanked out our luggage and crashed through the glass doors into the main lobby . . . and ran straight into a queue of more than a dozen people waiting to check their bags in.

'Oh, Christ . . .' groaned Buzz.

We joined the queue, every second or two throwing nervous glances towards the main doors. Too impatient to stand still, we moved around in tight circles, like two guys dying for a pee at a funeral service, cursing the slowness of the booking clerk who appeared to be having trouble with some old biddy about over-weight baggage.

'But they can't do anything now, can they?' I asked him, desperate for reassurance. 'I mean, not in *here*!'

'God knows. I wouldn't trust that Kohlman as far as I can throw him – which ain't far. They're tricky customers . . . could come up with anything. Jesus, what's that old dame taking with her – a fucking piano!'

A few moments later, to our immense relief, realizing the delay the old bird was causing, another check-in desk opened up.

Buzz was there in six strides, pre-empting everyone else in the line and drawing a flurry of muttered abuse. Onto the scales went the luggage . . . whizz, bang, wallop, our tickets were stamped, ripped asunder, handed back.

'Your flight is boarding now, gentlemen, so if you'd make your way to Gate Ten . . .'

'Buzz!'

He shot round, followed my quivering finger to the white Cadillac convertible drawing up behind our car.

He spun back to the clerk. 'Gate Ten?'

'Yes, sir, just follow the signs . . .'

We were off, eating up the concourse with giant strides, not daring to look back, weaving in and out of the straggling passengers and putting as many people as we could between us and *them*. Now a right turn onto an escalator and up to the elevated concourse leading to the boarding gates.

'Did you see them?' I panted.

Buzz shook his head. 'Not actually . . . but it must have been them.'

'Could . . . they follow us?'

'Sure, why not. This is a local bus trip. As long as the plane's not full, they can just buy a ticket and hop on.'

I groaned. 'So we're not safe yet?'

'Not until that damn plane takes off without them. Tell you what we're going to do, though . . .'

'What?'

'When we're on the plane . . . if we see them heading across the tarmac, we make a bee-line for the bogs and lock ourselves in. Then, at the very last minute, we nip off the plane and catch another one tomorrow.'

I grinned. 'Fantastic.'

'O.K.?'

'Spot on.'

We reached the security line-up and suffered eighteen further nervous breakdowns while waiting to be electronically scanned . . . yet, thank God, there was still no sign of Kohlman and Felicia.

'Maybe they stuck behind the old girl with the baggage,' suggested Buzz. 'But they'll hold the plane for them if they're buying tickets.'

We reached Gate Ten. Here we suffered another delay for inspection of boarding passes, but then we were through, descending a flight of stairs and half-running across a few yards of tarmac to the forward steps of the jet.

At the top we were greeted by two radiantly smiling airstews, one blonde, one brunette, so lovely we almost forgot Kohlman and Felicia . . . almost.

'Good evenin', gentlemen,' whispered the blonde, giving us the eyes. 'Smoking or non-smoking?'

'Sort of smouldering, right now,' grinned Buzz.

'A window seat, if possible, miss,' I cut in. 'Near the rear door.'

'Yes, can do,' she smiled, her eyes on Buzz. 'Follow me.'

'Anywhere,' sighed Buzz.

We followed her swinging chassis down the length of the plane, Buzz generously walking sideways to let me have an eyeful.

'How about here?' she said.

'Beautiful,' said Buzz. 'You blaze a mean trail.'

'Please fasten your seat-belts, we're almost ready for take-off.'

'Ready when you are,' he laughed, sliding across to the window seat.

She departed, treating us to another wonderful display of posterial calisthenics all the way back up the aisle.

'Oh, man . . .' sighed Buzz.

'Never mind her bottom, get glued to that window.'

'Oh, yeah . . . good thinking, Tobin, moving to the back. By the time they get to the top of those forward stairs, we'll be long-gone down these rear ones.'

'Good job one of us can maintain a clear head in the face of big tits and a belting ass.'

He chuckled lecherously and turned to the window. 'Hey . . . more people coming out now.'

Our recent light-heartedness drained from me like water down a plug-hole. Breathlessly, I waited for his commentary.

'The old bird with the excess weight problem . . .'

'So – she's through.'

'Two young guys who came in after us . . .'

A lengthy pause.

For the eighty-fourth time that night I looked at my watch. It was seven minutes to eleven.

'Seven minutes to go, Buzz . . . the longest seven of my life.'

'Hey . . . a man and woman coming out . . .'

'Oh, Jesus . . .'

'No, relax, he's only five foot two . . .'

'I don't think I can stand it.'

'Oh, Christ, a tall guy coming out . . . black suit . . .'

'Buzz . . .?'

'Could be, mate . . .'

I unclipped my seat-belt in preparation for a different kind of flight.

'No, you can start breathing again, it's not Kohlman . . .'

'Malone, are you doing this on purpose!'

'Aha!'

I jumped. '*What?*'

'A blonde just came out . . .'

'Ohhhhhh . . .'

'With two kids.'

'Malone, you bastard . . .!'

Another long, nerve-tingling pause, Buzz hunched at the window. Then suddenly he turned to me, his face split in an outrageous grin. 'Mate . . . they've shut up shop!'

I gasped. 'You mean . . .'

'Closed the doors, cock. We're home and dry!'

I collapsed, sagged, went quite dizzy with relief. 'Mate . . . I feel nine thousand years old.'

I leaned out into the aisle, watched the blonde with the kids come aboard, then, with unqualified relief, saw the brunette stewardess swing the forward door into place and lock it home.

Behind us another thunk and the rear door was closed. I turned to Buzz and held out my hand. 'Mate . . . we made it.'

'Well . . . let's say the chances are now pretty good, anyway.'

My face fell. 'What . . . d'you mean?'

'Well, we're not in the air yet. One time I was actually out on the *runway*, just about to take off, when the tower ordered us back to pick up some passengers who'd been delayed in the security line-up.'

'Now, Malone . . . don't fool around with this . . .'

'No,' he laughed, 'it's true!'

Down the aisle came the blonde airstew, checking that all seat-belts were fastened.

'You both nailed down?' she smiled.

'Only temporarily,' Buzz assured her. 'How soon can we get a drink?'

'Soon as we're aloft, I'll be around.'

She moved on, then returned to the front of the plane.

The engines rumbled into life. With crossed fingers I urged the jet into movement and, by golly, it worked. Out we trundled, taking an eternity to reach the runway.

'Yeah, this is where we turned back,' nodded Buzz, and I replied with a couple of extremely rude words.

But there was no turning back this time. The giant thrusters suddenly thundered into full power and we were off, racing down the runway . . . a quick tilt . . . and we were up, up and away . . . our spirits soaring with every foot of altitude.

Buzz burst out in hilarious laughter, thumped me on the knee, ripped off his seat-belt and shook my hand vigorously. 'We made it, you old bastard! Dammit it, we really pulled it off! I'm going to get pissed, smashed . . . I'm gonna be stinko all the way to Tahiti . . . and then I'm *really* gonna start celebrating! Here comes the light of my life now . . . miss!'

The blonde came up, smiling. 'You two look happy. You break the house or something?'

'Ha!' laughed Buzz. 'We shattered it. Kindly bring us a dozen small bottles of champagne – for starters.'

She laughed. 'You realize this is only a fifty-minute flight?'

'Yes . . . you can bring the second dozen in about twenty minutes.'

Grinning, she departed.

'Hee hee!' chuckled Buzz, rubbing his hands eagerly. 'Right, let's have a look at the pickings. By God, Tobin, we are going to have a right old time in Tahiti . . . we are going to live like lords . . . kings . . . potentates! Fifty women each . . . a super-luxurious hotel suite . . . the best food, cars, clothes . . .'

Shaking with excitement, I plunged my hand into my left pocket. 'Here, that's our roll.'

Almost contemptuously he whipped off the rubber band and stuffed them in his inside pocket. 'Peanuts. I'll give these to the stew for a tip. Come on, let's have a look at the other beauty.'

Reverently I withdrew Felicia's roll from my right pocket,

thrilling to the firm, fat feel of it and to the sight of that scrumptious five hundred dollars' worth of wrapping on the outside.

I weighed it in my hand, squeezed it, grinning like an idiot. 'Well . . . how much d'you reckon, old chum?'

'God knows,' he gasped, eyes like ping-pong balls. 'Thousands . . .'

'Do we open it . . . or dream a little longer?'

'Ohhh, Russell, we are going to have the time of our sweet lives. I've always wondered what it'd be like to be rich . . . I mean really, filthy, stinking, overwhelmingly, mind-bogglingly *rich* – even for a couple of days.'

'Yeah, me, too. Used to drive me nuts reading about people winning three hundred thousand pounds on the football pools and them saying it wouldn't change their lives . . . that they'd still go on living in the same terraced house in Fulham and . . .'

'I know, makes you sick. Well, we won't have three hundred thousand, but we've certainly got enough for three or four days of unadulterated paradise.'

'Shall I open it?'

'Yeah, go on . . . I can't stand the suspense any longer.'

'O.K. . . . on the count of three. One . . .'

I slipped my finger under the rubber band.

'Two . . .'

Slowly I eased it up the roll, paused at the very tip, and then . . .

'Three!'

I flipped it off.

Slowly . . . I released my grip on the roll, allowing its natural springiness to open it out.

I gasped. 'Buzz . . .!'

The inside note was another five-hundred-dollar bill!

'Jesuschrist . . .' he whispered, '. . . they're all *five hundreds*! It's *fifty thousand* doll . . .'

His voice tailed away, became a gulp, a groan, a whimper, accompanying my own plaintive moan as I thumbed the notes into a fan, exposing them one by one . . . for the dirty, rotten, stinking, cheating, thieving, conniving swine hadn't even had the decency to fill the roll with singles . . . it was all immaculately guillotined . . . toilet paper!

'Ohhhhh, bloody . . . fucking . . . hell . . .' gasped Buzz, his chin hitting the floor. '*Bog* paper!'

I slumped.

He slumped.

'We should've known.

He shrugged. 'Who was to *know*, her bloody diamonds were real!'

'Wanna bet?'

He shook his head. 'No.'

'Oh, Buzz . . .'

'Oh, rotting hell . . .'

Then the blonde was there with six small bottles of champagne and two glasses.

'Here y'go. This is a rare event – serving winners.'

'You'd better take them back,' sighed Buzz. 'Bring us two Cokes instead.'

'Hm!' she frowned. 'Hey, what happened to the two happy swingers that were sitting here a minute ago?'

'They baled out . . . without parachutes.'

'Hm . . .?'

'Buzz . . .' I said, beginning a grin. 'Think about it . . . we're still a thousand dollars ahead of when we started.'

He looked at me, thinking about it.

'And there was Josie . . . and Angela . . . and Pussycat.'

He frowned. 'Who?'

I ignored him. 'And we have had a couple of pretty exciting days in Vegas . . . and we've still got Tahiti coming up . . . and . . .'

He grinned the old indefatigable Malone grin. 'Yeah, we have, haven't we?'

'Gentlemen,' sighed the Stew, 'do you want this champagne or not?'

Buzz looked up at her, appalled. 'Mm . . .? Of course we want it. Whatever gave you the idea we didn't want it?'

She slid the tray onto my table. 'Boy, one thing we're always guaranteed on the Vegas run . . . a plane-load of nuts!'

As she departed, I poured a beakerful of bubbly and passed it to Buzz.

'Yeah,' he said, 'we didn't come out of it at all badly, did we? A free night on the town, courtesy of Qantas . . . an all-time thrill of hitting a big jackpot . . . a wild old night with Josie . . . *and* a thousand bucks expenses in Tahiti.' He grinned. 'Not forgetting, of course, six months' free supply of bog paper.'

'*I'm* more than satisfied,' I said. 'Cheers.'

'Cheers. Er, Tobin . . . I've got a sneaky feeling you're one up on me, somehow. What's this "Pussycat" thing you let slip?'

'Mmm . . .? Oh, that . . .'

'Yeah – oh, that.'

'Buzz, I couldn't possibly tell you. After your recent financial bereavement, this could conceivably throw you into such black despair . . . could bring you so close to the abyss of nervous breakdown . . .'

'New Year's night,' he muttered. 'While *I* was getting the treatment from Felicia, you were getting . . .'

'*I* can't help it, Malone, I have that kind of face. There I was, sitting all alone and minding my own business in the Flamingo bar, simply waiting to see the New Year in before quietly slipping off to my lonely bed, when suddenly up walked this *scrumptious* piece of . . .'

'Tobin . . .'

'Yes, Buzz?'

'Shut up.'

'Yes, Buzz.'

'And think of Tahiti.'

I grinned. 'You're too late . . . I landed an hour ago.'

'Terrific?'

'Fan . . . tastic!'

'Yeah,' he chuckled. 'Now, on that you *can* bet your bottom dollar.'

How all too often does reality fall short of the dream by many a disappointing mile . . . but not Tahiti.

It *was* fantastic.

Maybe when I get my breath back – and some more ink in my pen – I'll drop you a line and tell you about it. All right?

Tarra.

A selection of bestsellers from Mayflower Books

Novels

DELIVERY OF FURIES	Victor Canning	35p	☐
THE DEVIL AT FOUR O'CLOCK	Max Catto	35p	☐
MURPHY'S WAR	Max Catto	30p	☐
FANNY HILL (unexpurgated)	John Cleland	40p	☐
THE STUD	Jackie Collins	35p	☐
BLACK STAR	Morton Cooper	50p	☐
THE PRETENDERS	Gwen Davis	75p	☐
GROUPIE (unexpurgated)			
	Jenny Fabian & Johnny Byrne	40p	☐
STORE	Alexander Fullerton	40p	☐
CHIEF EXECUTIVE	Alexander Fullerton	50p	☐
THE MEDICAL WITNESS	Richard Gordon	40p	☐
LIKE ANY OTHER FUGITIVE	Joseph Hayes	50p	☐
THE DEEP END	Joseph Hayes	45p	☐
I, A SAILOR	Morgen Holm	40p	☐
I, A PROSTITUTE	Nina Holm	35p	☐
I, A WOMAN	Siv Holm	35p	☐
I, A TEENAGER	Tine Holm	35p	☐
LAST SUMMER	Evan Hunter	30p	☐
BUDDWING	Evan Hunter	40p	☐
THE PAPER DRAGON	Evan Hunter	60p	☐
LITTLE LOVE	Herbert Kastle	50p	☐
THE MOVIE MAKER	Herbert Kastle	50p	☐
ALL NIGHT STAND	Thom Keyes	35p	☐
BANDERSNATCH	Desmond Lowden	35p	☐
PUSSYCAT, PUSSYCAT	Ted Mark	35p	☐
THE NUDE WHO NEVER	Ted Mark	35p	☐
THE COUNTRY TEAM	Robin Moore	40p	☐
THE SEWING MACHINE MAN	Stanley Morgan	40p	☐
THE DEBT COLLECTOR	Stanley Morgan	40p	☐
THE COURIER	Stanley Morgan	35p	☐
COME AGAIN COURIER	Stanley Morgan	40p	☐
TOBIN TAKES OFF	Stanley Morgan	35p	☐
TOBIN ON SAFARI	Stanley Morgan	35p	☐
COMMANDER AMANDA NIGHTINGALE			
	George Revelli	35p	☐
RESORT TO WAR	George Revelli	35p	☐
AMANDA'S CASTLE	George Revelli	35p	☐
THE CHILIAN CLUB	George Shipway	35p	☐
THE GADFLY	E. L. Voynich	40p	☐
THE BANKER	Leslie Waller	60p	☐

THE FAMILY	Leslie Waller	50p ☐
THE AMERICAN	Leslie Waller	60p ☐
STRAW DOGS	Gordon M. Williams	30p ☐
THE CAMP	Gordon M. Williams	35p ☐
THEY USED TO PLAY ON GRASS	Gordon Williams & Terry Venables	40p ☐
PROVIDENCE ISLAND	Calder Willingham	75p ☐
ETERNAL FIRE	Calder Willingham	60p ☐
END AS A MAN	Calder Willingham	50p ☐
THE GOD OF THE LABYRINTH	Colin Wilson	50p ☐
A COLD WIND IN AUGUST	Burton Wohl	35p ☐
THE JET SET	Burton Wohl	40p ☐
GOAT SONG	Frank Yerby	50p ☐
THE MAN FROM DAHOMEY	Frank Yerby	60p ☐
THE DEVIL'S LAUGHTER	Frank Yerby	40p ☐
THE SARACEN BLADE	Frank Yerby	50p ☐
MY BROTHER JONATHAN	Francis Brett Young	40p ☐

War

SEVEN MEN AT DAYBREAK	Alan Burgess	35p ☐
RICHTHOFEN (Illustrated)	William E. Burrows	40p ☐
HUNTING THE BISMARCK	C. S. Forester	25p ☐
SURFACE!	Alexander Fullerton	35p ☐
HOUSE OF DOLLS	Ka-Tzetnik	50p ☐
THE LIEUTENANT MUST BE MAD	Hans Helmut Kirst	40p ☐
FIVE CHIMNEYS	Olga Lengyel	35p ☐
PATROL	Fred Majdalany	30p ☐
'HMS MARLBOROUGH WILL ENTER HARBOUR'	Nicholas Monsarrat	35p ☐
THREE CORVETTES	Nicholas Monsarrat	40p ☐
AUSCHWITZ	Dr. Miklos Nyiszli	30p ☐
ALL QUIET ON THE WESTERN FRONT	Erich Maria Remarque	40p ☐
THE HILL	Ray Rigby	35p ☐
CAMP ON BLOOD ISLAND	J. M. White & Val Guest	30p ☐

Romance

DANCE IN THE DUST	Denise Robins	35p ☐
BREAKING POINT	Denise Robins	40p ☐
MY LADY DESTINY	Denise Robins	30p ☐
BRIDE OF DOOM	Denise Robins	40p ☐
GOLD FOR THE GAY MASTERS	Denise Robins	35p ☐
TIME RUNS OUT	Denise Robins	30p ☐

Mayflower Crime for your enjoyment

THE TERRIBLE ONES	Nick Carter	30p ☐
WEB OF SPIES	Nick Carter	30p ☐
THE GOLDEN SERPENT	Nick Carter	30p ☐
THE WEAPON OF NIGHT	Nick Carter	30p ☐
THE EYES OF THE TIGER	Nick Carter	35p ☐
THE MAN WITH THE TINY HEAD		
	Ivor Drummond	35p ☐
THE PRIESTS OF THE ABOMINATION		
	Ivor Drummond	30p ☐
THE FROG IN THE MOONFLOWER		
	Ivor Drummond	30p ☐
THE CASE OF THE TERRIFIED TYPIST		
	Erle Stanley Gardner	30p ☐
THE CASE OF THE RESTLESS REDHEAD		
	Erle Stanley Gardner	35p ☐
THE CASE OF THE GRINNING GORILLA		
	Erle Stanley Gardner	35p ☐
THE CASE OF THE NEGLIGENT NYMPH		
	Erle Stanley Gardner	30p ☐
CAGE FIVE IS GOING TO BREAK		
	E. Richard Johnson	30p ☐
THE INSIDE MAN	E. Richard Johnson	30p ☐
MONGO'S BACK IN TOWN	E. Richard Johnson	25p ☐
DEATH ON DOOMSDAY	Elizabeth Lemarchand	30p ☐
CYANIDE WITH COMPLIMENTS		
	Elizabeth Lemarchand	30p ☐

All these books are available at your local bookshop or newsagent; or can be ordered direct from the publisher. Just tick the titles you want and fill in the form below.

Name_____

Address_____

_____

Write to Mayflower Cash Sales, PO Box 11, Falmouth, Cornwall TR10 9EN. Please enclose remittance to the value of the cover price plus 15p postage and packing for one book plus 5p for each additional copy. Overseas customers please send 20p for first book and 10p for each additional book. *Granada Publishing reserve the right to show new retail prices on covers, which may differ from those previously advertised in the text or elsewhere.*